THE
NAIL

An absolutely gripping British crime mystery full of twists

JANE ADAMS

Detective Inspector Mike Croft Book 5

Joffe Books, London
www.joffebooks.com

First published in Great Britain in 2024

Cover art by Dee Dee Book Covers

ISBN: 978-1-83526-540-6

PROLOGUE

Tuesday

For Ross Cahn, the nightmare had begun two years before, when a massive hand had come down upon his shoulder and a voice had said, "Seems like we have a mutual friend we want to be rid of."

Until then, Ross had been determined just to do his time and be gone. Yes, he still bore a grudge, was still happy to relay to anyone who would listen how this man had let him down and ruined his life but, as time had gone on, he'd realised that talking about revenge was one thing — acting on it another. Or at least, that's what he'd told himself. Over the following months this hulk of a man had dogged his steps, had planned what was going to happen when they both got out of prison, and there was a part of Ross that had been excited at the prospect, that had enjoyed the fantasy. But Ross had been well ahead on the likelihood of release, the big man hadn't even been in line for probation at that point, and Ross had been inclined, in his more hopeful moments, to believe this had been all just talk. He'd get out, Bri would still be inside. He'd go somewhere new, start again, and Brian would forget about him.

1

But Brian Hedgecock did not intend to forget and now they were both out, and Ross was in deep trouble. Though not as deep as the man Ross was clinging on to as though his life depended on it, which, considering the mood Bri had worked himself into, it probably did. It was bad enough that Ross had turned up on his own. That had never been part of the big man's plan . . .

And now here Ross was, alone with Brian and his victim, up past his neck and drowning.

Ross had known that Brian wanted to punish this man . . . Okay, so Ross had known that Brian wanted him dead, but knowing was one thing, actually seeing it happen — no, being part of it . . . Ross was sure he was going to throw up. Ross was capable of violence — that was why he'd been locked up in the first place. Rage had got the better of him and he'd hit out, almost killed someone, but this was something else. He should have run, long since disappeared, but could anyone get away from Bri, once he'd marked them?

"Hold him still, hold him fucking still!"

So, Ross clung on, hard, the fingers of one hand wrapped in the man's lapels and the other scrabbling for purchase in his close-cropped hair. A second later the hammer came down and a second after that the man was dead and Ross's accomplice was smiling as though all was right with the world.

"You can go now," he said, his voice suddenly calm. "I've just got to tidy up a bit in here and then I'll be done. I'll give you a call in a few days, sort out the rest of your money."

And Ross had nodded and then taken to his heels and run. What the hell had he just done? What the fucking hell had he just done?

CHAPTER 1

Wednesday

Morgan Springfield had moved to the area some eight years previously. He was an entrepreneur and ran a small engineering business making specialist machine tools for the aerospace industry. His body was discovered when his financial director arrived at work one morning and was surprised to find the place still locked up. Morgan Springfield was always first in and often the last to leave.

The colleague, Sid Patterson, had a key of his own. On that Wednesday morning in late November, he let himself in and turned his attention to the alarm, disconcerted not to be hearing the beeps that warned him he had only thirty seconds to unset it. Closer inspection revealed that the alarm had not even been set and then Sid realised that his boss was in fact already there. He could see him through the glass panel of the office door, sitting behind his desk.

Puzzled, Sid tapped on the door and then stuck his head around it, and the smell was the first thing that hit him. Stale urine and something worse.

Alarmed, thinking that his boss must be ill, but also realising with increasing shock that Morgan hadn't moved,

Sid began to cross to the desk and then stopped. He knew a dead body when he saw one and Morgan was definitely dead.

In a remote corner of his mind, Sid told himself that he should be handling this better than he was. That this was not the first dead body he had seen — but those bodies, he told that more rational fragment of his brain, had not been Morgan.

Sid seemed to be suddenly floating outside of himself. He heard a little whimpering noise escape from a cramped throat, felt the room spin. He grasped urgently at the door frame, steadying himself enough to stumble out into the foyer. Morgan was dead. How could Morgan be dead?

What to do? What should he do? Call an ambulance, call the police, call Cath, Morgan's secretary, see if she knew how Morgan could possibly be dead.

With an effort he pulled himself together. How the hell would Cath know?

"Come on, Sid, get a grip." The room was spinning again and he leaned heavily against the wall, still wondering whether he should call the police or an ambulance, and in the end he dialled 999 and asked for both.

"He's dead," he told the call handler. "How can he be dead?" Sid broke down, floods of tears pouring down his face as he tried to listen to what the call handler was saying to him, to give her the information she needed. Who was dead? Where? Was he certain? Had he checked for a pulse?

Sid realised that he was not making any sense; dimly he understood that he sounded in such a state that the handler had decided to err on the side of caution in case reports of death were premature. She told Sid that she would be sending both police and an ambulance to the scene. He heard himself thanking her and then wondered what good the ambulance would do. Finally, legs unable to support him, Sid sank down against the wall.

He was not sure how much time had passed before a patrol car pulled into the car park on the little industrial estate. This was closely followed by a paramedic. He could see them through the big glass doors, but seemed unable to move. When they came into the lobby, Sid was still sitting in the hallway, his back to the wall, his whole body shaking with cold.

Sid watched as the paramedic went into the office and then came out again only moments later. He watched as the man shook his head and then spoke in a low voice to one of the police officers. The second officer had taken one look at Sid and then returned to the car. He came back with a thick blanket, which he draped around Sid's shoulders. Sid pulled it tight.

"Thank you," Sid managed. He watched as the second officer peered through the open door and again engaged in whispered conversation that Sid didn't quite understand the purpose of. Morgan was dead — he was slowly beginning to accept that now. What more was there to say? He was startled when the second officer came back and crouched down at his side.

"Shall we get you out of here, sir? The young lady from the next-door office is making some tea."

Sid was abruptly aware of someone standing beside the entrance. Imogen from the architect's office in the next unit down. He accepted the police officer's help in getting to his feet.

"Did you touch anything, sir?" The officer's voice was quiet and almost casual. Was he that used to death, Sid wondered, that he could be so relaxed about it?

"Touch anything? No. I went just inside the door. I thought he was ill, then I realised he was dead. You can see he's dead."

"Yes, sir, you can. And then you made the 999 call?"

Sid nodded. He wanted to be out of there now. To get away. The policeman led him to the door and handed him over to Imogen. She put an arm around Sid and hugged him tightly, then led him into her own company reception.

"I saw the police car and the paramedic arrive," she said. "So I went out to find out what was wrong. The officer told me that something had happened to Morgan. Oh, Sid, I'm so sorry."

Sid was vaguely aware that he was crying again and that she was taking him into a little side room. That someone was handing him some tea, that he was curled up under the blanket in the corner of a small sofa and that Imogen was rocking him, hushing him like she might try to comfort a distraught child.

"He's dead, Immy. I found him dead. What if I . . . what if I could have done something? If I'd found him sooner."

But already Sid was starting to realise that there was more to this than Morgan suddenly dropping dead. The whispered conversations between the officers and the paramedic, the way the paramedic had not even taken time to examine the dead man. Then the other police cars arriving and the sound of Imogen agreeing that she would check with her boss, but she was sure the police could use the conference room until they got a mobile incident room sorted out. And looking at the clock on the wall and realising that time had passed and that he had finished several cups of tea and that he now urgently needed to pee. And crossing to the toilets, seeing the scientific support van arriving and realising that meant CSI and that meant that he was right and something more than a sudden death had taken place.

When he left the bathroom, Imogen was waiting for him in the lobby. She didn't ask if he was okay, just took him by the arm and settled him back on the sofa.

"They're going to get a detective to come to talk to you," she said. "And then they're going to arrange for you to have a lift home. Or I can take you if you like?"

"A detective? Immy, what's going on?" He felt he knew but his mind could not quite support that knowledge.

She hesitated as though not sure how to tell him. "They're saying it's a suspicious death, Sid. They think maybe someone killed him."

CHAPTER 2

Seth Harding was on duty as the crime scene manager that day and he stood in the office doorway studying the scene and waiting for the rest of his team to arrive. Morgan Springfield was seated in an office chair and his hands were resting on the table in a very odd and unnatural position. In Seth's experience, death did not creep up on people so gently that they had no reaction to it. Even when people died in their sleep the body tended to spasm and move and slump, and none of those things had happened to Morgan Springfield.

The paramedic who'd been on scene earlier had immediately noted that the dead man seemed to have been tied to the chair. He had also noted that life was long extinct, a fact confirmed by the police surgeon half an hour before Seth had arrived. Closer inspection had revealed that a cord had been passed across the man's chest, beneath his arms and tied around the back of his chair so that he could not slide out of place. You had to get up close to notice that, Seth allowed, and evidently Sid Patterson, who had found the body, had not gone close enough to the dead man that this was obvious. Whatever the cause of death, Seth thought, this positioning was definitely not natural. A second, narrow cord had been passed just beneath the chin to keep the head in place.

The paramedic had reported this to the police officer who had arrived at the same time, and the police officer had called it in as a definitely suspicious death. Seth had come over to deal with the preliminaries and assess what kind of team he would need on this — and, more pertinently, what kind of team could be spared.

By the time DI Mike Croft arrived with Detective Sergeant Jude Burnett, Seth was standing on the doorstep, his bony fingers wrapped around a mug of very welcome coffee. It was a cold morning, chilly even for late November and as he got older and his first grey hairs established themselves, Seth was aware that his body noticed the damp and cold a good deal more. He had no wish to start examining the scene alone, only to have to break off and brief his team. Better that they divided tasks at the outset. In the meantime, he had established a common-approach pathway, defined by metal plates, and taken some contextual photographs and video, something the investigative team could get to grips with straightaway. He was glad to see DI Croft. Seth had a liking for the man and for his sergeant, finding them both straightforward and easy to deal with. Mike would want to hit the ground running, he guessed.

"Definitely murder then," Mike commented after they'd said their hellos.

Seth nodded. "Can't guess at cause of death — the pathologist will have to work that one out or we might be able to see more clearly when we move the body. It's not immediately obvious from what you can see first off, I can tell you that. But it's a strange one. The body is posed, he's been tied in place like whoever left him wanted him to be kept in position." The victim had, Seth estimated, been dead at least eight hours — rigor was starting but not yet established. Body temp had been taken but he wasn't certain how helpful it would be in calculating time of death. Sid Patterson had told the police officers that the heating was usually switched off by the last person to leave and that it was switched on by an automatic timer at six thirty a.m. But if his boss hadn't left, the heating would have stayed on and Seth had noted how close and stuffy the small office was. It was a fact likely to skew any calculations based on the cooling of the victim's body.

He led them inside and opened the office door.

"Mr Morgan Springfield, found by a work colleague just before eight this morning. He owns this place, apparently. Last seen by the same colleague, Mr Sidney Patterson, just after six last evening. Mr Patterson told the first officer attending, Constable Pick, that at that point his boss was packing papers into his briefcase and preparing to leave. The briefcase doesn't seem to be here, but I've not looked further than the office, so . . ."

"You managed to find the kitchen though." Jude grinned at him, gesturing to the mug in his hand.

Seth smiled back. "As you well know, DS Burnett," he told her with mock pomposity, "the kitchen here is also off limits, being included in the definition of possible crime scene. Actually, the nice people in the next unit along made it for me. Sid Patterson is waiting for you there. He's pretty shaken up. The receptionist, Imogen Tandy, is looking after him but I think he'd really welcome the chance to go home."

"No other employees here?"

"No, apparently there are only three other employees who work onsite here, the rest are either freelance or based at a workshop just outside of Norwich. Constable Pick called them straight after he reported what he'd found, just to make sure they didn't turn up."

"Did he tell them what had happened?"

Seth shook his head. "Just that there's been a sudden death. Mr Patterson hadn't got close enough to the body to realise anything other than his boss being dead and Constable Pick has told him he'll have to speak to you before he tells anyone anything more, but I know the other staff are concerned and they've called him. He's having a hard time keeping all this to himself. Pick's out there somewhere—" Seth indicated the car park — "talking to the security guys and trying to fix a place to set up the incident room. Constable Frazer was with him but he's been called away. Not a lot for him to do until my lot get done with the scene and as you can see, they've not turned up yet. Two major RTIs this morning, so there've been holdups. I think that's where Frazer was headed to."

As Seth was speaking, a van pulled up into the car park. The rest of his team were finally arriving. "Good," he said. "Now we can get on with this properly."

* * *

Seth went outside to help organise equipment and Mike glanced once more at the body. Mike guessed that Morgan Springfield would perhaps have been in his mid-forties. His close-cropped hair was still pure black. With not a streak of grey in sight. He was lean and muscular, with the appearance of a man who tried to stay in shape. Whoever killed him must have either been a lot stronger than his victim or relied on the element of surprise — this tall, solidly built black man would not have been an easy target.

So, either someone known to the dead man or someone who carried no sense of threat. But then, who actually expected to be murdered in their own office? Do people really take the time to assess everyone coming through the door as a potential murderer?

"If you didn't look too closely, I suppose you might assume natural causes," he said to Jude. "The way he's sitting looks odd, though, even from here."

"It does, but probably immediately odder to those of us conditioned to look for the odd. Not many people encounter sudden death and even fewer a suspicious one. Shock is going to make anyone less observant. Boss, how about you stay here so you can catch Seth's briefing and look at the material he's already gathered for us. I'll go next door and talk to the poor guy that found the body. No sense both of us getting under the CSIs' feet."

Mike nodded, confident that Jude could take care of anything that came up. "I'll come and find you when the CSIs have got themselves sorted out."

Mike took up a position at the end of the short hallway while Seth and the team erected a small tent with work tables in the car park and ferried their equipment into it, laying everything out on the tables in some order that escaped him. He'd have offered to help, but knew he'd just be a hindrance, bound to put something in the wrong place. Finally, Seth beckoned for him to join them. On a laptop screen were images he had taken of the scene on his arrival. He scrolled through them slowly.

"At first sight, this could just about have passed as a sudden death—" he glanced up at Mike and his team — "which is what the man who found the body initially thought. He called emergency services and the call handler decided they should send out a paramedic, just on the off-chance, and the paramedics arrived around the same time as a vehicle patrol. That was at about eight thirty this morning. It became obvious to both that this was not a natural death."

He zoomed into the image of Morgan Springfield. "As you can see, there is a cord at the neck, holding the head against the headrest. A second cord beneath the arms tying him into his chair. The hands seem to have been placed on the table, presumably post-mortem."

Again, he zoomed in. Mike and the three CSIs all leaned in for a better look.

"It's an odd way to position the hands," Benny Zahn said.

Mike peered at the image. The dead man's hands were flat on the table and Benny was right — it did look very odd.

"Kyle, you're first in, stills and video and 3D-mapping. Benny, the other offices look undisturbed but do a quick scan for anything untoward."

"Could you take some photographs for me?" Mike asked Benny. "Then I can show them to the witness that found the body. DS Burnett will probably have finished with him by now, so if he can have a quick look to see if anything's been moved or taken that would be helpful before we get him off home."

"Sure." Benny nodded.

"Sheila, you'll be recording evidence and providing backup for Benny with the fingerprinting."

Sheila Ferris, Mike remembered, was the newest member of the team. She looked very young and just a little nervous.

He watched as they moved off, each with their assigned task. His own, just now, restricted to hanging around until he could enter the scene and take a proper look at the body. Left alone, he took another flick through the images on the laptop. Both hands rested on the table, the position deliberate and unnatural. It was as though the victim had been told to place his hands where they could be seen, or the killer wanted to convey something specific. To Mike's eye, it conveyed a sense of helplessness, of forced compliance. Or was that just his imagination?

He zoomed out and looked again at the body in its entirety. The view from the doorway showed the man seated, his lower torso and legs hidden by the desk. Seth had taken more images from the designated pathway and these showed his right side. The desk was not central to the room, with the left-hand side as Mike looked at it pushed up against the wall, though it seemed to be at a slight angle, rather than parallel to the wall itself. The desktop was remarkably clear. A low, wooden filing cabinet, in the corner behind the seat, was set with stacked wire baskets, and Mike could see a couple of files in the topmost one and various bits of stationery in a rack in the space beside them. On the desk was a lamp with a flexible neck, and a pen. That was all. The bareness of the surface struck Mike as strange, as did those items that remained.

Springfield had last been seen packing paperwork into his briefcase, an item that now seemed to be missing. Would the pen have also gone into the briefcase? If so, did that suggest that he'd been interrupted very soon after Sid Patterson had bid him goodnight?

Mike zoomed in on the pen. It was blue with a silver clip and a silver band around the middle. It looked like a fountain pen, so perhaps a preferred writing instrument, something more personal than a random Biro.

He studied Morgan Springfield's face next. His dark skin made it hard to define the congested flush that might suggest asphyxia, but Mike could discern no sign of swelling. The eyes did not bulge, the mouth was slack but almost closed, the tongue tucked inside the mouth where it should be, and not protruding. No, the cord around his neck was most likely just to keep the body in place and not the instrument of murder.

Looking at the pictures Seth had taken of the body side on, he noted the flatness of the feet placed on the floor, knees set square, the whole body arranged neatly and tidily, and then set in place with an oddly disturbing deliberation.

His perusal was interrupted by the return of Benny with the shots he'd taken of the other rooms. A second office, a storeroom, a small kitchen. Benny set about downloading these onto a tablet that Mike could take with him into the neighbouring business to show to Sidney Patterson.

"Looks strange, doesn't it?" Benny commented. "Kind of precise. Sculptural."

Mike nodded. It reminded him of something but he couldn't quite place it. *Don't push too hard*, he told himself. The memory or the connection . . . if there was one, would come to him.

* * *

DS Jude Burnett came over to Mike as soon as he came into the lobby. This was a bigger operation than Springfield's set-up, Mike noted, with a proper reception area and a very proper-looking receptionist.

Sid Patterson was visible, seated in a small side room and talking to a young man. The witness was deathly pale. "How's he doing?" he asked.

"I got one of the first aiders from the warehouse at the end to have a chat to him," Jude replied. "I've been trying to persuade him to go get checked out at the hospital — he's clearly in shock — but he just wants to go home. I've done with him now, so I think we should get a lift organised for him."

Mike nodded. "Just a couple of things I want to ask before we let him go. Where does he live?"

"He's in Norwich, just off the Aylsham Road, so it's only fifteen minutes or so away. I'll get on to it now. See if you can get him to change his mind about seeing a doctor. We're getting a mobile incident room set up. We've been promised it for later this morning or maybe early afternoon. Constable Pick thought it could go on the grass at the side of the car park so it doesn't interfere with the businesses too much. The crime scene being at one end of the row makes the logistics a bit easier anyway. You want me to call headquarters and start getting a team in place?"

Mike told her to go ahead, knowing she was perfectly capable of doing that without his supervision, and then crossed to the side room where Sid Patterson was waiting. Close up, he looked paler still. The young man who'd been looking after Sid excused himself, but Mike noted that he hung around in the lobby, glancing anxiously through the glass panel in the office door.

"Was Mr Springfield a friend as well as a colleague?" Mike asked gently.

Sid paused and then nodded. "We moved here to start this business just over eight years ago, though we'd worked together before that on different projects and — been friends since university — but in the last few months . . . well, it was becoming more than that. We'd started talking about finding a place together. The only thing holding us back was family. My family. They don't really know and they—" He broke off, stared down at his shoes.

How old was he? Mike wondered. Late-thirties at least, he'd have guessed, though right now the poor man was looking twice that. And his family didn't know he was gay?

"But you weren't seeing one another every night?" he asked.

"That's the thing." Sid's voice was so quiet Mike had to lean in to hear him. "I was visiting my parents. My sister had come over for a few days and I wanted to see her and the kids. Tuesday is . . . well, it's my day for visiting my parents anyway. It's got to be a sort of routine, I suppose. I wanted to spend time with Harriet and the kids with no pressure one last time before I told everyone about me and Morgan. I knew what it would be like after."

"So, you never saw him on Tuesday evenings," Mike said.

"No."

"And who might know that? That Mr Springfield was likely to be alone on a Tuesday night?"

Sid looked baffled. "I really don't know. Anyone might."

"And the time you left the office — was that the usual time?"

Sid Patterson nodded. "I told all this to the other detective."

He sounded, Mike thought, utterly defeated and weary beyond words.

"Detective Sergeant Burnett is arranging for you to be given a lift home. Is there anyone we can call to come and be with you?"

"I don't know. I can call a friend or something, I suppose. There are friends who knew about us."

Mike nodded. "Mr Patterson, can I just show you some pictures before you go?" He saw the look of alarm on Patterson's face and added hastily, "Not of Mr Springfield. Just of the other office and the kitchen. I just wanted to check if it looked as though anything might be missing."

Sid Patterson nodded.

Mike handed him the tablet and helped him to scroll through the pictures. It seemed to be taking all of the man's resources to hold the tablet steady.

"It all looks normal," he said.

Mike thanked him before asking, "Did Mr Springfield use a fountain pen? A blue pen with a silver band?"

Patterson looked confused and Mike realised it must have sounded like an odd question.

"Yes," he said. "It was a vintage pen he picked up in an antique shop when we were out one day. He liked to have old things that he could still use. His briefcase is vintage as well. Was the pen in the briefcase? I don't quite understand."

"The briefcase doesn't seem to be in the office, but the pen was on the desk, which is why I noticed it."

He could see the cogs whirring in Sid Patterson's head. "So whoever killed Morgan took his briefcase," he said slowly. "That's what you think?"

"We think it's possible. The papers you saw him packing into his briefcase — do you know what they were?"

"Um . . . end-of-month accounts and invoices, I think. VAT stuff probably — he likes to keep on top of things and he says that Tuesdays are good days to do the boring stuff because I'm not going to be there anyway."

Mike nodded again, noting the use of the present tense. Morgan Springfield was not yet dead and gone in Sid Patterson's mind, despite the shock of finding him lifeless.

"And the pen was on the desk? No, that's not like him. First thing he does is put the pen away. There's a little pocket with pen loops at the front of his case. Once the pen is in the briefcase, that's like saying work has really finished for the day. At the office, anyway. What was it still doing on the desk?"

What indeed, Mike thought. Was it relevant? Probably not.

The first aider knocked on the door and told Mike that the car had arrived to take Sid home. Taking charge, he helped the trembling man to his feet and led him out into the lobby. Mike made no objection but something was bothering him now. He told himself that everyone reacted differently to shock and grief, and to finding themselves in frightening and disturbing situations, but, given that Sid

Patterson and Morgan Springfield were an item, albeit a closeted one, it seemed odd that on finding the man he loved having apparently died suddenly that he had not gone to him. Touched him, felt for a pulse, tried to ascertain that he was definitely deceased. Not to have done so struck Mike as distinctly strange.

"Anything useful?"

Mike shook his head. "Jude, if you saw someone you loved dead, what would your first instinct be?"

She smiled. "You caught that too. Of course you did. He says he just stood in the doorway, that he realised immediately that Morgan Springfield was dead and all he could think of doing was dialling the nines. All of that could be perfectly true. Like I said before, panic and shock do strange things to people."

Mike nodded agreement, but it still bothered him as he watched Sid Patterson get in the car. If Mike had seen Maria or John or any other member of what he considered his extended family looking hurt or worse, wild horses would not have kept him from going to them, even had he been convinced there was nothing useful he could do.

Or was he being totally unfair. Sid Patterson was undoubtedly in shock. There was no denying the pain the man was feeling. Mike doubted anyone could feign that level of deep and aching distress.

CHAPTER 3

This morning, DI John Tynan, retired, was feeling his age. He liked bright November mornings and particularly appreciated this one, following on as it had from nearly three weeks of steady rain. He was out in the garden doing some general tidying and quite grateful that current environmental advice was to leave seedheads and dead flowers standing over winter. He had come to like their sculptural form on frosty mornings — and anything that saved his knees, these days, was welcome. Although it was chilly, he had taken a chair out into the garden, a straight-backed dining chair that he kept in the little conservatory behind the kitchen, and set it down on the brick path to enjoy his coffee. Today, John decided, was quite a contented day. He would be going over to see Mike and Maria as he always did on a Wednesday evening — having dinner with them, good conversation and the company of friends he valued probably above anybody else. And, in the meantime, here he was at ten thirty a.m., enjoying a quiet coffee in his slightly overgrown little garden and thinking about what he might plant next spring. Life, he reflected, was actually pretty good.

His thoughts were interrupted by the ringing of the telephone. Not many people phoned a landline these days, and the sound was faint, the phone being in the hallway at the front of the house. Somewhat reluctantly, John got to his feet, assuming that he would get to the telephone and discover that it was somebody trying to sell him something or persuade him to claim on for an accident he had never had in the first place. He half hoped that the ringing would stop before he got there and he could get back to his coffee in his garden.

It didn't. Instead it took on an insistent tone. John lifted the receiver — he had long since got out of the habit of announcing who he was and settled for a simple, "Good morning."

The voice on the phone sounded vaguely familiar as the woman asked, "Is that John Tynan?"

"It is," he said cautiously.

"Ah, good. I need to speak to you." She sounded brusque, anxious and irritated.

"And who are you?"

There was a small hesitation before she said, "My name is Johanna Pearson. I believe we met only once, but your . . . associate, Inspector Croft, will remember me better I've no doubt."

John frowned, the name was certainly familiar and if he concentrated he called to mind a tall, austere woman Mike had arrested for killing her husband. That had been about a decade ago, hadn't it? John had become tangentially involved and met the woman on a couple of occasions.

He was about to ask her how she had got his number, but then realised it was a stupid question — when he had first retired he had like most former and serving police officers been ex-directory, but as the years passed and he had changed the company he got his phone services from, it had seemed less important. She could have found him easily enough, his number at least. The remoteness of his little cottage made it harder for people to actually get to him.

"My probation officer says we can meet in her offices if it makes that more comfortable for you, but I do have to see you. I want to report a crime."

19

"Then phone the local police," John told her.

"That's the thing — it hasn't happened yet, or at least I don't think it has. Or at least . . . Look, I'm not sure what's going on, but I know it could be serious and I've spoken to my probation officer, and she agrees with me, and if you'd like to speak to her, she's here. But I'm asking you to meet me. I would ask Inspector Croft but I can't think he would take me seriously, whereas perhaps you might, *and* you might be able to persuade him that I'm not completely off my rocker."

"How long have you been out of jail?"

"I was released on licence three months ago. Hence the probation officer. Don't worry, I won't be doing anything else — I killed that husband of mine because he deserved it. I have no intention of killing anybody else."

"I'd like to speak to your probation officer," John said.

There was a small shuffling sound on the phone and then he was speaking to another woman who introduced herself as Liz Jenna, a name John recognised. The voice was familiar as well. She had not been part of the probation team when he had been a serving police officer — she was far too young for that and John reflected that she'd probably have been in nursery school when he retired — but the various committees he had served on since, concerned with youth crime and policing practices meant that they had met on a few occasions.

"Good morning, John," Liz said. "I'm sorry to ambush you like this, but I really do think you should meet with Johanna and hear what she has to say. It may be nothing, but if it does turn out to be important then . . ."

She left her next statement hanging, but the implication was that Joanna had something important to say that might prevent a crime and if John didn't act, how would he feel.

"All right, Liz, set up a meeting. It will probably have to be next week. I'm free Monday and Tuesday, or I could perhaps manage this Friday morning if you think it can't wait that long."

The truth was he had nothing on for the rest of the week, apart from dinner with Mike and Maria, but he felt the need to take back a little bit of control after, as Liz put it, being ambushed by a woman he had encountered but did not know. He felt the need also for time to refresh his memory before any meeting and to talk to Mike.

He could hear a brief exchange as Liz spoke to Johanna. "Friday at nine," Liz said. "Earlier if you can manage it. I'm busy from ten with things I can't reschedule."

In the end they settled for eight thirty. "Can you give me any idea what this is about?" John asked.

"It's about one of Johanna's children," Liz told him. "When she was sent to prison the family was split up, going into foster care and so on. The younger ones seem to have coped quite well but one of the older boys, well, we think he's got mixed up with something. Look, it's quite complicated and I'm already late for my next meeting, so see you on Friday, okay?"

She ended the call, so John supposed it would have to be okay.

"Now what's all that about," he wondered aloud as he went into the kitchen to make himself some fresh coffee now his original mug had gone cold. Then he settled at his computer to remind himself just what Johanna Pearson had done and to see what else he could find out about the family and the background to the case.

CHAPTER 4

Mike crouched beside the body of Morgan Springfield, examining the knots on the cords that bound him to the chair. So far as he could see there was nothing particularly unusual about them — simple, utilitarian double knots, designed to keep an already dead or unconscious individual in place, not to restrain them so that the murder could occur.

He straightened up, watching as the CSI under Seth's supervision cut the cord a few inches away from the knot, leaving that in place so it could be examined properly later on. The cord was carefully removed, bagged and tagged.

"There is blood on the chair headrest," Seth commented. "And what looks like a messy and irregular puncture wound to the back of the neck."

Mike moved around to where he could see. Seth was right — dried blood on the neck, staining the collar of the shirt and more on the headrest where it had soaked into the fabric. It was quite hard to make out as the chair itself was almost black.

"Stabbed in the back of the neck?" Mike said.

"At first sight it looks that way, which could have severed the spinal cord. My initial impression is that they had trouble extracting the weapon from the wound, hence the irregularity." He indicated to the CSI that they should cut the second cord. This was done and the body slumped forward slightly. Mike looked but there seemed to be no other injury to the back.

"Let's get him moved before rigor fully sets," Seth said. "The warmth of the room probably delayed it a little, but it's got going now so we want him out of here."

Mike nodded and retreated along the designated pathway back into the hall. Jude had been watching from the doorway. "Not a lot more we can do here," she said. "I've just had word that the mobile unit's on its way. Though it will probably be early afternoon by the time it gets here. I suggested Constable Pick gets himself some lunch and then settles in for the duration, and that we get back to HQ to brief the team. Babbages, the architect next door, said Pick can stop there so he's on hand, and the warehouse at the end of the row has a canteen and they say he's welcome to get lunch there, or there's a nice little takeaway place round the corner. He seems to be getting on very well with Imogen, the receptionist, so I don't think he'll find it any hardship."

"She's very pretty, and she seems friendly," Mike commented. "And it is time Pick started dating again."

"Dating." Jude rolled her eyes. "How old are you? Does anyone *date* anymore?"

"Too old," Mike told her. "And I wouldn't know, I gave all that up some time ago. I don't think Maria would approve."

Jude laughed. "You'd be very stupid if you tried. You matched far above your paygrade when you married her."

"I'm fully aware of that. I'm still just hoping she doesn't realise."

They were standing outside now, enjoying the unexpected sunshine even though there was no warmth in it. Constable Pick could be seen walking across the car park with a cup of takeaway coffee and a small brown carrier bag. Mike could smell bacon and realised that he was hungry and — glancing at his watch — that it was almost lunchtime.

One last check-in with Seth and another with Pick to make sure he had everything he needed, and he and Jude were off.

"Well, it's an odd one." Jude frowned. "Seth said there was a wound on the back of the neck?"

"Something narrow from the look of it, probably severed the spinal cord. But that's all we could tell."

"They've managed to fit the post-mortem in early tomorrow morning," Jude told him. "Hopefully that will tell us a little more. I spoke at length to Sid Patterson, but he couldn't think of any enemies and I had a chat to the staff next door and everybody seems to have liked Morgan Springfield. They described him as a cheerful and friendly type, so we'll have to do a fair amount of digging, I think."

"When you were talking to Sid Patterson, did you realise that they had become a couple?"

"Not at first, but it soon became obvious that his feelings for Springfield were more than for just a work colleague or even a good friend. I knew you'd be asking the question so I didn't push it; I was trying to find out as much as I could about Springfield's contacts, movements in the last few days, all the practical stuff. On the face of it, nothing out of the ordinary, but I have a list of friends and family we can check now to see if something turns up. No parents or siblings though. He was an only child. The father's dead, the mother moved when Mr Springfield went to university and Sid doesn't seem to know where she's living. He reckons they didn't even exchange Christmas cards."

Mike nodded, conscious as he often was that they made an effective double act. Jude knew how he worked and they had come to trust one another over the past few years.

"I suggest we get back to the office, start assembling the team," he said. "That way by the time the mobile incident room arrives we'll be ready. I'd like to get statements from the neighbouring units, starting with anyone on the early shift though," he glanced at his watch, "we might be getting too late in the day for that, if they finish their shifts at two."

24

"I'll give Evan Pick a call and he can make a start on that," Jude said.

He fell silent while she got on with that, thinking about who he wanted immediately and who else might need to be brought on board. Jude had finished with her call to Pick so Mike said, "Get hold of DS Jacobs — ask him to get over to the scene before Seth and his team leave."

She nodded. "Good idea, boss. Pick tells me he arrived on scene just after we left."

"You already called him, didn't you?"

"Thought you might want him to liaise with the CSI team."

"You after my job?"

"Eventually. I can wait. I've got Terry Gleeson on standby as the loggist. I've asked Seth to send anything they've got straight to him so he can make a start. He's also doing background on the victim and on Sid Patterson, starting with the public-domain stuff, ready for the afternoon briefing."

"You are definitely after my job." DS Gleeson was a good choice. He had an eye for detail and a memory for ephemera that had stood Mike's investigations in good stead before. DS Amit Jacobs could read a scene as well as any CSI and, more to the point, interpret what he saw in a way that could convince the average copper he was on to something. As a PoLSA-trained search adviser, he was also invaluable in directing less experienced officers, doing so with far more grace and care than many Mike had worked with.

He frowned, that sense that he'd seen something like this before nagging at him though the memory stubbornly refused to coalesce. "We'll need to put out a press statement before the evening news," he said. "I'll brief the press office. Fortunately, Springfield's unit was at the end of the row so we can cordon that section of car park but we're still going to need a barrier at the end of the street — and soon, before the media get wind or Pick will be fighting them off." He glanced at her. "Don't tell me, already in hand."

"Hopefully, being organised as we speak. I've got Pick arranging that. He suggested we get a couple of the probationers involved, reckons it will be good experience for them." She grinned at him. "What would you do without me."

"Oh," he said. "I've definitely trained you up well. So, thoughts. Anything that immediately comes to mind?"

"That this is a cold killing," she said. "And the staging took time. It was precise and calm. There's no passion here, no anger. I'd go as far as to say it was almost businesslike. I can't believe it's the first time he's done it."

"Definitely he? A woman might have got close enough to inflict that wound. Might be capable of posing the body. It would take some degree of physical strength, but if he was already seated when they killed him—"

"True, but my money's on it being a man. It looks too . . ."

He waited while she sought the right word.

"Picky, fussy, fastidious."

He laughed. "Nice word. And women can't be fastidious?"

She thumped him on the arm.

"And now assault on a senior officer."

"You had it coming. No, a woman could have done it. Not restrained him, perhaps. Morgan Springfield was a powerfully built man, big but not fat — he'd have fought back if he'd seen what was coming. And there might be defence wounds somewhere on the body, bruising that won't be possible to see until the post-mortem, but from initial observations I'd say he'd either not suspected anything until it was too late or it happened too fast for him to react. And that wound to the neck — it suggests his killer knew what they were about. Like I said, it's cold, passionless, economical. Like they just wanted to do what was absolutely necessary to obtain a body. Like the purpose . . . the satisfaction was in what came after, not so much in the taking of the man's life."

That, Mike thought, was a chilling assessment, though it chimed with his own thoughts.

"All random speculation, of course," she went on. "But you did ask me what I thought."

"And I value that," Mike told her. "Did Pick say anything? Tell you what his impressions were when he first saw the body?" Constable Pick was a far less experienced officer, but Mike knew him to be observant and thoughtful — except when he was playing darts, then he was all killer instinct. Mike encouraged his team to think for themselves and to share those thoughts, however fanciful. He believed very firmly that if the team was used to kicking ideas around — challenging them, discarding, selecting — then there was less likelihood that an investigation would develop tunnel vision.

"He said he looked like he was waiting for someone," Jude said. "Like someone had just knocked on his door and he'd looked up, ready to tell them to come in."

It was an interesting observation, Mike thought. He cast his mind back to when he'd first looked at the body through the window in the office door and, yes, he could see what Pick meant. Morgan Springfield seemed to be looking straight at him. Mike frowned. He remembered that the desk itself wasn't facing the door, not directly. It was positioned towards the left-hand side of the office space, as viewed from the doorway, so that whoever was seated at the desk could see the calendar and the various clipboards and charts hung on the wall but would have to look slightly to the side to be looking directly at the door. The charts seemed to detail the various jobs that were in process, and, presumably, at different stages of completion. They hadn't made much sense to Mike — though he'd not made a thorough examination — but he guessed they'd been set up so that someone who knew what he was looking at could make an instant assessment of work in progress.

But Morgan Springfield hadn't been looking at the charts on the wall, he'd been looking straight at the door.

Mike recalled that the desk had not stood parallel to the wall. "They angled his desk and his chair," he said as they pulled into the car park at headquarters at Wymondham that they shared with the fire service. Mike hadn't liked the brick-and-glass edifice the first time he'd seen it and he'd had no reason to change his opinion since.

"So," he added as he got out of the car. "He'd be looking straight at whoever came to the door first."

"Perhaps his killer wanted everything to look normal at first," Jude suggested.

"Normal would have been facing the wall, turning his head to see who had knocked on the door, opened it or whatever. No, the killer wanted whoever found him to see his face, full on, to get the full impact of his set-up," Mike said. Somehow that thought chilled him more than the rest of the morning's events had already done. It was such a precise move, so fastidious, as Jude had said, and whoever had done it would have had to have stood by the door, looked back at the body, maybe repositioned the victim to get the position exactly right. He felt, suddenly, as though his belly was full of ice.

CHAPTER 5

By the time John arrived that evening, Mike was home and helping out in the kitchen. John took it upon himself to set the table and open the wine he had brought. Mike and Maria's house was a second home for him and he knew they felt the same about his little cottage.

Mike and Maria lived in a particularly ugly, particularly symmetrical house of brick and flint that squatted low in a very beautiful garden. It had been the garden that Maria had initially fallen for and then, when she'd got into the house itself, the bright airy rooms had convinced her. It might not be pretty, but it was a friendly house, the central hallway lit by a stained-glass window Maria had had commissioned for above the door that cast yellow and green and blue onto the worn flagstones. Only two rooms led off, one on either side. A living room with a massive French stove enamelled in teal, that the previous owners had restored, was on one side of the hall and on the other a big farmhouse kitchen, with a scrubbed pine table that was used for dining. This was set close beside the deep-silled window. In summer, when the kitchen window was wide open, the scent of lavender, pinks and roses drifted in. On this wintry November evening, the scent of herbs mingled with the aroma of fresh bread, not long from the oven, that Maria handed to John to put on the table. Maria had discovered baking during lockdown and most Wednesdays produced something that smelled wonderful and tasted even better.

"So, you've had a busy day," he said as Mike took his place at the table beside Maria. John poured the wine. "I heard on the radio driving over that the victim is Morgan Springfield?"

Mike nodded. "Did you know him?"

"No, I knew of him. I know Imogen, the receptionist from the company next door. Her mother and Grace were friends; they worked together for a while."

Grace had been John's late wife. It was, he thought, still painful to talk about her or, more particularly, to mention her in casual conversation, even now. "Imogen's mum is younger than Grace was, of course, but I've known Imogen since she was a little girl and I still see her parents from time to time. Morgan Springfield came up in conversation on a couple of occasions. Imogen really liked him."

Mike nodded. "It seems that everyone did."

"Apart from whoever killed him, presumably," Maria commented.

"We don't know for certain that the killer had an opinion."

John looked keenly at his friend. "Oh," he said. "And what leads you to that conclusion?"

"Probably nothing, I'm probably just speculating. No, that's not right. It's the way the body was posed, the deliberateness of it. Most people are killed by people they know and who know them. Nine times out of ten it's a spur-of-the-moment thing. It's messy and sudden and often instantly regretted. This wasn't one of those times."

John waited to see if Mike would say more but he returned to his meal, eating ravenously as though he'd missed lunch and was making up. Knowing Mike, that was probably the case. He'd most likely tell him more later, John thought, as much as he felt he could, anyway. It was years since John had been a serving officer, but the job still linked them and Mike knew that whatever he said would go no further. John was happy to know he had often been of help, albeit informally.

His comment on the act of killing often being an impulsive one made him think of Johanna Pearson. "I had an odd phone call today," he said. "It was from Johanna Pearson. You remember her?"

"It would be hard to forget." It was Maria who replied first. Mike had simply raised an eyebrow, registering surprise. "Once met never forgotten. Is she still inside?"

"No, she's out on licence — she was calling from her probation officer's. I've agreed to meet with her early on Friday morning."

"And why is that?" Mike reached for his glass.

"She thinks her eldest son might be mixing with the wrong crowd and heading for serious trouble. She implied that some sort of criminal activity was in the offing and that she had information." John frowned. "I think she'd have liked to meet sooner but I'm afraid she caught me in a cussed mood, so I said I was busy until then."

"She's lucky you agreed at all," Maria said. "Why did you? You don't owe the woman anything."

John shrugged. "I know, I suppose a little bit of me feels responsible. I inadvertently brought her the evidence of her husband's guilt, didn't I? She'd probably have gone on believing in his innocence and not bashed his brains out in front of witnesses, the way she did."

Police witnesses, John remembered, who had come to deal with a disturbance at the Pearson home, one of many that had occurred over weeks that summer a decade ago.

"It was hardly your fault," Maria commented. "You were merely doing a good deed."

"And you know what the proverb is about good deeds," Mike said provocatively. "How they never go unpunished." He shook his head and John knew he was remembering that strange episode and the even stranger man Johanna had killed. Eric Pearson, a primary school teacher, had been accused of inappropriate behaviour with a group of his young students.

They'd claimed he had taken improper photographs of them, an accusation Pearson had strenuously denied — a denial his wife had believed. Pearson had claimed that he was being harassed and set up because he'd had evidence in the shape of a journal — that the police had thus far ignored, according to Pearson — implicating various high-profile individuals in a paedophile ring centred on several children's homes. These individuals had not been arrested or charged or even investigated, and certainly not been involved in the court cases that had been ongoing. Pearson had averred that the police had been remiss, negligent, even. That they had been afraid to challenge individuals who had power and influence, and whom Eric Pearson had claimed he had evidence against. He'd claimed — no, really believed — that he'd been persecuted because he'd posed a genuine threat to those he'd accused.

It had been an agonising situation for so many, John recalled, and he remembered the overwhelming feeling that neither the police nor the courts had been truly prepared for the scale of the accusations or the evidence in the cases that had actually made it to prosecution. Eric Pearson's accusations had been made at a time when such cases were also being brought in the Midlands and in Northern Ireland, and he suspected that Eric Pearson and his so-called evidence must have felt like a step into overwhelm. And the behaviour of Pearson himself had been guaranteed to alienate any who might have been sympathetic. Forced out of their own community, Pearson and his family had moved from place to place, leaving trouble and bad feeling in their wake until that final house, in that quiet little close that had been anything but after the Pearsons arrived.

"He was a very unpleasant man," Mike said. "From what I remember he put the locals' backs up when he started photographing their kids."

John nodded. "And then someone realised who he was and what he'd been accused of and all hell broke loose." John doubted anyone would remember who had thrown the first stone and broken the first of the Pearsons' windows, but the local police would have vivid memories of the weeks that followed and John's totally innocent errand that brought such dreadful consequences about.

Eric Pearson's brother had died. There'd been boxes of family photographs and general knickknacks that had been due to go to Eric. John had been asked by a mutual friend if he'd give the nephew a lift to deliver said boxes and, though John had heard all about Eric Pearson's escapades, he had agreed. Perhaps, he admitted to himself, he had been curious about the man who was causing such determined mayhem. Curiosity, John acknowledged, could be a terrible thing. He'd had no idea that in among the innocent possessions had been evidence of Eric Pearson's own guilt.

"So," he said, shifting his focus from the old case to the new. "What bothers you about this particular murder. Apart from there being a dead man, of course."

Mike laughed. "Apart from that."

John helped Maria clear the table and fetch dessert as Mike described the scene that had confronted him that morning. One advantage, he thought, of having such a sociable kitchen was that conversations didn't have to stop between courses.

"And you've no idea what's jogging your memory?" he asked. "I don't recall anything local where a man was found posed and tied to his chair. It's the sort of thing that would stick in the mind."

"I agree," Mike said. "So, I don't think it's anything as obvious as that."

Conversation ceased for a moment or two as they all considered the problem and Maria asked, "You've no idea what Johanna Pearson might be concerned about?"

John shook his head. "Only that she thinks her son might be headed for a fall and we can imagine, my dear, how possible that is, given the trauma the lad went through and the breakup of his family. Presumably he spent the rest of his childhood in care and the later part of his teens fending for himself and we both know the statistics that follow."

"There are exceptions." Maria countered this almost automatically, John thought. Time was she'd have defended the social care system against even the smallest slight, but that was before she got worn down by the constant pressure of it all. John knew that.

"Most foster carers do a good job and these days every effort is made to place kids with families, and the aftercare is better than it was."

"If by that you mean better than non-existent," John said, "then you're right, but these kids often get the rawest of deals, however much anyone tries to correct that."

Maria nodded. "It's not perfect, I'll grant you that. And it's tough for those who try to pick up the pieces."

"That's the truth," John said with feeling, knowing that one of the reasons Maria had switched to part-time working was that her job as a psychologist brought her into far too much contact with those broken by one failed system or another. She had become as burned-out as some of her clients.

"Who's the probation officer?" Mike asked.

"Liz Jenna. I know her slightly. I like her a lot."

Maria nodded. "She's one of the good ones. And the fact that she thought it was worth you speaking to Johanna Pearson is . . . worrying. Liz isn't one to act out of impulse or be railroaded by a persistent client, if she didn't feel she'd got a valid concern."

"Perhaps I should have agreed to an earlier meeting. Perhaps I should have insisted she speak to Mike," he added mischievously.

Maria laughed.

"Oh, no, you don't," Mike said. "I saw enough of the Pearson family ten years ago. I think I've got enough on my plate without that."

John left a short time later. Sometimes he stayed over at the squat little house, knowing that the spare room was always ready for him in much the way that his own, smaller guest room was prepared should it be required. Tonight, however, he wanted to be home. He recalled the state of the Pearson house, the state of siege the family had endured and the sympathy he had felt for the children. It filled him with an odd disquiet and, irrationally perhaps, he wanted to check that his own little sanctuary was safe and sound and peaceful.

He parked the car in the spot against the fence and stood for a moment listening to an owl in the spinney beyond the garden and the soft susurration of wind in the leaves. Then he went inside and stood silently on the flagstones of the hall, listening, registering every familiar creak and tick as the cottage settled for the night.

And then he locked the front door and, after a moment's hesitation, he shot the bolt home.

CHAPTER 6

Mike lay in bed unable to find a comfortable position. His body felt weary but his mind refused to shut up and let him rest. He lay listening to Maria's soft breathing. She, at least, was sleeping better these days — there had been a time when she had twitched and fidgeted and talked in her sleep — that was when she'd actually managed to settle — and woken still exhausted and emotionally drained.

In an effort to turn his thoughts from the day's events, he thought about what John had told him about Johanna Pearson. It was like John to get involved, though the woman had been interesting, he supposed, and they had all felt sorry for the children.

Mike recalled the first time he had met John Tynan. Already retired, John had come to see him about an old case. A child had disappeared under circumstances that echoed events from twenty years before, when John had been a serving officer. That first disappearance had remained unsolved and that had troubled the older man throughout his time in the force and into his retirement. John and Mike had become friends. Bonding initially, he supposed, over shared concerns, over his informal involvement in this second case and the final resolution to the original mystery, that Mike had uncovered. It had been a friendship that had grown and developed over the years and one Mike and then Maria had come to treasure.

Johanna Pearson: John had only met her once or twice from what Mike remembered, but she was the kind of woman who made an impression. She and Eric and their brood of five children had previously lived in what Mike supposed would be described as a religious commune. A group of farming families had bought land a couple of generations before, erected a small chapel in what had been a stable block and had lived life their way ever since. They called themselves the Children of Solomon, though Mike had never bothered to find out why. By the time he'd got involved with the Pearsons, they'd left the community because of the accusations made against Eric. Johanna and the children would have been welcome to stay, but the community would not countenance the behaviour Eric had been accused of. There had been a number of children in the very family-oriented set-up, Mike remembered, and, given the climate of accusation that had been prevalent at the time, he could not bring himself to blame them for shunning one of their own who had been accused of inappropriate behaviour with children in his care. The accusations might have rebounded on them. There had been absolutely nothing to suggest that the Children of Solomon had been guilty of anything apart from wanting to escape the rat race and do things their way. Those who'd lived close by regarded them as good neighbours, several of the women had belonged to the Women's Institute and every summer they'd held a fundraiser for a local charity or good cause, usually a fete of some sort on their lawn at the front of the house. Mike had gathered that they'd been simply another in a long line of small religious or philosophical communities that had fetched up in the area, East Anglia being a region given to nonconformist worship, and no one Mike's team had spoken to had had a bad word to say. They'd managed to be separate without being separatist, though he could well imagine that an allegation such as that made against Eric Pearson would have filled them with dread and might have had the locals speculating about their slightly peculiar neighbours.

As it turned out, there had never, so far as he was aware, been any ill feeling or any hint of rumour from their neighbours regarding the Children of Solomon. They had acted swiftly to remove Eric Pearson and been outspoken in their condemnation of his alleged actions. Had they stood by him, things might well have been different.

They had also been part of the local scenery and, he guessed, a valued part of the local economy for so long that only incomers looked askance at them — and, Mike could imagine, they likely soon had their attitudes corrected.

But Johanna had chosen to believe her husband when he protested his innocence. Solid evidence had been thin on the ground. The family had left, been housed in temporary accommodation and begun an eighteen-month odyssey of settling, encountering trouble, settling again, then once more encountering accusation and anger. From what Mike had seen, Eric had not been one for keeping a low profile and Johanna had been full of what she'd felt was righteous anger.

So, what was troubling her now, he wondered.

Finally feeling that he might be able to sleep, Mike turned on his side.

He awoke abruptly an hour later. The clock on the bedside table told him it was almost two in the morning. He had been dreaming, and as so often happened in his dreams his body had been hovering above the ground and floating close to the ceiling. He realised that he had been back at the murder scene. In his dream he had been peering down at the top of Morgan Springfield's head, examining the desk from above, floating across to examine the stack of filing baskets on the cabinet. And then it came to him, that random memory.

It wasn't the position of the body, Mike realised, sitting up now and staring across the darkened bedroom. It was the pen he had remembered. The pen placed close to the left hand. Was Morgan Springfield even left-handed?

The previous victim had been sinistral, Mike recalled, though the pen placed so deliberately beside the hand on an otherwise empty desk had been largely ignored in that earlier enquiry. "So?" his boss had said. "There is a pen on a desk. Big deal. People do usually have pens on their desks." The crime scene manager had remarked on it and the photographer had taken images in context but once the pen had been fingerprinted and revealed nothing out of the ordinary, it had been forgotten. In fact it had never seemed important to anyone but Mike. And, he had come to consider as time passed, the only reason it had seemed odd to him was that he was still new to this kind of investigation and in some ways still greener than cabbage. He had decided long ago that he was probably just trying too hard and seeing significance in a random object that simply wasn't there.

Maria stirred and Mike lay down again, ready to sleep now that this little mystery had been solved. He would request the files tomorrow, just to be certain there really was no significance, just to reassure and pacify that younger version of himself who had observed meaning in everything.

"What is it," Maria asked sleepily.

"Nothing, just having trouble sleeping," he told her, but she had already drifted back into slumber and he knew would not recall even asking him the question.

CHAPTER 7

Thursday morning was clear and bright with a pale-blue sky still pink at the horizon. Jude stretched and peered out of the gap between the curtains. She wasn't overlooked, living on the top floor of a low-rise block in a street that was mainly houses and, if she craned her neck, she could glimpse the rise of Mousehold Heath. Jude didn't really like sleeping in the dark, so her curtains were rarely fully closed. Beside her, Seth Harding roused and blinked sleepily.

"Hi," he said.

"Hi, yourself. Did you sleep well?"

He chuckled. "Must have done."

This was the first time he had stayed over and Jude wasn't sure if she was happy about that or if she half resented having to share her early morning with someone else. It was not a thing she'd done for five years now, not since what she thought of as her last proper relationship had gone south. Dramatically. Because of that, the relationship — if that's what it was . . . she supposed it must be? — wasn't yet in the public domain.

At least Seth was not given to drama, Jude thought. A calmer, steadier individual would be hard to find. On the calmness and steadiness scale he probably compared to her boss.

"I suppose we should get up," she said, but made no move to do so. Instead, she lay back down beside Seth and settled into the crook of his arm, deciding that, on balance, she was happy to share her early morning after all.

Later, when she came out of the shower, he told her that her phone had chimed and while he went off to have his own shower, she checked her messages. There were two from Mike.

One just said mysteriously, *It was the pen.*

What pen? Oh. She thought about the crime scene, about the tidy desk and the victim's hands laid out flat on the table top. The blue pen with its silver band beside the left.

That pen.

The second message asked her to look out an old case in the archive. *I know we can arrange for the files to be sent over,* Mike wrote, *but if you could take a quick squint, see if it's worthwhile doing.*

Will do, she texted back and then set about getting dressed.

"Were you around for the Gary Gibson murder?" she asked as they ate breakfast together. It was strange, sitting down with someone and having an actual breakfast conversation. Then, "No, you'd have still been at university then. We're going back a couple of decades, I think." Seth, at thirty-eight, was five years older than she was.

Seth frowned. "No, but the name rings a bell. Local businessman. Found in his office. I vaguely remember it from the news, but that's about all. Why?"

"Mike wants me to look at the files, particularly at the crime scene photos. He's got a bee in his bonnet about something being familiar."

Seth raised an eyebrow. "Interesting," he said. "He did seem bothered by something." He picked up his phone and did a search for Gary Gibson, then turned it so Jude could see. "Eighteen years ago," he said. "Mike would probably have been a DC or possibly a DS?"

"A DC, I'd guess. He got his promotion to DI just before he was transferred here," she said. "Landed straight into a

41

child-abduction case. That's ten years back, just a bit before I joined up." Jude had been part of a fast-track program for graduates and had joined the force just after completing her MA and realising that a deep dive into Restoration Theatre, fascinating though it was, might not immediately convince prospective employers that she was a good fit for their jobs.

Thinking back, she knew that she had on the one hand hit the ground running as a detective constable and on the other hand been completely ignorant of even the basics — or at least the basics in practice and not just the theory. She'd had to catch up fast. She supposed that at some point soon she'd have to position herself for promotion to inspector, but felt oddly reluctant to do so. Truth was, she was comfortable where she was and close to her team. And very fond of her boss.

"Did he say what was bothering him?" Seth asked, and Jude felt suddenly uncomfortable with giving him the specifics. Felt suddenly that she should not have mentioned Mike's interest, even to someone as involved as Seth was as senior CSI. She shook her head. "Only that he remembered something."

"Right, well, I'd best be off." He leaned in to kiss her and she could see that his mind was already on work, his to-do list occupying his attention. She didn't blame him; she too was shifting into work mode.

"Be interesting to compare the crime scene data from back then with what we collect today," he said. "Much of what we do as routine now was either not done or in its infancy. First officers attending weren't even routinely taught how to preserve a scene until the late nineties–early noughties. Odd to think that, isn't it?"

It was, she agreed, and moments later he had gone and she was gathering her things together ready to leave. She paused and texted Mike. *Am I looking for anything in particular?*

No, the reply came through a few minutes later. *Just get an overview. If on that basis you feel the files are worth requesting then we'll have them brought over. If I'm chasing shadows, no harm done.*

When did you ever chase shadows, Jude thought. If DI Mike Croft had a feeling that something was off, then she'd bet her flat on him being right.

* * *

Across town, Mike watched as DS Amit Jacobs compared the images on his tablet with the crime scene. Morgan Springfield's body had been removed the previous afternoon and in an hour Mike would be going to the post-mortem. Everything else was as it was, apart from the bright-blue, silver-banded fountain pen, which now resided in an evidence bag somewhere, waiting for the fingerprint officer to get to it. Mike would bet on it having been wiped clean or just have its owner's prints upon it.

"Seth thinks the killer must have come over to him when he was already sitting down," Mike said. "Killed him, tied him in place. That would have been easier than striking at a standing man and then lowering a body into the chair."

Amit nodded. "That would only really work if the killer caught him as he began to fall and that death was instantaneous. There don't appear to have been defensive wounds?"

"Not that we could see. Of course the PM might reveal something but most likely Seth is right and the man was sitting down."

Amit glanced around. "Why is there no second chair in here? Nowhere for a visitor to sit."

"Jude wondered about that," Mike said. "Sid Patterson said there was always a second chair in here, usually set against the wall over there." He pointed to a space beside the filing cabinet.

"So, if a visitor came in and wanted to sit down, either Mr Springfield would have fetched the chair and placed it, or the visitor, if they were someone familiar with the set-up, would have come over and fetched it for themselves. Either scenario would provide opportunity."

Mike nodded. "Morgan Springfield would have had his back to the visitor for a few seconds — that could have been

43

long enough for a killer to strike. Or, he brought the chair over and set it down, which would also have exposed him for long enough to have been stabbed in the back of the neck. So, where's the visitor's chair now? And why was it moved?"

"Do we know what kind of chair we're looking for?"

Mike shook his head. "I'll see if I can find out."

"CSI have printed them all anyway. It will be easier to figure out more precisely what happened once we know the angle of attack," Amit said. "After the PM."

Mike nodded. Hopefully the post-mortem would provide some useful answers.

Amit glanced again at his tablet. "So the pen was by his left hand. Was he left-handed?"

"Apparently not." Mike had confirmed that earlier in the morning. "So either the killer made a mistake, was making a particular point, or it has no relevance whatsoever. He could have just, I don't know, picked it up off the floor and set it on the desk."

He noted the appraising look that Amit cast in his direction, but he made no comment. Mike knew his interest would have been logged, filed and would be brought out for consideration later. He decided he would share the reason he had particularly noted this and told Amit about the previous case.

"It's probably nothing," Mike added.

"But best to cover all bases. Be interesting to hear what Jude thinks."

* * *

What Jude was thinking was that she really needed to bring a duster and a pack of wet wipes with her when she was sent to do a job like this. It was as well she didn't have a dust allergy.

The computer log had provided her with a shelf number and Alison Tucker, the archivist, had scanned the records, calculating how many boxes there might be. A murder case generated a great deal of material and it was likely Jude would require a bit of expert help, just to prioritise her initial review.

"You know," Alison said. "There's not so much here as you might think there should be. Only three filing boxes and a few pieces of bagged evidence. I wonder if the boxes have been split up for some reason and some of it stored elsewhere."

"Why might that be?" Jude asked.

"Well, there could be several reasons. If there was a lot of forensic stuff, that's sometimes put in specialist storage."

Jude nodded. Blood, organic materials and possible sources for DNA might well be kept elsewhere, but that still didn't account for the lack of paperwork. The enquiry dated from a time when computers were just starting to play a major role in recording and collating, but, even now, when everything was logged electronically as a matter of course, it was still far from a paperless process. Initial notes were often on paper, witness statements were noted down by hand; background information was often also paper-based, so everyone could lay hands on the relevant documents quickly. Crime scene photographs and other visual evidence — pictures of the victim, the suspects, the relatives, screen grabs from CCTV. Then there would be the media packs and press clippings and all the random detritus that any large team of people, all focused on the same concerns might create. She agreed with Alison — three boxes for a murder investigation did seem light.

"So . . ." Alison led the way along the rows of stacked shelves and Jude sneezed, then sneezed again. She reached into her pocket for a tissue.

Alison smiled sympathetically. "There's supposed to be all these fancy environmental controls, temperature, humidity and all that bunk, but nothing seems to stop the dust getting in. You do get used to it, I suppose, but my first month here it was like I had hay fever. Antihistamines help. Ah, here we are."

They had paused at the end of a row of heavily stacked shelves. Grey boxes with labels facing out, additional labels below them on the racking. Alison ran a finger along the shelf, checking the label and then cross-referencing with the boxes. "Yes," she said, sounding surprised. "Just the three."

"Could . . ." Jude sneezed again. "Sorry. Could they have got mislaid or mislabelled or mixed up somewhere else?"

"Very possible. Though if anyone asks, of course not. We *are* very careful with all data in our care. The problem is a lot of the older stuff was shipped over from other storage areas, a lot of them in local police stations, rented warehouses and the like when this purpose-built unit was set up. Some of it was in a right state. Quite a bit of it was improperly labelled, not to mention improperly kept." She paused, frowning. "But this lot isn't that old, is it." She examined the date. "Eighteen years ago. These are the original boxes by the look of it and they're in okay condition, so you'd think they'd all have arrived together and stayed together. Anyway, let's put them on the trolley and get them, and you, out of here."

Gratefully, Jude nodded. They lifted the boxes onto the wheeled trolley Alison had brought with them and headed for the exit.

A little later, Jude had washed her face and reapplied her lipstick, glad that she wasn't given to wearing much in the way of make-up. She had accepted an antihistamine from Alison and was now settled in a small side office assessing what she had. Her DI had asked her to look at the crime scene photographs first, see if his memory had been faulty or if the similarities in the crime scenes were accurate. She was glad to find that these were all collected into one place and, placing the other boxes on the floor, she set these out on the table and began to examine them.

This murder had also taken place in an office, though at first glance that seemed to be the only similarity. Skimming through the records, checking the location, she discovered that this office space was on the second floor of a six-storey block on the outskirts of Norwich. It was less tidy than Morgan Springfield's space. The bin needed emptying and the wire baskets on the top of the filing cabinets were stacked high with folders and loose sheets of paper.

A table off to one side had a kettle, mugs and the makings for tea and coffee set on a tray. Beside that, a row of box files took up most of the space. The victim was seated behind his desk, very upright in his chair — though Mike had not mentioned him being restrained, as Morgan Springfield had been. Jude looked more closely and realised that the chair had been tucked in tightly, so the man's body was effectively trapped in place. His head had flopped forward, but careful positioning seemed to have ensured that the body had remained upright.

Was that relevant? Had the killer — if it was the same killer and, given the time lapse between the two deaths, Jude wondered about that — simply improved his technique and now discovered that a length of twine or cord would improve his display?

But it was the desk that led Jude to the reluctant view that Mike might be on to something. Reluctant because, hell, who wanted a serial killer on their patch? In comparison to the clutter and relative disarray of the rest of the office, the desk was remarkably clear. The desk lamp was switched on and illuminated the dead man's hands resting on the surface of the desk. A pen lay by his left hand.

"Shit!" Jude said.

CHAPTER 8

Sid Patterson stared at the kettle. He wanted coffee but somehow the connection between wanting coffee and what to do with the kettle could not be made.

"Come on, Sid, get a grip."

But Morgan was dead and someone had killed him. Someone had actually come into Morgan's office and taken his life. How did you get a grip on that?

Luce came into the tiny kitchen, her six-foot-five frame filling what was left of the space. She reached past him and filled the kettle then set it to boil.

Oh, Sid thought, that's what you did with it. But Morgan was dead so what did any of it matter.

"Sit," Luce said pulling out a chair for him. "You think you could manage some breakfast?"

He sat down, tried to process what she meant by breakfast.

"Toast," Luce said. "I'll make some toast and see where we go from there."

"Thank you," he managed. He remembered something. He should be going to work. Luce should be going to work. He must have said this out loud because Luce said, "I've called in and got the day off. I'll have to go to the club tonight, but I've asked for my set to be switched to earlier, so I'll only be gone a couple of hours."

"You didn't need to do that." Though he was grateful.

"Oh, yes, I did." Luce crouched down beside him and Sid gazed into the carefully made-up face. How did she look so good at this time of the morning? What time was it anyway? Here he was, still in his dressing gown, still not showered, his eyes still raw from the hours of crying that had only stopped when sheer exhaustion caused him to collapse into a heavy sleep.

"I've asked Tracey to come and sit with you until I get back tonight," Luce said.

"You didn't have to do that," he said again.

"Yes, yes, I did. You have friends, Sid, people that care for you and that know just how bloody besotted you and Morgan were. You think we're going to leave you alone to deal with that?"

Luce gripped his hand and he squeezed back. Her grip was firm, reassuring, understanding. Sid had known Lucille Connolly for years, since before he'd left the army, since before his head had imploded. Since before he'd started to come to terms with who and what he was. Luce had been there for that too and Sid was profoundly grateful. And just now he would probably have crawled off into a corner and given up if Luce hadn't taken charge.

He watched as Luce made tea and then toast, placing it in front of him, thick with butter and marmalade. The tea was hot and strong and slightly sweet. Luce always did make a good brew, Sid thought.

Gingerly, he picked up a slice of toast and nibbled at the corner. He was surprised to discover that he could still be hungry. Morgan was dead; Morgan had been murdered — how could Sid be hungry? It seemed like a betrayal, that he should still want and need the things that sustained life now Morgan was gone.

"Eat," Luce commanded, softly.

Automatically, Sid obeyed.

Once he had eaten he was ordered into the shower and when he emerged, there were clean clothes laid out on his bed.

Luce stood in the doorway and nodded approval. "That's better."

"What time is it? I thought I heard the phone."

"It's half past ten and so you did. Someone from the police will be over later this morning. They asked again if you needed a family-liaison person, and I told them you did not."

"No, I don't want a stranger in the house." He slumped down on the bed, shocked at how much just eating breakfast and taking a shower had taken out of him. Sid glanced up at Luce remembering that Luce had been going to be their best woman when he and Morgan married and the tears threatened again.

Luce came over to him and Sid found himself engulfed in a bearhug, the like of which only Luce was capable. "Oh, God, Luce, what am I going to do?"

Luce stroked his hair, hushing him, the powerful arms pulling him into a tighter embrace. "Get back into bed and try to sleep. Get dressed later, if you feel like it."

"You said the police were coming?"

"Someone will be; they didn't say when. I can deal with that. I'll wake you when they arrive."

Gratefully, Sid lay down and Luce covered him with a quilt then quietly closed the door.

Yesterday had been so unbelievably bad on every level that it was possible for something to be bad. You read about murder and violence in the news, but you never thought it would happen to someone you loved. Not someone like Morgan. The police officer who had driven him home had asked who he could call, and Sid had got the impression that he wouldn't leave until someone had arrived to take charge. The first person Sid had thought of was Luce. Luce had left work and been with him within the hour.

Luce worked part time in an estate agents, arranging mortgages and advising clients on, so it seemed to Sid, everything from understanding their legal packs to the cheapest place to get new carpet. Sid had the impression that there wasn't much Luce didn't know. About anything.

Three evenings a week, Luce sang in a small jazz club, her low, smoky voice reminiscent of the times when jazz clubs were also low and smoky.

Yesterday, Luce had asked all the questions Sid would never have thought to ask and then, later, knowing that Morgan's death would be on the news, and that Sid's family knew he worked for Morgan, Luce had helped him make the call.

The call that Sid had been certain would have cut him off from them. The call that was meant to tell them that he and Morgan were an item, that they were to be married and that his family were invited if they could put their prejudices aside for long enough to come.

All of that had to be said and on top of that Sid had to tell them that none of it would happen because Morgan had been killed.

He remembered his mother's shocked silence. His father's bemused questions. Then Luce taking over and telling them quietly but firmly that Sid had lost the love of his life. They would either have to accept that and be helpful or they could just keep out of the way.

"The choice is yours," Luce had said.

They had not called back and Sid was in no doubt as to which it would be.

CHAPTER 9

Mike arrived at the post-mortem after the examination of Morgan Springfield's body had begun. The clothing had been visually examined and then removed, enclosed in evidence bags ready to be sent off to be swabbed and taped. Hands had been removed from their coverings and fingernails scraped — he had clean nails, Mike was told, short and neatly trimmed, so there had been nothing much to show for the exercise. His height and weight had been recorded, along with his black heritage; the fact that he was forty-three, that he was well nourished and well muscled, and had a small appendix scar on his abdomen.

The body was then more closely surveyed before it was washed down.

"You should look at this," Roy Nicholls, who was carrying out the post-mortem, told him. His assistant was holding a sheaf of photographs from the crime scene and Nicholls was studying an image of the back of Morgan Springfield's neck.

"Seth suggested the killer had difficulty extracting the weapon," Nicholls said. "I'm inclined to agree. Bruising has continued to develop post-mortem and as you'll see, there are distinctive marks around the wound."

Mike studied the photographs and compared them to the back of Morgan Springfield's neck. There was now heavy bruising below the wound, a long solid streak of it, rolling down his spine.

"It looks . . ." Mike paused, his first thoughts seeming absurd.

"It looks as though someone used a lever or a claw hammer or something similar to extract whatever they had driven into his neck," Nicholls said. "They rested the hammer, or whatever it was, on the back of the neck and levered the . . . well, I'd have to speculate that it was a large nail, out of the wound and they didn't have an easy time of it. Hence the jagged marks around the edges of the wound and the bruising on the neck. I'll have to get some equipment together and look for a best match, but on the face of it . . ."

Mike nodded. On the face of it, what Nicholls was saying made a lot of sense.

* * *

By the time Mike left, it was after ten. He called Sid Patterson to let him know that he would need to speak to him later that day, but it was a woman who answered the phone. A woman with a deep, melodious voice and a calm manner and Mike, remembering what the PC who had driven Sid Patterson home had told him, guessed this must be Lucille Connolly.

"Sid's in the shower, then I'm going to suggest he gets some more sleep," Mike was told. "Do you know what time you'll be arriving?"

Mike did not. He suggested it would probably be late morning or early afternoon. He would take Jude with him, he decided.

Lucille Connolly said she would still be with Sid, whatever time it was. Mike thanked her and ended the call. So, who was Lucille Connolly? he wondered.

He drove back to headquarters and sat in the car for a moment before entering, gathering his thoughts. His mobile rang. It was Jude.

"Anything?" he asked.

"Unfortunately, yes. I'm bringing over everything I can find."

"Can find?"

"Mike, how much evidence was there, can you remember? We've come up with three filing boxes. Fortunately, one of them contains the crime scene photos but frankly—"

"There should be more than that," Mike confirmed. "Is the post-mortem report there?"

"Not that I've seen, but that should be on record elsewhere. Alison reckons it's possible things got misplaced or misfiled in the move. She's going to do a search for me, but have you seen the size of this place? That could take a little while."

His thoughts returned to her first response. "You said 'unfortunately, yes'?" he said cautiously.

"You remembered the pen, but there's quite a few more similarities in the crime scene. You'll see what I mean when I get in."

Mike was not sure whether he should be pleased that he'd remembered right and that his instincts as a new detective, all that time ago, had been valid, or displeased because similarities meant a possible pattern, which meant a possible serial offender, which meant . . . well, he didn't want to go there right now.

* * *

Jude arrived just as the very late morning briefing had begun. She'd co-opted a constable to help her carry the boxes in and they now set them down quietly on a table at the back of the room.

Mike glanced over and nodded a greeting. Seth had the floor and was pointing to a crime scene photo on the electronic whiteboard, a recent fixture that Mike seemed determined to make full use of. Jude fished the photographs from the old case out of the box and found one that showed a very similar shot. The body, side on, the shot taken from a high enough angle that it also showed the desk top. Gary Gibson's writing instrument of choice had not been a blue fountain pen with a silver band, but a common-or-garden Biro; however, the positioning of both pen and desk lamp were the same and that of the body similar enough that, in Jude's view, it defied random chance.

"As you might be able to see," Seth was saying. "Mr Springfield has been carefully positioned and then bound in place." He switched to another photograph, this time of the cord used to tie him around the neck and beneath the arms, an arrow with a reference scale pointing at the knots.

"There's nothing unusual about the cord. It's the kind usually sold for hanging pictures and can be bought at DIY shops, stationers. The little corner shop on the end of my road sells it, on a rack alongside safety pins and sewing thread, in little plastic packets. So, in itself it's not helpful, or won't be unless you find some in the course of your enquiries. The ends have been cut, probably from a bigger hank, with a knife, rather than scissors, and the lengths used to bind Mr Springfield to his chair are a substantial length. There's a possibility of matching the cuts, but I'm not holding my breath."

"The knots look very ordinary," someone commented and Seth nodded. Living this close to the sea, Jude had noted that it wasn't particularly unusual to see various sailors' knots in the casual run of things and they did turn up at crime scenes. That didn't seem to be the case here.

"These are just very ordinary knots," Seth confirmed. "What is more interesting—" he switched to another image of the desk and the body, this time taken from the doorway — "is that the desk has been moved slightly out of position so that it more directly faces the door. Indents in the carpet suggest that it was usually positioned so the side was up against the wall."

"So, someone wanted whoever came to the door to get a full view of him," another officer suggested.

"I can't speculate," Seth said, then speculated anyway, "but it looks that way."

When Seth was done, Mike stepped up with the pages of the post-mortem report that had been emailed. "We're obviously going to be waiting on the toxicology results for a day or two, but initial indications are that the cause of death was a penetrating wound to the back of the neck, that severed the spinal cord between the C2 and C3 vertebrae." He touched his own neck to indicate. "The blade was narrow and rounded. So, imagine something like a stiletto or even a sharpened knitting needle or, most likely, a long nail. The angle was slightly upwards. I've got some helpful drawings here, but if you imagine that it passed between the vertebrae and then continued into the brain stem, so the pathologist thinks Mr Springfield may have been bending forward when the blow was struck."

To indicate, he reached for a nearby chair and bent down as though to pick it up. He again touched the back of his neck. "So, something like that angle. Death would have been pretty much instantaneous."

He paused. "This next bit is informed guesswork, but it's likely whoever drove in the spike did so by hitting it with something, probably with the flat end of a claw hammer."

"Why a claw hammer?" Jude asked. "Were there marks on the back of the neck? Did they remove the blade?"

Mike nodded. "Exactly that. The post-mortem images will be sent over later, but it looks like our killer drove the spike in with a hammer. Then withdrew it with the claws. The marks against the skin, post-mortem bruising having developed overnight, are consistent with that kind of action."

A murmur of distaste and disgust fluttered around the room. It was bad enough that this man had been killed, but somehow the deliberation of that final act made it worse.

Though it hadn't been the final act, had it. The extraction of the murder weapon must have taken place before Morgan Springfield had been tied into his chair and set up like an installation in an art gallery.

Jude had intended to speak privately to Mike about the Gary Gibson murder, but now she picked up the bundle of photographs and made her way to the front of the room and handed them over. Mike glanced at the top picture and then at her. He passed the picture to Seth and indicated to Amit that he should also take a look.

Jude saw the shock register on their faces as they took in the similarities.

"Yesterday, when I first saw the crime scene," Mike said, "I noticed something that rang a vague bell. The way the desk had been cleared and the pen positioned next to the victim's left hand. Morgan Springfield was right-handed. Late last night, or rather about three o' clock this morning, I realised what memory had been jogged. This morning I sent DS Burnett to take a look at the case files on the Gary Gibson murder. It was about eighteen years ago and remains unsolved."

Jude could see from their reactions that some of the older officers remembered.

The image was passed from hand to hand. Jude watched as officers examined the picture and compared it to the one Seth had put back on the screen. The mood shifted with the realisation that they now might have two deaths to deal with instead of one — one being bad enough. That the killer had evolved his methods since the Gibson death — the Springfield scene spoke of efficiency and practice. Of confidence. The realisation that then followed was that it was rare for such a killer to be dormant for such a long period between murders. Were there more unsolved deaths in the intervening time, deaths that would have to be examined and connected and integrated into the current investigation, or had the killer been prevented from further actions, perhaps by a long spell in prison.

"What was the murder weapon in the Gibson death?" The question came from Amit.

"I've not laid hands on the PM report yet; it wasn't in the boxes and the archivist suspects that some of the evidence boxes may have been misfiled when they were moved into permanent storage. The post-mortem results should be on record separately though, so hopefully I can get a copy sent over from the local hospital. According to Alison, at records, they should have duplicates."

Amit nodded.

"Prioritise that, please," Mike said. "If the cause of death was similar then the similarities become more than circumstantial."

A pen and a lamp and the odd hand position wasn't enough to be certain, Jude reminded herself. Then added silently that they were all kidding themselves if they claimed there wasn't a link. If the similarities weren't already striking.

"I was part of the team that worked the Gary Gibson case," Mike said. "Back when I was a DC." He explained how it had come to mind when he had looked at the Springfield crime scene, though it had taken him a while to recall the circumstances.

One of the older officers spoke up. DS Carrington was close to retirement. "I know it was an unsolved," he said, "but wasn't there a rumour about an affair. That the wife wanted out and paid her new fella to get rid of the husband."

Mike nodded. "That was the angle the media played. But the boyfriend had a solid alibi. Gibson was known to us, domestic violence reports. The wife was hospitalised a time or two from what I remember, but didn't want to press charges. She finally left and was living with her new man by the time her husband had died. She'd filed for divorce, I think. I'd need to refresh my memory. I can't recall there being any solid leads or any clear suspect once the wife and her boyfriend were cleared."

"Who was SIO?" Jude asked.

"That would have been DI Foston," Mike told her.

The name meant nothing to Jude.

"Retired and buried long since," DS Carrington commented. "Poor bugger only got about five years' retirement then had a massive heart attack."

A murmur travelled around the room as those who had known the man recalled the funeral and the pity of it all.

"So, we need to track down the remaining records on the Gibson case, prioritising the PM report. We also need to contact anyone who worked the case, see what they recall. Jude, if you could take care of that."

Jude nodded. She knew that the creating of a major-incident team would have to be accelerated, the media handled, cold cases reopened and, most likely, liaison with other forces. Had there been other murders where the victims had been staged like this then someone would have called them to mind. No, if the killer had claimed other victims, then they were not to be found locally. Jude recognised these same thoughts in the expressions of her colleagues.

The game had changed.

CHAPTER 10

The door to Sid Patterson's house was opened by a tall and rather imposing woman with dark, wavy, shoulder-length hair and brilliantly blue eyes, who introduced herself as Lucille Connolly, "Though most people call me Luce. Come along in. I'll get Sid."

Mike thanked her and he and Jude followed Luce inside. She directed them into a small front room and told them to make themselves comfortable. Then she paused at the door and said, "As you can imagine Sid's in bits. Go as easy on him as you can, okay?"

Mike nodded. They heard Luce go upstairs, presumably to fetch Sid.

He looked around. The front living room was small, as was often the case in terraced housing, though this was on the larger side for that kind of building. A deep bay window was occupied by a small sofa and an open book lay on the window-sill. He could not make out the title from where he sat, but the alcoves either side of the fireplace housed bookshelves.

"Someone collects vintage Penguins," Jude said and Mike saw that she was correct, noting the orange, blue and green spines and also the shelf of yellow-jacketed hardbacks that reminded him of his childhood. He had discovered the

Gollancz yellow covers at his local library and soon realised that whatever book was dressed up in the plain yellow jacket was likely to be worth reading. He had worked his way through Dorothy L Sayers, Daphne du Maurier, the short stories of Cornell Woolrich and Guy de Maupassant and discovered what remained one of his favourite books in Joe Haldeman's *The Forever War.*

He got up to see what Sid Patterson had been collecting, struck by a sudden fellow feeling for the man that caused him to momentarily forget why he was there, in Sid's living room.

Footsteps on the stairs, Luce's firm and steady, the second hesitant and slow, caused him to turn and return to his seat, suddenly guilty as though having been caught in the act of doing something vaguely inappropriate.

As he turned away, his attention was caught by a selection of photographs on the mantelpiece. There was a picture of Sid, alongside an older couple and a woman around his own age. He guessed this must be the sister. Beside that, a photo of a much younger Sid and to Mike's surprise he was in uniform. So, Sid had been a soldier? The third picture was a group photo of Sid and Morgan and three others, standing outside the unit where Morgan's body had been found. Morgan Springfield held a bottle of what Mike took to be champagne and they all had raised glasses in their hands. The company opening?

No pictures of Sid and Morgan alone, but if Sid had not come out to his family, then that was not surprising.

Mike had intended to retake his seat before Morgan and Luce returned, but his perusal of the photographs had distracted him and he was still standing beside the fireplace when they came in. Sid glanced at him and then came over. He reached out, his fingers gently touching the picture of Morgan Springfield. He was shaking.

"The day we moved in," he said. "Morgan was so happy."

Gently, Luce took him by the shoulders and led him to the seat beside the window. "Is this where I ask if anyone wants tea and you," she directed her glance at Jude, "say you'll come and help and then we both go into the kitchen and you ask me a lot of questions?"

Mike blinked, momentarily surprised. Jude was quicker to respond. Of course she was, Mike thought.

"Works for me," Jude said. "Shall we go then?"

Lucille Connolly laughed and, Mike thought, looked at Jude with more interest. Even Sid managed a half smile. Mike saw Luce taking note of that too and the slight nod of satisfaction. Mike knew grief — he knew how it cut you to the core, sliced your soul, removed all certainties you might have thought you had and he guessed that Luce knew this too. That Luce also knew that any tiny relief from that fog of utter despair was to be valued and that a half smile was a sign that Sid might just survive.

Mike waited until Luce had sailed from the room, Jude in her wake, and then he said, "So you were in the army?"

Sid nodded "The Royal Mechanical and Electrical Engineers, based at Lyneham. I left school, didn't know what to do with my life so I joined up at seventeen. My father was in the forces and I knew it would please him. Or I thought it would. Truthfully, I enjoyed most of it. It might sound strange, but it gave me time to think, to figure out what I actually wanted to do, filled the time I might have just spent drifting. When I left, after eight years, I went to university as a mature student, studied engineering and met Morgan in my final year. He'd also gone to uni as a mature student but he was doing a PhD by then. We first met about eleven years ago. I was twenty-eight and he was thirty-two, and it was love at first sight." He laughed. "We worked together on and off after that, became good friends. Morgan had a couple of relationships, none of which lasted. And as for me, I still couldn't admit to what I felt or even that I was entitled to feel like that. My family were . . . the way I'd been brought up was . . ." He sighed. "It was Luce that helped me get past that, but I still couldn't tell Morgan how I felt.

"We moved here to start the business, but it was another seven years before I finally came clean, and when I did, he was all, 'Yes, I know. I was just waiting for you to tell me.' He just had this wonderful smile and this great, raucous laugh. He'd fill the room with it and people would turn around and look at us and that would just make him laugh all the more."

Sid shook his head, disbelieving, and his next words came out harsh and hard. "Who the fuck would do this to him? Who the hell would kill a man like Morgan?"

The sudden change of tone, the fury and pain of it was understandable but Mike thought he also glimpsed some other side to Sid Patterson. Then it was gone and Jude and Luce returned with tea and biscuits, Jude carrying a folding table on which Luce set the tray.

"So." Luce took a seat next to Sid. "Do you know any more than you did yesterday?"

Mike thought of all the possible stock responses he could give. Discarded all of them. "Truthfully, not much," he admitted. "Mr Patterson, would there have been a chair for visitors in Mr Springfield's office?"

Sid looked puzzled. "Of course. The office was small — well, you saw that. Morgan liked to keep things tidy and uncluttered, so he kept a folding chair next to the filing cabinet. When he had visitors, it only took a moment to . . ." He trailed off, his gaze suddenly elsewhere, and Mike knew that he was remembering the office from the morning before. The position of the desk and Morgan's body and the absence of the chair.

"It wasn't there, was it? Did his killer take the chair away? That's just absurd."

"We don't know if the killer removed it," Mike said. "But, no, it wasn't in the office."

"There were two red folding chairs in the storeroom and a couple more in the kitchen," Jude said. "Was the one in Mr Springfield's office the same as those?"

Sid nodded, the expression on his face now bewildered. "Cath Tilling, that's our PA, she shares an office with me, the larger one next door to Morgan's. Mostly it's just Cath in there. I'm out for a lot of the day seeing customers, liaising with the manufacturing side and that sort of thing. Officially I'm the finance officer, but it's a tiny company so we were both jacks-of-all-trades too. Morgan did more when we were first setting up but the past year or so he's been able to concentrate more on research and development. We picked up a couple of major new contracts that needed specialist tooling and our current set-up wasn't large enough to handle the whole process. We had to get the laser-cutting and drilling done elsewhere; Morgan thought it would work better if we could bring that all in-house so we were looking at expansion . . ." He broke off, his burst of enthusiasm faltering as he suddenly remembered that none of that would be happening now, or at least none of it would be happening for Morgan. Mike felt for him.

"You were asking me about chairs." Sid's voice was small again, his body seeming to shrink. "There should be two in the storeroom, one in Morgan's office, one in the office I share with Cath, four in the kitchen, though usually two of those are propped against the wall."

Mike nodded. "So, eight in total."

"Yes, though I don't recall we've ever needed all of them. Morgan bought them as a job lot, I think, when we were setting up."

"And what other interest did Mr Springfield have, outside of the business?"

This elicited a burst of laughter from Luce. "What wasn't he interested in? That would be a shorter list."

Sid smiled sadly. "Morgan was one of those people who had excess energy to burn. Always doing, always getting involved, always saying yes to people. It could be . . . exasperating at times. He'd take on so much, but it all seemed to get done, somehow."

"I know it's hard," Jude said. "But could you both make us a list of all the things Mr Springfield was involved in, places he might have visited recently, contact details for business associates and friends and anything else you think might be useful to us."

Luce was regarding them both with narrowed eyes. "You think Morgan and his killer knew one another?"

"It's possible Mr Springfield and his killer crossed paths somewhere," Jude said. "If Mr Springfield was an active member of the business community, if, as you say, he had a variety of interests and involvements, it's possible that they could have met."

"Because whoever killed him knew that Morgan was often last to leave on a Tuesday evening," Luce said. "Because Tuesdays he was often alone."

Mike saw Sid Patterson's body grow rigid. "Other nights I'd have been with him. We'd often meet with friends. I think I mentioned that Tuesdays he did paperwork? He'd gather everything he needed and take it home with him. I'd leave around five thirty, Cath would have gone, Morgan was often still around until after six. His killer knew that?"

"It's possible," Jude said gently. "We have to look at all possibilities."

"I was supposed to have this one last Tuesday to see my parents and my sister before I told them about Morgan and me. This was the last Tuesday we wouldn't have left together. The last night . . . If I'd been there, Morgan might not be dead."

He buried his face in his hands, body shaking again. To Mike's surprise Luce said sharply, "Sid, if this bastard wanted Morgan dead, he'd have found a way to kill him no matter what. You and Morgan didn't live in each other's pockets. He'd have found a way and found a time."

Sid took a deep breath and nodded. He lifted his head and wiped the tears from his cheeks. "You're right," he said, though Mike could see he'd still not accepted the truth of it, that he was merely clinging on to any temporary relief Luce's words might bring. That in reality he would face a whole lifetime of guilt that he hadn't been there on that particular Tuesday night; that the killer must have known their routine. He could see Sid processing all of this and the slow realisation dawning more forcefully that, "This was someone Morgan knew? Someone we both knew?"

"Perhaps not *knew*," Jude said. "But perhaps someone whose path he crossed. The more we know about Mr Springfield's movements in the days and weeks before his death, the more we know about his contacts and friends and activities, the more thoroughly we can build a picture."

"Because right now you don't have a clue as to who killed him," Luce said flatly.

"Not yet," Mike told her, knowing that anything less than honesty would be despised by both Lucille Connolly and Sidney Patterson. He was reluctant to invoke that emotion in two people he was inclined to like.

"Not yet — but we will. And perhaps you can help us do that," Jude added, and Mike saw just a little flicker of light and hope come into Sid Patterson's eyes.

"We'll work on it today," he said. Luce nodded and Mike could see that she was grateful to Jude. It was something they could do, something Sid could focus on, something better than just drowning in grief and despair, even if in the end it didn't help at all.

In the car, Jude said, "I like her."

Mike nodded. "And how did the interrogation in the kitchen go?"

Jude laughed. "It was mostly about who needed sugar and what biscuits we should choose. I asked again about having a liaison officer and Luce said she had it covered. That she'd be spending the day with Sid and other friends would be rallying round to help out. I asked how long they'd all known one another. Luce has known Sid since they were both in their early twenties — they met at a friend's twenty-first. Sid was still in the army then. He stayed with Luce, had a room in her house, when he went to university."

"And does Miss Connolly have a family she has to get back to?" Mike asked as he started the car.

"No, she's untethered and unattached, as she put it. I got the impression there had been someone but not recently. She said she was *now* untethered and unattached, so—"

"He knew his killer."

Jude glanced at him. "You're sounding very certain. I mean, on balance I agree with you, but—"

"Whoever killed him knew his routine."

"And could simply have kept him under surveillance."

"So how did he pick Morgan Springfield? You only surveille a possible victim once you know they exist."

"He could have spotted him in the street one day, had a eureka moment. That does happen."

"Springfield was tall, fit, strong. Not your usual random victim. He could have fought back and the killer might have found himself in serious trouble. Morgan Springfield didn't think twice about turning his back on the killer."

"And how many times in the day do you turn your back on complete strangers? We automatically make the not unnatural assumption that most people we meet aren't psychopathic nutcases out to get us."

"But if a stranger came into your office and you were the only one there. Not just rang the bell on the outer door, but actually walked into the unit and then came into your private space, would you not be a little more wary? Would it not cross your mind that you should watch your step?"

"Probably," Jude conceded, "and yes, I'm with you, he had almost certainly already met with his killer in a situation that meant his guard was down. But if what Sid and Luce said is true, we could find ourselves with a very long list of contacts to work through."

They fell silent for a few minutes, considering the situation and then Jude said, "What do you make of him?"

"Sid Patterson? I don't know. Like you, I'm inclined to like both of them. Lucille Connolly seems to be an interesting woman and I get the impression that she and Sid and Morgan Springfield were very close. She doesn't strike me as the type of person who would choose friends who are . . . I don't know . . . not worth her attention. No, that sounds really crass, but you know what I'm trying to say."

Jude nodded.

"But there was a moment, I don't know, just a second or so, when I saw something else in Sid Patterson. Something harder, something almost feral."

He was aware of Jude's raised eyebrow when she looked at him this time. He knew this might sounded fanciful and there were few people to whom he would have expressed such an opinion. Well, probably just two others — John Tynan and Maria. But he knew he could trust Jude with it and that she would log the thought, take it seriously.

"Maybe something left over from his army days," she said. "Or maybe the thing inside him that caused him to join up in the first place." She shrugged.

"Not just to please his father, then?"

"I'm sure that was part of it. But how many young men and women crash out before basic training is done. How many fail to pass out in the end? You have to have what it takes to adapt to army life — that has to be in there to start with, I would have thought."

Mike nodded. He didn't personally know anyone or have anyone in his family that had chosen a military career. It wasn't a Croft thing. But he supposed that was exactly the point that Jude was making — it *had* been a Patterson thing. "It's a bit chicken and egg."

But it bothered him, just a little. So, Sid had been a soldier, had probably seen dead bodies, had known immediately that Morgan Springfield, the man he loved, was dead. He had been trained, Mike supposed, to control his impulses and his emotions. Mike, who admittedly knew little of soldiers and soldiering and military discipline supposed that this was what the army did — it taught you to separate your emotional responses from your rational ones. But did it teach you not to go to the man you loved, to check that he really was dead?

Mike knew he would have done, and it still nagged at him that Sid Patterson had not. He did not in any way doubt that Sid's grief was real, but it did . . . what? What did it make him doubt?

Mike often credited the women in his life — and by that he meant Maria and Jude — with mind-reading talents and, as if on cue, Jude said, "Do you think Sid Patterson had reason to expect trouble? That it was less of a surprise when something happened to Morgan Springfield? That he was almost not surprised to find him dead?"

"What makes you say that?"

Jude shrugged. "I can't really say. It's like, he's not just grieving. And there's no mistaking that — the man's in bits. And it's not just that he's angry. I mean we've both seen victim's families enough times to expect anger. It's a natural-enough emotion to feel when someone's taken a life, even when that's an accident. But there's something about Sid's anger that's more than that. Different to that. It's like he's keeping a lid on it but it's building like a pressure cooker. Luce knows it too."

"Oh, did she say something to you?"

"No. It's more a feeling. It's more, just how watchful she is, like she's waiting for something to go off. Like . . . like she's watching to make sure she's out of the way when it does."

Mike nodded, much as he was able to say things to Jude that might be regarded as fanciful and even absurd, he was profoundly grateful that she was able to do the same. Often these random observations had led on to other, less random thoughts. To ideas that had firmed into theories and then into action.

They were pulling into the car park at police headquarters now and Mike glanced at the dashboard clock. It was quarter past four. Once they'd got upstairs, it would be time to assemble the troops for the afternoon briefing. Financial records, both business and personal, background checks on employees and on the victim — and on Sid Patterson. Anything of interest turned up from interviews at the adjacent factories and the small housing estate beyond. Anything useful from CCTV — though Mike, having been on site, had already worked out that there were enough blind spots for a whole gang of murderers to have slipped unnoticed into Morgan Springfield's work unit. Most CCTV was set up to watch over the valuables of specific companies, not to watch the comings and goings of random pedestrians or even random motorists. The car park itself did not have a dedicated camera and Springfield Developments didn't have one at all — after all, there was little to steal. So far as Mike could make out, only one computer remained in the building overnight and that was the one used by the PA. Sid had a laptop that travelled with him, as had Morgan Springfield — though that, of course, had disappeared with the briefcase. It was possible the killer would try to sell it on. If they got lucky, he'd attempt to flog it at a local pawn shop.

"Penny for them," Jude said.

"Not worth it. But I reckon Terry Gleeson is going to need help with all the background info we're going to generate."

Jude nodded. "I'll get some help organised."

CHAPTER 11

Friday

According to the clock on Sid's bedside cabinet it was now two in the morning and he was not immediately sure of what had woken him. He had been dreaming of Morgan and woken with tears on his face but, as he lay in the dark, he realised that the thing that had filtered through into his dream and dragged him back into wakefulness was a memory.

Sid sat up and listened to the silent house. The familiar clicks and creaks that any old house makes, comforting sounds, and the less familiar but still comforting sound of the radio on very low in the spare room where Luce was sleeping. She had always slept with the radio on, tuned to something classical or occasionally jazz, or at least she had in the years since Sid had known her. Hearing the music put Sid in mind of an older memory, not the one he had woken with but a much more welcome one and for a moment or two he indulged in that memory instead, even though it hurt just as much.

He'd lodged with Luce and three others during his last year at university, and he and Luce, being the eldest of the group, had taken on the role of joint housemother. The house had in fact belonged to her. It had been the family home and when her mother had passed on, Luce had inherited the run-down barn of a place. Letting out rooms helped her to cover costs and made up for the fact that she was often working two jobs while she tried to get her singing career established.

Eventually she'd just sold up and used the cash from the sale of the sprawling, draughty old place to buy herself a one-bedroomed flat and put some money in the bank. Her singing career had taken off and she'd even released two albums, which had both sold well, but she said that she had in the end found touring too lonely and now she seemed happy to have an ordinary day job and regular local gigs. Sid and Morgan had known there was more to it than Luce had let on, but she had made it plain that the matter was closed and that was that. Luce, for all her generosity of spirit, had stories she did not want to tell, just like Sid and Morgan and most other people of Sid's acquaintance.

Sid's memories of the old place were happy ones, especially as it was there, at one of Luce's parties, that he had met Morgan.

Sid leaned back against the headboard and turned the memory this way and that, examining it as he had done so many times over the years, recalling the first sight of the tall man standing in the doorway, scanning the room for familiar faces. He had been so beautiful, Sid thought. Not handsome, that word seemed cold and trite and Disney. Morgan was more than that. Sid, though he only admitted this to himself much later, had been smitten.

Reluctantly he let that memory go and turned back to the one that had woken him. It had been on a Wednesday morning, about three weeks before Morgan had died. Sid knew it had been a Wednesday because he had not been with Morgan the night before. Morgan had come in late to work and it had been obvious to Sid that something had been very wrong. His partner had been agitated and upset and even sharp with Cath when she'd told him that a client had phoned and needed a call back. Sid remembered how he and

Cath had looked at one another in surprise, wondering what the hell was wrong. Morgan was never sharp with Cath — he was rarely less than considerate with anyone.

A few minutes later, Sid had brought coffee for them into Morgan's office, set the mugs on the desk and taken the folding chair from beside the filing cabinet.

"Now, you going to tell me what's wrong or are we going to have to hire a new PA?"

He was joking of course — Cath was as concerned as Sid was at the uncharacteristic outburst and was very fond of her employer. Her friend.

For a moment, Morgan looked at him with incomprehension written plainly across his face. Then he sighed. "I'll tell her I'm sorry," he said. "My bad. The day got off to a lousy start."

"What happened?"

Morgan paused, coffee mug raised halfway. "I ran into someone I'd almost forgotten I'd ever met. He hadn't. He seemed to think I'd done something to him and was ready to argue about it in the middle of the street. It upset me, that's all."

Sid was troubled by the vagueness of this. "Was it an ex?" he asked tentatively.

Morgan shook his head emphatically. "Oh, no, no, nothing like that. This was someone I tried to help. Apparently it wasn't enough."

Morgan's phone rang and he took the call. Sid left him to it. Morgan apologised to Cath and seemed to have recovered his mood. The incident passed, and though Sid tried to raise the matter a time or two, Morgan seemed to have got over his annoyance and upset and the matter was dropped.

Sid had forgotten about it until now. What if . . . what if this had something to do with Morgan's death? What if this argument had been what got him killed?

Sid knew he was probably not thinking straight but the need to make sense of what had happened meant that what was probably a trivial incident now attained massive importance.

Luce, waking to find a very agitated Sid at her bedside, was less convinced.

"Sid, it's . . . almost three o' clock in the morning. Go back to bed. If you still think it's important in the morning, I've got DS Burnett's number, and we can ring her."

"Who?"

"Jude, the young woman who came with the inspector."

"Oh, yes."

Feeling a little foolish and somewhat guilty about waking his friend, Sid went back to bed. Luce was probably right — likely this was nothing and she was definitely right that no one would want to be woken in the middle of the night with news that Morgan had been upset one morning when he'd come into work, especially as Sid could tell them so little about why he had been out of sorts.

Sid lay down and tried to sleep, but it wouldn't come. What did arrive, in place of oblivion, was a slew of memories that at first seemed unrelated. Sid's brain seemed dead set on disturbing his sleep and filling his head with doubt and uncertainty. Flooding into his memory came a whole surfeit of tiny incidents, little discrepancies: cancelled meetings, sudden phone calls that led to Morgan leaving the office or, occasionally, even leaving Sid on their evenings together, or mornings when he'd woken and Morgan had already left. At the time they had all been explicable, all been normal, and Sid had been blissfully unconcerned, but now, these random incidents preyed on his mind. What if the man he loved had been cheating on him? No, there was no affair, Sid was certain of that. But what if there had been things that Morgan was deliberately concealing?

Like what?

Sid didn't know but he also knew that he could not sleep.

He went downstairs and made some tea. He retrieved his diary and a notepad from his briefcase and, sitting at the kitchen table, he began to write, starting with the incident when Morgan had come in late for work and then all of the other tiny but awkward discrepancies he could recall in Morgan's behaviour.

Yesterday afternoon, after the police had left, he and Luce had started to put together the lists they had asked for.

Morgan's friends, his family — not that there was much of that, just an uncle he rarely saw and a couple of cousins — his interests and all of his social, business and even cultural involvements. Sid fetched that now and continued to add to it, returning to his new list from time to time as he thought of another incident — a random phone call that had seemed to last too long for it to actually be a wrong number. The sudden change of plans when Morgan had decided that a favourite pub was no longer a place he wanted to drink at. His keenness to stay over at Sid's place more often than at his own. Even the talk about relocating to a bigger office, when the unit they were in was, unlike the manufacturing set-up, perfectly adequate to their needs. Had whoever had upset Morgan continued to hassle him?

In the weeks before he had been killed, Morgan had been restless and troubled, but Sid had not realised just how much, because Morgan had been so very careful not to let it show. Sid was certain of that now — Morgan had been really worried about something but had been hiding it from the very person who would have moved mountains and drained lakes if that might have put things right. Why had Morgan not confided in him? Perhaps if he had, Morgan would still be alive.

Sid looked at the stacks of paper set out on the kitchen table and thought he could almost glimpse a pattern in all of this, but, after three hours of writing and list-making, his mind was too tired to see it, even if one was actually there.

* * *

"Sid? What is all this?"

Sid felt Luce gently shaking him awake — he'd fallen asleep at the table. He looked down at the notes he had compiled and remembered that small sense he'd had that there was a pattern, a clue, an answer to why Morgan had died. Whatever he had half seen was gone now.

"I want to find who did it, Luce," he said. "And I want him to die."

CHAPTER 12

Friday

John was very surprised to find that Johanna's oldest son was present at their planned meeting. He must be, John thought, in his early twenties now, with dark hair like his father and pale-grey eyes like his mother.

He was, John realised, regarding him with a degree of suspicion. "What's this?" He addressed the question to his mother. "I'm here because Steven said you'd got something you needed to say to me. I'm *only* here because it was important to my little brother — I never agreed to meet him."

It was always odd, John thought, to hear the name Steven mentioned and Mike Croft not be involved. Mike's son had been Stevie and he had been just twelve years old when he had died in a hit-and-run accident. It felt strange that another boy, one approaching adulthood, could own the name.

He refocused his attention on Paul as the Pearson boy turned back to him. "I remember you. You came that day with my cousin Sam and brought those boxes over."

John nodded. "So I did." The boxes that had inadvertently led to his father's death. If they'd been left in the

76

storeroom of their old home, then Johanna would never have found the negatives and never have killed her husband. He could forgive the young man for feeling that, in some vague way, all of this had been John's fault. Did he also blame Sam?

"Do you see much of Sam?" he asked, keeping his tone carefully neutral.

Paul shrugged. "Time to time. He don't have much to do with any of us though, not since he left and married out."

Married out, John thought. "You still see yourself belonging to the Children of Solomon?"

Paul studied him for a moment, his expression hard to read, but John thought Paul looked as though he might be regarding him as a collector might view some kind of exotic but slightly repellent insect. "They took us in after what happened. The younger ones and Steven are still there." Abruptly he turned his attention back to his mother. "So, what do you want to say?"

Johanna seemed taken aback by the tone as much as the question.

"I wanted to see you," she said. "I wanted to talk to you. Paul, I've been worried. These past few years you've been—"

"I've been what? Like you know what I've been. How would you know what's been going on in my life? You left. You abandoned us. You weren't even there."

"I was in prison," Johanna said flatly. "There was very little I could do. But . . ." She reached out for his hand and then drew back sharply as he pulled away. "But I'm out now," she continued, far too eagerly, John thought. "I can help you."

"Help me! What the fuck do you think you can do for me? What do you think I need you for?"

"Paul! We don't use language like that!"

"You don't get to tell me what I can say or what I can do. You hear me? I'm an adult now. You've got no rights in this, not anymore."

"Paul." Johanna's probation officer's tone was professionally reasonable, but John could tell that was going to cut no ice with this angry young man. But what precisely was he so angry about? The cause, John sensed, was something precise, something particular.

"No, he's right," Johanna said. "I don't have any right. He's a grown man and I missed his growing-up. But, Paul, I didn't abandon you. I did what I believed and still believe was right. I couldn't risk your father hurting any more children. I couldn't risk him hurting you."

"How do you know he hadn't already," Paul asked.

Johanna looked as though she'd been slapped. She raised a hand to her mouth as though to contain the emotions, the words that threatened to come pluthering out.

"And did he?" John asked, knowing she could not ask for herself, knowing she must have wondered all these years.

"No," Paul said. "He never laid a hand on any of us and if you'd been any kind of wife you'd have known that. But, no, you killed our father and you abandoned us."

"I found those pictures," Johanna said, her voice rising in anger for the first time. "I saw what I saw. I know what he did."

"And it never occurred to you that someone else might have put them there. Might have been trying to pass the blame."

"It did occur to me. I went to speak with your Sam. You remember." She turned to John. "You drove me out there."

"I did."

"If you thought Sam had anything to do with it, or would have known anything about it, then you're more stupid than I thought," Paul told her. "But someone else put them there. If you'd really thought about it for two minutes, you'd have known that. Where did those boxes come from? Where did that fucking ornament come from? Did it not occur to you that Dad didn't have the owl to hide the negatives inside? It was still at the house, and that stuff wasn't even his. He only got it after his brother died."

Looking at Johanna's face, John could see that these thoughts had occurred to her. That she must have wondered if she'd got it right. It seemed though that Paul was done with her and finished with this meeting.

He got to his feet. "I came because it was important to Steven, not because I wanted to see you. Stay away from me," he added, spitting the words with such venom that Johanna quailed. And then he was gone, the door slamming and his angry footsteps echoing on the uncarpeted stairs.

"*Did* it occur to you?" John asked. "That your husband may not have been the one to hide those negatives?"

She turned an impatient, distracted look in his direction. "Of course it did. I'm not entirely stupid, Mr Tynan. But the negatives showed images of the children my husband was accused of interfering with. The photographs the children claimed he had taken had gone missing, so they said, not that I believed they had existed in the first place." She sighed. "As it happens, he would have had plenty of opportunity to hide the negatives before we left the community. I now believe that is what he did. I didn't believe any of it until that moment. I didn't believe the children. I didn't believe he had ever taken those pictures and so I didn't believe that they could have gone missing. They hadn't existed, so how could they be lost. And then I found . . . what I found. And I knew I had to do something."

"You could have let the law take its course," John said. "This was new evidence. Your husband could have been charged."

She sighed again and slumped back into the uncomfortable chair. The grey eyes had dulled, John noted, the fire gone out in them. She looked older than her years, strained and tired and defeated. Was that truly the first time she had doubted her husband? Knowing it was probably a bad idea, he asked her anyway and saw the flame return to the eyes, the flush to the cheeks as she turned on him.

"What sort of woman do you think I am?" she demanded. "The sort that would stay with a monster?"

"I don't know you," John reminded her. "We met only briefly and, to echo your son, I'm here today because Liz felt it was important I come, not because I feel I owe you anything."

He paused. This was getting them nowhere. "All right, so let's think about this. What motive did you think the children might have? The ones that accused your husband?"

"I thought . . . I wanted to believe that someone had put them up to it. He had the capacity to rub people up the wrong way sometimes. I thought he might have upset someone."

"Upset someone enough that they would orchestrate that kind of accusation? Forgive me, but that sounds a little far-fetched, don't you think?"

She shrugged. "People can be full of spite — you must know that. You were once a police officer. Or I thought it might have been a misunderstanding. Children can misinterpret things. Or that it was a story that had got out of hand. All children lie on occasion, even those who've been raised to know it's wrong. They panic or they worry about getting into trouble or they lie to protect someone. Small children don't have the experience or the judgement to find their way out of problems. It's the job of the adults in their lives to help them. But even the best parent can't anticipate every eventuality."

The fire had died again and she no longer met his gaze. She *had* suspected, John thought, and now she blamed herself twice over. For believing her husband when he'd first been accused and for bringing her own children into danger because of him. No wonder she'd broken under the strain and lashed out with such dramatic consequences.

"You must have been deeply hurt and deeply angry," he said quietly.

"Oh, it went beyond anger. Believe me, I was enraged. He had lied to my face and I had been foolish enough to believe him. To make excuses for him. He had lied to our children. Worse, far worse, he had endangered our family, so now it was my job to protect them."

"But killing Eric meant you were taken away from them," said John. "Killing him meant you lost your right to protect them. It would have been better to have reported the matter to the police. Mike would have moved mountains to help you, believe me."

"You think so? I have no trust in the authorities. Oh, no doubt Inspector Croft is the sort of man who means well, but, no, this way I could be certain of my husband's punishment. And as to that meaning I had deserted my children? Well, I had failed them already, hadn't I? I no longer had the right to call myself their mother, Paul was right in that."

John considered for a moment, noting that at no point during the conversation had she called Eric Pearson by his name. It was as though she could not bring herself to speak it out loud. "Isn't forgiveness part of your faith?"

Her head jerked up. "You think I should have forgiven him!"

"No," John told her gently. "But I think perhaps it would have been better for all concerned if you'd forgiven yourself."

As he walked away from the meeting, John could not help but wonder what had been gained. He had gone with the intention of speaking to Johanna purely because Liz Jenna, a woman whose judgement he respected, had thought Johanna's concerns worthy of bringing to his attention. Not worthy of going straight to the police though, John noted. There was about all of this the sense that Liz was relying on John to dictate her next move; that she didn't want to make any rash decisions off her own bat.

John was safe — he was retired, had no job to protect or axe to grind but he had knowledge, experience and connections, should they prove necessary. He knew he was being used, was prepared to forgive that if it was in a good cause, but was it?

He had been surprised to find Paul at the meeting though and as it was, Paul had stormed off before anyone had been able to talk to him about anything and John, rather guiltily, found he had not been too unhappy with that outcome. Did he really want to be involved with the Pearsons and their troubles? Unfortunately, not being involved might not be an option.

Johanna seemed to have changed her mind as well. When John had spoken to her about forgiveness she had stared at him, as though she could not believe he was daring to utter those words. Her face, white and pinched, lips narrowed and bloodless, had told him that he really had crossed some invisible line. She had risen from her seat, taken her coat from the hook on the back of the office door and left without another word.

"Well, I handled that well," John said sourly as Johanna's footsteps receded on the stairs.

"Believe me, you did no worse than I've done," Liz Jenna told him. "She's not the easiest person to deal with. Angry at the world and most of all angry with herself."

John nodded. "Do you know exactly what she was worried about? When you asked for this meeting, I understood there was some specific problem, some risk of criminality—"

"Oh, there is or at least there might be and, well, since you were brought here on that basis, I suppose . . ."

He saw her hesitate. Johanna had been prepared to talk to him but now she'd left without passing on what she suspected and Paul had also exited so precipitously, was there any need for her to say more? Was it even ethical for her to do so, now her client had left?

John sighed. "Truthfully, I'd as soon leave this alone unless you really think—"

"John, I don't know you well, I think we've met what, half a dozen times on various boards and committees, but I've come to respect you, both in terms of your professional judgement and your common sense. So, please, just bear with me. The truth is I feel there is cause for concern but what I'm not sure of is how much I can say without Johanna's express permission, and I don't think that's going to be forthcoming now."

"She seemed very intent on speaking to me earlier this week. I have to say I was surprised to find Paul here today."

He let that thought hang and fell silent for a moment, waiting to see how her inner conflict would resolve.

"So was I," she said at last. "As you heard, it was apparently his younger brother, Steven, who persuaded Paul to at least come to the meeting. Johanna had been trying to persuade him since she spoke to you but he wasn't having any of it. Ironically, it was Steven who started this whole thing off. He confided to his mother that Paul had told him things . . . he was scared his brother might be involved in something really serious or at least know about someone who was."

"That's all a little vague." John was feeling impatient now. If she was going to spill the beans, then why didn't she just get on with it? If she wasn't, then he'd as soon go home and get on with his gardening.

She nodded, acknowledging that. "Okay, so you may or may not know that Paul served a short sentence in a youth-offending centre and his probation officer happens to be a close colleague of mine. I thought . . . I thought if Johanna wanted to talk about him then it might be as well to involve Paul in the conversation. So, I spoke to Jo, my colleague, and she had a chat with Paul, suggested if he had anything to say to reassure his mother — and you — that there was nothing to worry about then perhaps he should show up. Up until a couple of days ago he was . . . declining the invitation. Steven apparently convinced him it would be a good idea to just clear the air and get Johanna off his back." She sighed. "Fat lot of good that did."

The pair of them were resorting to far too many clichés, John thought. He'd noticed people often did that when they were hedging around an issue. "I got the impression that he wanted to punish her far more than that he might want to get her off his back. He's a very angry young man. Being the eldest, I suppose he felt responsible for the younger ones in some way?"

"I think he did. He took it upon himself to look after them, I suppose."

"And what happened to the Pearson children? Can you tell me that? Did the community take them in, as Paul said?"

"Yes, they did. The relatives stepped up and so did the rest of the community. Jumped through all the official hoops and did everything we asked of them so they could be considered appropriate guardians. And it worked out well. Not for Paul, in the end, as he found it hard to settle, but Steven and the other two have done well. Daniel was too young to really remember any of what went on and Evelyn is very attached to her auntie. They've managed to live quiet lives. Poor little Frankie, of course — he died a couple of years after Johanna killed Eric."

"How did he die?"

"Oh, it was terribly sad. Meningitis. His family rushed him to the hospital as soon as they recognised what was wrong but . . . He was only eight. The local papers got hold of the story, did a feature on the 'tragic family' or whatever."

"Johanna must have been devastated."

"I'm sure she was. I'm sure everyone was."

"And apart from that, the media have left them alone?"

"Mostly. There's been the odd thing, as you might expect. There was a piece done on the family, a couple of years after Eric Pearson was killed, around the time that Frankie died, so the attention must have felt doubly hard. The press was interviewing neighbours and such like, and people who had known them before they left the community. The Children of Solomon wouldn't speak to anyone, quite understandably, their one and only concern in all of this was to protect the children. All of this happened around the time the last of the court cases ended, you know, to do with the children's homes."

John nodded.

"And then on the fifth anniversary of Eric Pearson's death, I think it was, so Paul would have been seventeen, there was a follow-up article in the local paper. It wasn't front-page stuff or anything, more of an editorial or a think piece, but it must have been painful and it brought the kids back into the spotlight. I know that Paul was furious; it was his reaction that got him into trouble. He went to the editor's house, set fire to his front gate and his car, scared his family, threatened the man. Anyway, he was still a juvenile at that point so he did a stint in a young offender's centre and then finished up in an adult open prison. So far as we know he's behaved himself since. He holds down a job and lives independently, so—"

"Oh? Look, you never said what made Johanna think her son was heading for further trouble. I'd assumed they were still in contact and that he must have confided in her but judging by this morning's performance . . ."

"Well, quite." She glanced at her watch. "Look, John, I'm really sorry but I've got a meeting I can't skip in about ten minutes. I'd hoped I might be able to get you all together and then leave you to it for a while." She grimaced apologetically. "I know, not very professional, but this meeting wasn't exactly official . . . more—"

"Covering your backside just in case," John said cheerfully. "No, I do understand. But seeing as you've got me here—"

"You deserve an explanation. Look, I'm going to have to think about this, speak to my manager and talk to Johanna again. Now she's chosen to absent herself, there are issues of confidentiality that definitely apply and just now they—"

"Trump vague ideas regarding events that might never happen," John finished for her. "All right, Liz, but let me ask you this. If Johanna's fears turn out to have foundation, is anyone at risk? Could your lack of action lead to someone getting hurt or—" he registered the flicker of anxiety in her eyes — "something worse?"

"John, I really don't know. At least, I don't know anything for certain."

A knock on the door disturbed them both. A young man opened it and tapped his watch. He smiled at John and then hurried away.

"Your meeting," John said.

"I'm sorry, John, and I'm sorry to have dragged you over here for nothing." She began collecting papers together and thrusting them into an already overstuffed bag, her relief at having an excuse to shelve the conversation painfully obvious.

John, feeling a little put out, took his leave.

He walked slowly back to where he'd parked his car. The meeting had bothered him more than he had expected and he wasn't entirely certain why. Nothing much had happened. Though perhaps that was it — his unease was driven by what had not taken place. He still had no idea what the meeting was meant to be about. Was it a matter that could safely be ignored? It was, he realised, something that would nag at him until he found out, one way or another.

CHAPTER 13

Angrily, Johanna Pearson wiped the tears away and strode off down Palace Street. What had she expected? Had she really believed that this man, whom she'd met on what, two brief occasions, would be willing to help her? No, she was on her own with this. On her own yet again.

Johanna paused, her chest tight and that now familiar feeling that she was choking on her own breath threatening to overwhelm her. She hadn't taken much notice of her route when she had left the probation offices but now she realised she was on St Andrews Street and the doors of St Andrew's church stood open. Johanna stumbled inside, made it to a seat close to the back where, shielded by a substantial pillar from casual observation, she flopped down onto a pew and closed her eyes.

Her chest still cramped painfully, restricting her breathing so that she felt light-headed and sick. She struggled to remember the advice she had been given to try to ground herself when suffering from what she had been told were panic attacks. Johanna wasn't sure she liked the description — it made her feel weak and helpless — but she hated whatever took over her body when this happened, however you wanted to describe it. *Focus on what you can see and touch and smell, all*

87

the concrete stuff, she told herself. *Count your breaths.* What happened if you couldn't breathe and could not remember how to count? She forced herself to look at the impressive stained-glass window behind the altar, examining the colours, the blues and greens and flashes of red, though they danced in her vision and made her feel giddy and she was forced to close her eyes.

Johanna rolled her fingers into fists, dug her nails into her palms, focused on the pain. On occasion she had actually drawn blood, but it helped her to direct her thoughts, helped her to calm down enough that her lungs no longer felt as though they had collapsed and forced every tiny drop of air from her body. She opened her eyes, forced herself to look at what was going on around her. Forced the sense of utter helplessness back down.

Close to the altar, two women were arranging flowers. Chrysanthemums, stems of eucalyptus, late-flowering dahlias, a little past their prime but still beautiful. She guessed they must have been grown in containers and taken into a greenhouse to extend the flowering past the first frosts. This was something Johanna had done when she had lived with the community. She had a soft spot for the blowsy, vibrantly coloured flowers and had found that with a little care and planning she could keep a few in flower all through November and sometimes beyond. Did anyone bother to do that now? she wondered.

The women were chatting, quietly, companionably. One woman laughed at something the other had said. Johanna envied that casual intimacy. When had she last had an actual friend?

Her first weeks in prison had been a blur. First on remand, then her court appearance — she had pleaded guilty of course, there had been enough witnesses to what she had done to make anything else impossible, even had she wanted to, and Johanna was far too honest to even have considered denial had that been a possibility.

She had done what she had done and that was that.

Reluctantly, she had agreed to allow her legal team to suggest that the balance of her mind had been disturbed. She'd had to acknowledge that was probably the truth. Blind fury, the desire to protect her children, rage at what her husband had done and the pain of knowing that he had lied and lied and lied . . . what had been the sum of all that if not an imbalance in the mind.

Slowly, after her initial weeks of incarceration, her senses had seemed to have returned to her and then she had despaired. Locked away from family, from loved ones, unable to explain or to seek understanding from those she had sought to defend. Would Eric have harmed them? Had he done anything to her children? Johanna felt that she would have known. They had all lived so closely together, first at the community and then thrown together in the inadequate accommodation the council had offered until eventually they had been rehoused. No, there had been no opportunity, even if Eric had been inclined — she was sure of that and for that at least she was grateful.

The strange thing, Johanna thought, was that the crime she'd been imprisoned for had to some extent protected her inside. She had killed a man that everyone believed had abused children. Johanna still did not know if Eric's activities had extended to anything beyond the taking of photographs but bad enough that the images showed the children naked — surely that spoke for itself?

She had come to realise that she was something of a celebrity and though that had eased her path in that new and alien environment, she had hated the implications. She was a murderer, she could not deny that fact, even if others might think her actions had been justified.

As time went on, she had settled into the prison routine. She was no stranger to communal living so being thrown together with this disparate group of women had not been in itself such a challenge and she had slowly realised that she could be useful, almost a mother hen to the younger women who had come to share her situation as much because of what had been done to them as because of their own actions.

As she allowed these memories to drift through her mind, Johanna calmed. She had been useful — Johanna felt that she'd been born to be useful. The need to be needed had shaped her life, was the foundation of her personality, her motivation, her very being. Being back in society she had found *that* the hardest thing to deal with — that she was no longer useful, no longer needed by anyone, not even by her own children. They had their new families now, were cherished and cared for, and Johanna would have had no desire to uproot them just because she was now free, albeit on license.

But Paul was different. He had gone astray. It was the responsibility of the parent to bring the strays back into the fold. The image she had cleaved to lifelong, of Jesus, of God, was as the shepherd who would not leave even one of his lambs to the mercy of the wolves.

She realised that people might have laughed at that, but Johanna held this belief sincerely, totally, because she loved her children, and her entire upbringing in the community had taught her that it was the duty and the purpose of a parent to love their children and to keep them safe.

Johanna looked up as footsteps came towards her. One of the flower-arranging women, holding a small tray on which was set a mug, a tiny milk jug and some packs of sugar, was heading her way.

"Hi," the woman said. "You looked like you could use a cuppa."

For a moment Johanna stared at her and then, reminding herself of her manners, she managed a faint smile. "Thank you," she said. "It's been a bit of a morning."

"I'm Elsie, by the way."

"You look too young to be an Elsie," Johanna said, the words coming out before she could stop them.

Elsie laughed. It was a warm and unaffected sound. "The old names are coming back," she said. "But I was named after a great aunt. She died a few days before I was born."

"Ah," Johanna said. She supposed that would explain it. She was grateful when the young woman set the tray down on the pew and took her leave, her act of kindness not intrusive. Johanna didn't think she could have coped with further expressions of concern or curiosity.

The tea looked strong, the way Johanna liked it. She added a little milk and one of the packs of sugar, stirred the mug and then closed her eyes, the tea clasped between her hands, the mug almost painfully hot but somehow soothing.

It was a good cup of tea.

Afterwards, she took the tray back to the front of the church and found the two women in the vestry. "Thank you," she said.

"Any time." Elsie's smile was so kind and so genuine that Johanna almost wanted to confide in her, to talk about her troubles as so many of the women she had been incarcerated with had spoken to her. Johanna was a good listener. But this woman was a stranger and anyway Johanna was not so good at telling her own story. She thanked the women again and then took her leave.

Despite her moments of what she saw as weakness, Johanna knew herself to be a strong woman, a determined woman, someone who carried things through and with or without anyone else's help, she was going to save her son. From whatever or whoever it was he needed saving from.

* * *

"Where have you been?" Ross Cahn asked.

"Nowhere. Had a meeting with the probation officer."

"That's not till Tuesday."

Paul sighed at the challenge. Resorted to a version of the truth. "Johanna's probation officer. She'd been on about me seeing her, reckoned she wanted to put things right between us or some such crap. Wanted us to have a proper relationship. I was sick of the hassle, so I went along to tell her to fuck off."

Paul threw himself into a chair, trying for sulky but unbothered, knowing that his interrogator would be watching him closely.

"She's got some balls, your old lady. Whacking your dad in front of witnesses like that. Balls, but no sense," he added.

Paul could not help but agree. He really couldn't understand why Johanna had acted as she had. Okay, so she was mad with Eric for having lied to her, so hand him over to the police, or, if she really wanted him dead, wait until she got him alone some place. "Stupid," he said. "Really, fucking stupid."

Ross Cahn laughed then got to his feet and shrugged into his coat. "So, leave well alone," he said. "She's out of the picture. You've got other things to concern yourself with."

Didn't he just, Paul thought as the man left. He looked around the scruffy little room, the uncomfortable sofa on which he'd slept for the past three weeks because this other had insisted he always be on hand when required. What the hell was he even doing here?

The urge to go and speak to May, his own probation officer, and tell her what was going on, or what he thought might be, was almost overwhelming. He pushed the idea aside. May was all right, genuinely meant well and was doing the best she could for him, but what the hell could she do with this situation? He was actively associating with known criminals, breaking the terms of his parole. He'd be back inside before his feet could touch the ground and be no safer in there than he was out here. No, if you signed a deal with the devil, you'd best remember that the devil could reach you anywhere.

CHAPTER 14

Friday

"Johanna, how are you? It's good to see you."

David Laughton stood aside and opened the door wider. She stepped past him into what had once been her home but where she now felt she was a stranger. She had been here twice now, to see the children. Had found them happy and content and loved and left knowing that, despite the joy she had felt at seeing them and the hugs and kisses they had all exchanged, they were no longer hers.

"Evie and Daniel are at school, but Steven is here. I'll let him know."

It jarred for a moment, the mention of school. Back in the day they had educated their children onsite and occasionally brought in tutors if anyone seemed to be struggling, either to teach a particular subject or to grasp it. Eric had set up a small laboratory and they had done experiments. Sometimes they had taken their experiments onto the bit of waste ground, where an outbuilding had been demolished, and Eric would make things go bang or they would send pop bottles skyward, launched by compressed air. When she'd arrived, she had noticed that the bit of waste ground was now home to a large greenhouse. And now this talk of school.

"David, I need to talk to you first. Please."

"Of course, come on through to the kitchen. Have you had lunch? I was just about to make a sandwich."

It was late, she thought, at past two o' clock, for him to be eating lunch. She caught sight of her reflection in the hall mirror as they passed, noting her own pale face, more heavily lined than seemed right for a woman of her age, the lines accentuated by the lack of flesh on bone. She had lost weight in that first year of incarceration and never quite managed to regain it. She guessed the suggestion of lunch was more because she looked in need of sustenance than because he really wanted to eat. Some small part of her rebelled at being patronised. But the idea of doing something normal, eating lunch with a man she had once counted a friend, was something she desired so much that it was almost more than she could bear and it was this emotion that won out. She nodded, managed to thank him and then followed him through to the communal kitchen where she had once felt so at home and now felt like an intruder.

"How . . . how are they getting on at school?"

"Oh, very well. Daniel took to it from the start. He's a really sociable child. Evelyn was very quiet for the first few terms, as we told you when we wrote, but she's got a couple of very good friends that come here regularly and, as you know, she's talking about university in a year or two. She's undecided whether to go straight on from school or do some voluntary work for a year. I think she could use a break from studying. Daniel's just made his GCSE choices. Chalk and cheese, as you know. Evie is all science and Daniel's never happier than when he's making something or got a paintbrush in his hand."

"Thank you," Johanna managed to say, "for all the letters, all the news. It . . . helped."

She sat quietly as he made tea and prepared sandwiches. She realised suddenly that the place was unusually silent. She supposed it was that in her day there would always be the voices of children as a background to whatever noise the adults made. That the big kitchen where everyone pitched in to prepare the communal evening meal was rarely empty. Families and couples catered for themselves at breakfast and lunch, but the evening meal was something to be shared and the chatter and chaos as everyone caught up with one another, talked about their day, congratulated or commiserated, was Johanna's favourite time, or had been.

"Where is everyone?" she asked. Usually the place would be bustling with life. Even if the children now went to school, there had always been the more distant voices of the adults working in the garden. Someone, somewhere, was bound to have had the radio on. When Johanna had lived here, the children would have been having a music lesson at this time of day. Music and song played a big part in the community and just about everyone played something, even if, like Johanna, there was no particular talent for it. It was the participation and the enjoyment that mattered. She was reminded, painfully, that it was more than a decade since she had even attempted to play anything. There had been no music for them after she and Eric and the children had gone away. Now, in this place that was at the same time familiar and unfamiliar, all was quiet, just the ticking of the kitchen clock, louder than Johanna could remember it ever being.

He hesitated. "This is a much smaller community now," he said. "People left . . . after . . ."

Johanna's head jerked up. "After the accusations. After I killed Eric?"

She could see in his eyes that he had no wish to hurt her, that he still cared deeply for Johanna who had once been at the very heart of their extended family, but he knew her too well to lie.

"After that. People worried about the impact all of it would have. About the possible implications."

"So how many remain?"

"Well, there are . . ." He sighed. "Johanna, a lot's changed. There are fourteen of us now, including six children

95

and another on the way. Julia, Gordon's daughter, you remember her? She's due in about a month."

So, Daniel, Evelyn, Steven . . . not Frankie. Poor little Frankie was dead and gone. She remembered getting the news that he was seriously ill and the prison governor making arrangements so she could go to him. But it had been too late. She'd never got to say goodbye, though she'd been allowed to attend the funeral service, along with two guards, one of whom had wept openly as the little coffin had been lowered into the ground.

The Children of Solomon didn't hold with cremation and her erstwhile community had stood the cost of the burial. Johanna had been grateful for that.

"So," she asked. "Who is still here? I know Judith and her family left for York." Judith had been Eric's niece. She had recently been married and had been expecting her first child when Johanna had killed Eric. It had been considered best for everyone if the new family made a fresh start elsewhere.

"And they are thriving," David told her. "Three children now and Judy works in the farm shop. She took some courses and now also deals with the community accounts."

"*They* still educate their own children," Johanna said.

He ignored the disapproval in her tone. "They have a large enough community to have a schoolhouse."

"I heard they opened their school to outsiders?" Johanna could not keep the concern from her tone. "Was that wise?"

"Not the school, no, but they run courses on organic farming and now on regenerative agriculture. As you know, we've been using these techniques since Norman Luther founded our first community. It seems it's now become fashionable again." He smiled at her. "So, who is still here that you would know. Well, Gordon and Esther are still here and their Julia married Ruben and Mary's boy. You remember Aaron? And, of course, Joseph and Ann, and Mark and Hanna."

She nodded. They were the couples who had fostered her own children. They were relatives of hers and had stepped up immediately to care for her brood as though they had been their own. She could not fault them — it would almost have felt better if she could. There had been a time when all the families in the community had been related in some way, either with those who lived here or those that lived in the other two enclaves, those in York and Scotland. Here, the main house had been converted into small apartments and there were a number of farm cottages and various conversions of farm buildings on what had once been a big estate. When the original families had pooled all of their resources to buy this place it had been semi-derelict, but soon it had been thriving and now, now it seemed to be in decline. And it was her fault. Eric's fault.

Impatiently, she pushed her mug away, feeling now that to have accepted his invitation to eat and drink with him had been foolish. There was no going back to the way things had been. She had now only the most casual claim on his friendship. No, not even that — on his friendliness and con-cern, the same friendliness and concern he would have shown towards anyone. It was nothing like the connection they had shared before. "It seems everything has changed since we left," she said, unable to keep the bitterness from her tone.

He regarded her thoughtfully for a moment and then countered, "Everything changed *because* you left. Because of the manner of your leaving. No," he held up a hand for silence as she tried to object, "Johanna, no blame has ever attached to you and certainly not to the children. We under-stood that you felt you had to follow your husband, even if we didn't agree. But we had to protect ourselves. You made your choice, Johanna, and so did we."

Angry words threatened to spill out. She closed her lips tightly, trapping them. She could not blame David or the others. They had given her the option of remaining and she and the children would have been protected and cared for. She had chosen to believe Eric . . . had wanted to believe him . . . had . . .

"I could not believe he might have done something so terrible," she said softly. "How could I believe it? Then when

I discovered the depths of his deceit, David, I couldn't bear it. I made my decision. I passed my judgement. I took action against him, and I stand by my decision."

"As is proper." It was one of their founding precepts that you passed your own judgement and you dealt with whatever followed, much as Solomon would have done had the child he had threatened to kill died at his hand. He would have had to live with the repercussions, had the child's mother not spoken up and saved its life by relinquishing it. Once a decision was made, you lived with the consequences and those consequences were that Johanna, even now, had no place here.

"So," he said gently. "What brings you here today? You know that Paul is gone from us, that there is nothing we can do for him."

"I know. I wanted to speak to Steven, to see if he could tell me more. David, I know that you can't do anything, but I need to know what led up to him being—"

"How can we know, Johanna? He's not lived with us for the past year and before that he was in prison. Well, in a young offenders' centre and then the prison. We visited, we did all we could to look after his interests, but once he was released and was offered the option of coming home or of moving into a hostel he chose not to return. He made his decision, Johanna, as was his right."

"He'd not yet reached his majority. He was not yet twenty-one. He was still a child."

"Not in the eyes of the law. Not in his own eyes. We have no right to compel him or anyone to return — we don't lock our children up, we don't force them to accept our beliefs and our ways, you know that. We encourage it, of course, but sometimes it becomes clear that they must go their own way and, yes, sometimes that happens before we would wish it to." He sighed. "Your Steven wants to stay. He's happy here, working on the market garden and dealing with the customers in the shop. And we're glad to have him. Your Evie, well, she's a different story. She has plans for university and beyond and though I hope that she will keep her options open and come back to us, we can none of us be certain of that."

"Then tell her she can't go!"

"Johanna, we have no moral or legal right to do that. We have suggested she makes no final decision until she graduates, but . . ." He spread his hands wide to express his helplessness.

He stood then and began to clear the table. "How did you get here?"

"I caught a bus and then walked the rest of the way."

"Then I'll get Steven to give you a lift back to Norwich," he said. "I'll put your sandwich in a bag so you can take it with you. You and Steven can talk on the way. Perhaps we can arrange another weekend visit so you can see the children? I know Evie and Daniel have been asking."

Have they? she wondered, though it was nice of him to say it, she supposed. Her last meeting with Daniel and Evelyn had been enjoyable but it had also underlined just how much of their growing-up she had missed. Evie would soon be eighteen, have taken her exams, be going off to wherever. Daniel, who'd been little more than a toddler when she'd been forced to make her decision to kill his father, was a confident teenager. The community had done all it could to keep her in contact with them but she had found it so painful when they had come in on visiting days that she had almost despaired. And then she had been moved so far away that visiting was difficult, and contact had been reduced to frequent letters and the occasional telephone call. Where did she fit into their lives now?

"Thank you," she said.

She waited in the hall until her second eldest son appeared. Steven hugged her and kissed her gently on the cheek. She followed him outside and he opened the car door and saw her settled.

He looked well, she thought, and content. He was tall — she had been taller than Eric and her own father had been well over six feet, and he seemed to have inherited that trait. "So," she said. "You're happy here?"

"I'm doing fine," he said. "I always loved this place."

"I'm so sorry I took you away."

"You've said that before and I told you I've forgiven you."

"And I'm grateful."

"And you, I can see that you're unhappy. What are you going to do now?"

Now you're out, he meant, *now you can start again*, but Johanna wasn't thinking long term just now. "I'm going to get your brother's life back on the right track," she said and as he started to object, "that's my decision. I've made up my mind."

* * *

Johanna sat in her small room at the hostel and stared at the piece of paper in her hand. It was a grim, grey little room with a single bed, a miniscule table and a chair that tried to bridge the gap between dining and desk and comfort and managed none of them. A table-top oven and hob stood on what passed for a kitchen counter. There was a sink and some cupboard space and Johanna had bought some brightly coloured mugs and plates to try to add a splash of light to the overwhelming grey. It had been a mistake — the rainbow colours somehow intensified the blandness and deepened the overall air of depression that settled in the space. She thought of all the others who had occupied this room before moving on. Their despair and confusion had seeped into the fabric of the place until it wrapped like fog around the shoulders and the feet of any occupant, like a cold and careless 'duty' hug or a half-seen snake determined to trip the unwary, misty and ill-defined but still dangerous.

Her conversation with Steven had yielded little of use. He had given her an address that Paul sometimes stayed at, sometimes used for letters to be sent to though occasionally official stuff was still arriving at the community house. She had been disturbed to realise that this was not the address he had given to the probation service. That, she thought, could lead to real trouble for him. Bank letters warning him about an overdraft, semi-threatening missives from credit agencies and debt collectors had been arriving at the community house until a solicitor's letter had been sent, warning them to desist. So far as Steven knew, he no longer had a permanent residence anywhere. It was something, she supposed, that he was still maintaining contact with his PO, even if the young woman dealing with him didn't actually even know where he was living, though Steven supposed Paul kept that from her. He had an official address, a flat that had been organised for him a month or so after he'd been released, but Steven didn't think he'd stayed there for long.

He had also provided the names of friends and associates Paul had mentioned and tried to suggest where Johanna might find them. It was clear though that Paul had not been a major element in Steven's life for the past year or so.

"I visited every visiting day while he was in the young offenders' centre," he'd told her. "He could have been out sooner but he got into a fight and by that time he was old enough to be transferred to an adult prison. That changed him — if he'd come out when he should, I think he'd have been all right, eventually."

"It's my fault," Johanna said.

"No, it's not your fault. Your actions led to him feeling like you'd abandoned him and he just got angrier. But he never believed . . . Eric . . . was guilty. That was the biggest problem. You made a decision and acted on it. That had consequences. Paul made the decision that he wasn't going to believe any of the evidence. That's had worse consequences than anything you did."

"What else could I have done?"

He turned his head to look at her, his expression one of disbelief. He held her gaze for so long that she wanted to tell him to keep his eyes on the road.

To her relief, he turned his attention back to his driving and signalled a left turn. They were on the outskirts of Norwich now, just a few minutes away from the hostel, and after that her chance would be gone. "Steven, I—"

But he'd not finished. "What could you have done? You could have told the authorities, had him arrested. That way he'd have been the one in prison and you . . . you'd have stayed with us. Oh, don't get me wrong, we've been well looked after, loved. We couldn't have been more loved, but it's not the same, is it? We wanted you there. We wanted that. You promised us everything was going to be all right and even through the worst of times when there were bricks flying through the windows and even as he . . . Eric . . ."

"Your father—"

"You think I can call him that? Really?"

"No, I don't suppose you can."

"Even as he became more and more demented. Oh, don't get me wrong, we were all too young to understand just how out of his tree he was. But we trusted you to make things right. You were the strong one, the one holding what was left of our lives together and then you went and . . ."

They reached the hostel and he pulled up into a space about a hundred yards away from the entrance. She could see that he was close to tears.

"I got it wrong," she said quietly. "I failed you all." Which was why she couldn't afford to fail now. She had to save her eldest son from whatever harm he was getting into. "You're happy at the farm?" she asked. "You'll stay? David says that Evelyn will be going on to university. That she'll probably not come back."

"Evie will make her own way in the world. She'll find where she belongs and we'll all be proud of her. Daniel, too. He's a lovely kid and the only problem anyone will have with him is getting him to finish what he starts." He was laughing now and Johanna relaxed a little. "He's hopeless," Steven went on. "Gets distracted so fast. Everyone's really patient with him though and he'll be fine."

"David tells me he loves his art. I had his pictures on my walls. It helped a lot. The pictures and the letters."

"I'm glad. I really am. Johanna, we never wanted to cut you off, never wanted you to feel that we had forgotten about you but—"

"But I wasn't there to be mother." She nodded. It hurt. His use of her given name, rather than 'Mother'. It felt like a knife being stabbed into her belly and twisted. Pain radiated from there throughout her body. Who knew that pain could be so bad? But she couldn't blame them — they had been children; they had needed to be loved and to love in return and they *had* been loved. Of course they had grown close to their new families. Johanna knew how the community worked; she knew that the interests of the children were paramount. This was why the accusations against Eric had been so profoundly felt, so utterly damaging. Had he killed someone, had he murdered an adult, that would have been dealt with, could, depending on the circumstances, even have been forgiven. But to exploit and damage children, well, that was beyond forgiveness, at least by the families that formed the Community of Solomon.

"Has Paul confided in you? Steven, I want to help him, but I need to know more. He told me things. Then he got scared and told me he was making them up."

"Maybe he was. Johanna, of all of us, he took all this the hardest. He felt he had to become the parent, I suppose. He was the one with the most anger."

"I know." Among all the letters and cards and pictures and phone calls from her children, Paul's contribution was defined in terms of absence. Nothing ever said, no excuses made, he made that choice and that choice was to limit his interaction with her. She had hoped, once she was released, that things would be different and, indeed, he had agreed to meet with her. They had talked. He had told her things that worried, frightened her even.

"It's not occurred to you he might have been lying," Steven asked her. "That he might just be punishing you?"

Johanna nodded. "It occurred to me, yes. But I know fear when I see it. Paul is afraid."

Steven sighed. The car engine was still running, as if he expected her to get out so he could drive away. He killed it and they sat in the sudden silence, broken only by the occasional car passing along the narrow street.

"What did he say to you?" Steven asked.

Johanna relaxed, just a little. She would get her hearing — perhaps she would even get her son to help her.

"He talked about a man he had shared a cell with for the last few weeks of his sentence. About how he knew this man would be released a few weeks after Paul. How this man wanted to involve him in something serious. In a murder."

Steven sighed, turned in his seat and looked at her. "Ross Cahn," he said. "He told me the same thing. Then he told me he was making it up. That he'd not seen Cahn since he got out. There's no reason to believe he's here, Johanna — Paul finished his sentence in Bristol. It made visiting hard, but we collected him when he got out and Ross Cahn came from somewhere in Kent, I think. He'd have gone back there or maybe London. What would he be doing in Norfolk?"

"He's scared, Steven, and he told me this Cahn man — he wanted someone dead and he wanted Paul to help him."

"Wanted who dead?"

"I don't know. But he told me Cahn was threatening what he'd do if Paul didn't help him."

Steven restarted the car engine. "Look," he said. "I know you don't like me to swear but my brother is full of shit. Has been for a long time. He's lied and he's cheated and he's tried to cause trouble for just about everyone he's come into contact with. David and the others. They all tried to help him. Gave him chance after chance but in the end the . . . anger, it just seemed to . . . In the end he actually attacked someone, set fire to their car, their garden gate, threatened them and their family."

"The newspaper editor."

Steven was shaking his head. "He threatened the editor but the person he attacked and whose car he set fire to was

Tom Andrews, a journalist, and the article he'd written wasn't sensationalist. It was . . . I think he wanted to be kind. He wanted to know we were all okay, that there could be a *good* news story come out of all the crap. Well, Paul, he went spare."

Johanna frowned at her son. "You say he attacked this man? I thought he just set fire to his car. I mean, I know that's reprehensible but—"

"No, Mr Andrews had just pulled up to his house. He was getting out of his car when Paul chucked a petrol bomb at him. Then he chucked another one into the car. Mr Andrews was lucky not to have been really badly hurt. His wife had been looking out for him and she opened the front door. Mr Andrews ran inside and they called the police. Paul had been drinking. He was drunk and he was on something—"

"I know he'd been taking drugs." Johanna could not keep the distaste from her voice. "I didn't know the details. I never saw anything about all that in the news."

"Mr Andrews played it down. He met with David and some of the elders and he said he thought we'd all suffered enough and that he had no intention of hurting any of us further. His editor wasn't pleased but Mr Andrews was adamant. He's a good man. The police brought charges, of course, but Tom Andrews actually wrote a statement for the courts asking them to take into account what Paul had been through and he told the court he'd got no intention of stirring up more hate. It could have been really bad, for all of us. Evie and Daniel started having nightmares again."

"It was good of him, I suppose," Johanna said, though she had a low opinion of journalists and wondered what this Tom Andrews thought he would gain.

"He's never asked for anything," Steven told her. "But I think Paul would have found it easier if Mr Andrews had pushed for heavier charges. It would have justified his anger. One of the police that came said it could have been treated as attempted murder and not just criminal damage. Mr Andrews said he'd been almost in his house when Paul had attacked the car but it wasn't true."

"How do you know it wasn't true?"

"Because David and Mr Andrews talked to us all about it. They wanted us prepared for more trouble, just in case."

"This Tom Andrews might have been lying."

Steven shook his head. "He wasn't. Paul was proud of what he'd done. He said he was doing what Eric would have done. Like Eric, standing up for justice, and that he remembered what Eric taught us to do. You remember all those bottles lined up by the window? And the stink of petrol. Johanna, how could you have let him do that?"

"No one could stop Eric once he'd got an idea in his head," she said softly. "Besides, I thought he was in the right."

"And that justified him in making Molotov cocktails? In making us help him. In throwing them into the street? In burning people?"

"Who had been attacking our home!" she reminded him angrily.

"And that made it right? No, of course what they were doing was terrible. I can remember being scared, all the time. But he made it worse." He sighed. "Look, I've got to go. I need to get back. You take care of yourself, okay? And leave well alone with Paul. You won't do any good, getting involved. And if Paul is involved in something criminal and you get mixed up with those kinds of people, you could be sent back to prison, Johanna, so just think about that."

She could feel his impatience for her to be out of the car. By the time she reached the door to the hostel, he was driving away. But at least now she had a name, something and someone she could research. She also had the name of the journalist — the cause of Paul going to prison in the first place. She would be sure to speak with him, find out what his game really was. Clearly, he was fooling David Laughton and the others in the community — fooling her children into believing that his interests in them were not malevolent — but Johanna knew better than to trust people like him.

He made his money by exploiting the misery of others — that was what journalists did. Why was this one going to be any different?

CHAPTER 15

Saturday

In the communal room at the hostel was a computer that the residents could use for job applications and email, but this was not suited to Johanna's purpose. For one thing it was often in use — even in the dead of night, the darkened lounge flickered with YouTube videos or games. On the Friday night there had been no opportunity for her to log on.

She had a mobile, a fairly basic, prepay smartphone that the Children of Solomon had supplied her with when she had been released and which she used mainly for texting. She preserved her credit carefully and though she knew she could use the Wi-Fi in the hostel, she still found searching for anything complex too awkward on the small screen, and was frustrated with the restricted versions of news and access that seemed to come with the territory.

Noting her frustrations, one of the support workers had suggested to her that she try the local library. She could get herself a library card, borrow books and make use of the internet. The support worker had also suggested she look at the various job sites or maybe ask the librarians for information on free courses she could access to build her skills ready for the workplace.

Johanna had refrained from telling this very young woman, who clearly looked upon her as some kind of barely educated dinosaur, that she had taken every course on offer while inside, had volunteered to teach others to improve their reading and writing skills, and in some cases basic mathematics, and even become a listener, dealing with the troubles and concerns that assailed everyone who had been separated from whatever family, friends and support system they may have had outside. Though she had been struck by the number who had none, or at least none that mattered or could actually be helpful.

It had been a slap in the face, one day, when a girl she had been helping had commented that she was probably so good at listening because she knew what it was like to have no one. The comments had not been mean or intended to hurt — it had in its own way been intended as a compliment — but Johanna had spent the rest of the day reeling from the truth of it.

She could account for practically every minute of the near decade she had been inside. Not the first year so much, that had been spent simply dealing with the despair, with the reality of her situation, with the brief court appearance at which she had pleaded guilty, though with the mitigation of diminished responsibility. At the time she had been astonished and indignant that this had been admitted as mitigation as easily as it had but then she had seen the photographs of herself, snapped as she had entered and left the court, and wondered at the pale, almost emaciated zombie staring in such bewilderment at those gathered outside.

"I took a degree in business and computer sciences in prison," Johanna had told the support worker as gently as she could when really she wanted to yell at the young woman, tell her not to make such crass assumptions. "Then I applied for funding and did my MA."

She had been held up as an example of what rehabilitation could achieve, Johanna remembered resentfully, acutely aware that the word "rehabilitation" required there to have been some habilitation in the first place. Frankly, she had rarely met anyone either in the secure unit or the main prison population or the category D institution in which she had served the final three years of her sentence to which that might have applied. Prisons, Johanna thought, seemed to be full of those who society, parents, authorities and medical professionals had failed from the outset. For whom habilitation had been a complete myth — so how could they possibly hope to be rehabilitated?

Johanna knew that she was probably being unfair. But she found it hard to remain objective after all this time.

Her studies and what was termed her altruism, had helped her with the parole board. She had refused to apply for parole before, feeling that in some way she was undeserving. Johanna knew that she had been in receipt of advantages that many of the other women could only have dreamed of. Johanna had grown up in a loving home, had believed she had a loving marriage, until circumstances were to prove otherwise. She had been educated and her education had been broad based, covering not just the basics but, as she got older, been led by her own interests. She had loved her children and been loved by them. For the first thirty-five years of her life, Johanna felt she had been privileged.

And then it had all fallen apart. Eric had been accused, they had left their home, they had wandered almost three years in the wilderness and taken their children into danger. And for nothing — that was what Johanna found so hard to bear. What she found so unforgivable. Had her husband truly been innocent and that innocence been proven, then she and her brood could have resumed their lives, returned to the safety of their community and moved on. Eric's lies had robbed them of everything. He had deserved to die.

But had her children deserved to have been deprived of their mother? In the cold light shed by ten years of imprisonment and loss, Johanna knew that she had made the wrong choice. She should have put her children first, given the evidence to the police and hoped it was enough for Eric to have rotted in prison for the rest of his natural life. She had to live with that misstep now and there was very little Johanna could do about it.

She consoled herself by acknowledging that while she might not be totally happy about the choices her younger children might make, if Evie went off to university and Daniel perhaps chose a career in the arts — though perhaps he could be prevailed upon to see that as a part-time occupation and continue to serve the community. To keep himself safe? Though even if her children chose a path that Johanna was not entirely happy with, she knew that they would be making those choices from firm and loving foundations and that the community would guard and guide them for as long as it could.

Three of her children were safe. One, sadly, was no more. That left Paul.

Johanna sat at one of the computers in the library and stared at the screen. She was tempted to find the article that this journalist, Tom Andrews, had written about them and which had so angered Paul. No, that could wait. First of all she needed to know about Ross Cahn, the man he had served his final weeks with and the man that Paul had told her was leading him onto potentially very dangerous ground. If she could find some evidence that she could take to the police, perhaps she could make things right. Johanna had already decided that this time she would have to act in a more conventional manner, if only because she had to be honest with herself and admit that taking on a younger man, with a view to putting him out of her son's life, might not be within her capabilities. It was one thing to bash Eric over the head — she could still feel the smooth shape of the heavy glass paperweight in her hand and the memory of how it had felt when she had caved in Eric's skull. It would never leave her. She'd been told that she'd struck him in just the perfect spot — though not for Eric, of course. By chance he had been in the act of turning towards her, the side of his head slightly exposed and she had caught him hard on the temple. Had she struck the back of his head the thickness of his skull might have saved him. Or not. Johanna had been standing slightly above him as he'd taken his first step onto the staircase and rage had given her arm additional heft and force. Her full weight — the full weight of her intent — had been behind that blow.

Johanna put the memories aside. This Ross Cahn would be another kettle of fish entirely. Johanna was ten years older and feeling every one of them. She was hurtling towards fifty and though she knew that this was no age, not in real terms, it seemed old. David, the leader of the community, was over seventy and still hale and hearty and working as many hours as he'd ever done. Those living in the safe haven of the Community of Solomon often lived to very great ages indeed and most enjoyed healthy and happy retirement, retirement being a gradual process that took place according to the needs of the individual, rather than some arbitrary pensionable age.

She typed the name of Ross Cahn and was surprised at the number of results that came up. Clicking on the first, she was taken by surprise.

The report was eight years old and was the kind of feel-good filler piece that was bread and butter for local news outlets. It showed an award ceremony, honouring young people who had served their local community in some special way. At first she assumed this must be another Ross Cahn — though Cahn, with that spelling, was such an unusual name, so surely . . . She searched for another photograph of Cahn and found one associated with the court reports from his sentencing. Steven had been convinced that the young man came from Kent, she remembered, but he had that wrong. Ross Cahn was definitely a local lad and this was also most definitely the boy in the picture of the award ceremony.

Carefully, she compared the picture of the ceremony with that of the other photograph, taken only eighteen months later at Ross Cahn's court appearance, the picture having been snapped outside the court. A young man with his hand raised as though to shield his face from scrutiny — just a little too late to prevent the photograph being taken. There was no doubt, this was the same person and, when she read the details of the report, the reference to previous good character and service to his community were mentioned, the judge essentially telling Cahn that someone with his advantages and obvious abilities should be ashamed of himself.

Johanna searched for other information on the court case. Serious assault — the victim, a young woman called Priscilla Eames, who had been nineteen at the time of the attack, still in a coma three months on — possession of drugs with intent to supply. Other, more minor offences.

She had a number of tabs opened now and she returned to the picture of the award ceremony. Six young people posing for a picture, clutching envelopes and little boxes that she assumed must contain their prizes. At the front of the group Ross Cahn, then eighteen years old, looking happy and relaxed, a rather goofy smile plastered across his face, body turned slightly awkwardly towards the photographer, shook hands with the businessman who had put up the monetary element of the awards. The businessman was tall, well built, black and, Johanna thought, robustly good-looking. He too was smiling broadly, and Johanna got the impression that both he and Cahn were genuinely glad to be there, at the ceremony, giving and receiving what was well deserved.

She read the names captioned beneath the photograph. Only Cahn's was immediately familiar to her. Although . . . where had she read that name before? She knew it was in the past day or so. Surely it was not . . .

Swiftly, she searched for Morgan Springfield and stared in horror at the news of the man's murder.

CHAPTER 16

Mike sincerely wished that he could have taken the Saturday off, but this early in the murder investigation it was obviously impossible. He consoled himself with the thought that had he been at home, the Saturday morning would have involved a trek around various garden centres, Maria set on looking for winter bedding for the large terracotta pots outside the front door. John had stepped into the breach at the last minute and Mike knew that the older man would in fact enjoy the experience and that the morning shopping would end in lunch in a country pub and might even drift into afternoon tea. That part of it Mike would have enjoyed, but he'd be the first to admit that although he enjoyed the garden he wasn't exactly into the process of gardening. Maria tended to call him in when she needed something chopping down and even then she shadowed him, pointing out exactly where to cut rather than trusting to his discretion.

So, instead of choosing primulas and winter pansies and whatever evergreens she might have picked out, Mike was ensconced in an examination of financial records, while Jude, together with DS Terry Gleeson, examined random information thrown up when the area had been canvassed and the lists that Lucille Connolly had dropped off for them that morning.

She'd apologised for the length and the somewhat random nature of the final scripts.

"Sid quite literally wrote down everything and everyone he could think of," she'd said. "He remembered something. Morgan coming in one day very distressed and saying he'd run into an old acquaintance and the man — at least Sid thinks it was a man — accused him of letting him down in some way. You might want to talk to Sid about it. The date and everything he can remember about the incident is on the last page. It might be nothing, but—"

"Thank you," Mike said. "I'll give him a call when we've been through all this." He looked at the bundle of papers in the folder Luce had given him and thought that might take some time. "Thank you both for doing this," he said, meaning it. "It can't have been easy."

She nodded. "Not to start with but once Sid began, I don't think he could stop. Look, it may not be helpful, but I suspect you'll be getting more of the same. Sid's desperate to do something. He feels so damned helpless."

Now, Mike glanced over at Jude and the others. DS Gleeson had done a long stint in community policing early in his career and he still kept up his old contacts. People liked him — a rare accolade for a copper, Mike often thought — and Terry Gleeson genuinely cared about the community where he had grown up. A quick glance at Sid's folder had told Mike that there was a lot in it about organisations Morgan Springfield had belonged to and the associations he had made. There would be people in there that Terry knew and would therefore be able to approach on a more personal level. Likely they'd tell Terry more than they would a stranger.

It was likely that by Monday morning the team would have dramatically increased in number. Those above Mike's pay grade were assessing the likelihood of the Gary Gibson case being directly connected to the killing of Morgan Springfield. Mike was acutely aware that for now there was no direct evidence. There were similarities that convinced him it was at least worth considering. But was that enough to warrant putting a major-incident team together? One murder could be dealt with in-house, as it were — two would trigger a greater response. Was that response disproportionate given what they presently had?

As Mike had been reminded by his bosses, yes, the Gibson case was unsolved but it was also eighteen years old and neither HOLMES nor the Police National Computer database, or any other, had turned up a similar staging in the meantime. Just now it was all so much coincidence.

Mike had not been surprised at the response, but he was keeping the Gibson case actively in mind and knew his colleagues were doing the same.

The financial records from Springfield's company seemed straightforward. They'd be examined by a forensic accountant later, but he wanted to have a glance through, just to familiarise himself with essential background. The bank account looked healthy, the start-up loan Morgan Springfield had borrowed had been repaid early and Springfield's being a limited company, the financials were a matter of record at Companies House. The only surprise, for Mike, was discovering that Sid Patterson was a partner in the company, albeit a junior one. Morgan had not just been his employer as Mike had first thought. A brief examination of the records, together with helpful notes from their accountant, informed him that in addition to the start-up loan, Morgan and Sid had both sunk their savings into the business. It seemed their risk had paid off.

Until now.

Could Sid be implicated in Morgan's death? Did he want control of the company? Mike dismissed the idea — it was one that had to be asked but Mike was convinced that Sid's grief was genuine. Besides, you weren't looking at a multimillion corporation here. The company was doing well, with a healthy turnover and assets in the shape of machinery and the usual office equipment. They employed staff, mostly on a freelance basis, which Mike assumed must keep costs down, the only real exceptions to that being Cath, the PA and the specialist toolmakers. Mike had only a vague idea of what these three employees would be doing but assumed that as they were employed full time, it must be central to the business model.

He was distracted from his perusal by a call from the front desk. A woman had come in and was demanding to see him. Her name was Johanna Pearson.

Mike groaned. It was enough that John had chosen to involve himself in this woman's probably imaginary concerns, but here she was, asking for him. His first instinct was to fob her off with an excuse or even to send Jude. Jude was good with troublesome people. His second was that seeing her might be the quickest way of getting rid. The Pearson business brought back nothing but distasteful memories and also, he felt that overall it had not been well handled. Nothing had gone right — there had been deaths, there had been the revelation of high-level police corruption. The fallout had been unpleasant to say the least.

"Problem?" Jude asked, glancing up.

"Just an inconvenience. I hope." He looked at his watch, noting that it was almost lunchtime, and then went reluctantly downstairs and into Reception.

Johanna Pearson was standing beside the desk. Mike's impression of her had always been of a woman who was tall and thin and a little uncomfortable in her own skin. He remembered that she had thick, dark hair pulled back into a knot at the nape of her neck. It seemed to Mike that she was taller and thinner than ever and the dark hair was now streaked with grey. She still wore the long skirts she had worn in their previous encounters and her jacket was buttoned tight, even though it was warm in the lobby. She looked older, Mike thought, reminding himself that a decade had passed and that for Johanna Pearson it would have been a hard one.

"Mrs Pearson. What can I do for you?"

"Inspector Croft. I hope you can listen." She studied him thoughtfully as though she was as aware of the years passing him by as he was of her. He found himself hoping that he had aged better and then felt the thought was cruel and unworthy. What was it about this woman that raised his hackles, caused him to go on the defensive? Mike wasn't sure but he did not like the way this woman made him behave. He did not like himself when he was around her.

"You wanted to speak to me? Mrs Pearson, I'm in the middle of a murder enquiry—"

"I know. That's why I'm here."

She thrust several pieces of paper in his direction. Computer printouts of news items, Mike saw.

"Please, just look at them."

Mike sighed but flicked through the pages. Morgan Springfield giving an award. He was smiling and looked relaxed and happy, and Mike felt a sudden sorrow, that this evidently vibrant man had been taken from the world so violently.

He was surrounded by a gaggle of six young people, all looking equally happy and clutching large white envelopes and wooden boxes.

Johanna pointed to one of them. "His name is Ross Cahn and I believe he was involved in killing Mr Springfield."

Before Mike could ask why, she jabbed at another printout. This concerned the attack on a young woman called Priscilla Eames. "Look, this proves he's violent. See what he did to her."

Frowning, Mike read the brief article. Cahn had been arrested. The young woman had been struck with a hammer and was lucky to be alive. Cahn was reported as saying that he'd lost his temper but had offered no other excuse or explanation for his actions. There was a picture of Priscilla Eames. Dark haired, pretty, late teens, smiling out at the photographer.

Mike frowned, reminded for a moment of the murder of Morgan Springfield. While it was true that hammers featured in both attacks, the MOs of the two assailants were quite different. There was nothing to suggest a definite connection.

"I'm sorry, Mrs Pearson, but this doesn't prove he went on to kill anyone."

"It shows he was capable!"

"Capable, probably, but—"

She jabbed her finger angrily at the images of Ross Cahn outside the court. Ross Cahn's victim, Priscilla Eames, finally released from hospital but still requiring care.

"I'm sorry, I don't quite understand."

"Cahn knew Mr Springfield."

"A lot of people knew Mr Springfield."

"Oh, don't be so obtuse, man. He made threats. He threatened to kill someone when he got out of prison. My Paul told me, they shared a cell just before he was released. Oh, he didn't tell Paul who he was going to kill, but isn't it obvious? Just look! The man is dead and Cahn threatened to kill someone. He wanted Paul to help."

Mike stared at her for a moment as the wheels clicked into place. So this was what she'd wanted to tell John Tynan about — that her son's cellmate had made threats and now a man he had briefly met, at an awards ceremony eight years before, had been murdered. Ergo he must have been responsible.

"Mrs Pearson, thank you for your concern and for bringing this to my attention, but—"

Johanna glared at him. "Why is everyone so reluctant to listen!"

Mike was aware of the desk sergeant looking their way, barely able to conceal his amusement. Of a young couple coming through the double doors, clearly perturbed by Johanna's raised voice. Mike sighed. "I can give you ten minutes," he told her and led the way through to a small interview room off the reception area.

Johanna followed, head held high and long skirt swirling. "I don't have much time either," she told him. "I had to catch a bus to get here and they are few and far between, these days. So unless you're prepared to offer me a lift, I also need to be quick."

That suited Mike just fine. The idea of offering Johanna Pearson a lift was not one that appealed either.

"So," he said. "Tell me what happened with Paul. I understand you planned to speak to John Tynan, but that the meeting didn't quite go to plan."

Johanna dismissed this with a wave of her hand. "I thought he'd hear me out, but our meeting was unsuccessful. Then I wasn't sure what I should do, so I spoke to Steven. He's my second eldest."

Mike nodded, pushing aside the memories that threatened to invade, as they always did when he heard of a child with that name.

"Paul had talked to me, you see, told me that the last few weeks he spent in prison, this man Ross Cahn shared a cell with him and he told him things. Cahn wanted someone dead; he wanted Paul to help him. Paul was naturally upset by this, distressed—"

"Did he report the conversation?"

She frowned at the interruption. "No. Do you honestly think anything would have been done if he had? You've clearly not spent time in jail."

Clearly, Mike thought. He gestured for her to go on. "Paul was released first. This Cahn told him that when he got out he was going to find Paul and that Paul was going to help him."

"To kill someone."

"That's what I said." She glanced impatiently at her watch. "Yesterday I spoke to Steven. Paul had confided in him too, told him about Cahn, but he had also insisted, with both of us, that he had been making this up. Steven chose to believe that — I do not. Paul was frightened. I know fear when I see it."

Mike nodded. He gestured towards the printouts. "So, you wanted to find out about this Ross Cahn."

"So, I went to the library and I found him. The first thing I found was from when he won the prize. Morgan Springfield awarded the prizes."

119

"To six young people," Mike said, pointing to the picture.

"Five of whom did not subsequently go off the rails." Johanna's voice was stern. "Then I found reference to his arrest and court appearance. He beat that poor young woman so badly she was in a coma for months. That's proof that he's violent."

"But not proof that he had anything to do with Morgan Springfield's murder. Johanna, no, listen to me for a moment, please. Mr Springfield probably didn't even meet these young people until the evening he presented the awards. It's likely he never saw them again. Now, I promise you, I will pass your information on and Ross Cahn will be spoken to if he's returned here. But do you even have any evidence that he's come back to East Anglia, never mind here. Has your son had any contact with him since he was released?"

She opened her mouth to speak and then reluctantly shook her head. "I don't know."

"So, Mrs Pearson, I understand that you were alarmed by the possibility. You're worried about your son, of course you are. It can't have been easy for any of you. I promise to add this to our background checks and to ask the probation service if Mr Cahn has made his way back here. That his PO needs to at least have a word. It's possible, don't you think, that Cahn just wanted to seem harder than he was. That he was mouthing off to try to protect himself. Adult prison can be a difficult place for young men. It could all have been posturing."

He could see she wasn't convinced and, to be fair, why should she be? Mike didn't know the truth of the situation any more than Johanna did.

"I suppose that will have to do," she said, standing up, and he was suddenly pained by how defeated she looked.

Mike might not actually like the woman, but he could spare a degree of sympathy. Life had not treated Johanna Pearson well.

After she'd gone, he returned to the incident room and dropped the printouts on his desk. Jude looked up from her work. She raised a quizzical eyebrow. Mike grabbed a chair and scooted it over to the table where Jude and Terry Gleeson were working. "Are you familiar with the Pearson case, about ten years ago, so the pair of you would still have been . . ." Actually, he wasn't sure what they would have been. Jude probably just finishing university, Terry . . .

"Doing teacher training and realising I didn't like kids. Though it wasn't called teacher training then, it was something like early years development."

"Really?" Jude's astonishment echoed Mike's. Terry was an affable guy, well liked and easy-going, but somehow Mike could not imagine him in a classroom.

"Like Jude, here, I finished my degree and looked at joining the police. Actually, I looked at taking a bridging course and becoming a solicitor. But my uncle is a solicitor and I did work experience at his offices. Hated that too." Terry grinned. "But sure, I remember the Pearson business. Hard to forget if you lived around here."

"I'm a blow-in, remember," Jude said.

"It was at the same time as all the revelations about child abuse in children's homes," Terry said. "This chap, Eric Pearson, he reckoned he'd got some kind of journal that revealed names of offenders. People who didn't work in the homes, but who were allowed access. He'd had accusations made against him, from what I remember. Photographs?" He looked at Mike.

Mike nodded.

"Anyhow, he was making a lot of noise and also causing a disturbance where he lived. Or being at the centre of one, anyway. No one seemed to know who started it all, but it went from name calling and bad feeling to stone throwing and petrol bombs. Nasty business. Anyway, his missus found out that he'd been lying to her about the kiddie porn and wacked him over the head. Killed him."

"Lacking in nuance," Mike said, "but accurate in outline."

Terry Gleeson grinned at him. "So, what about it?"

"Mrs Pearson was released on licence about a month ago. While she was inside her kids were looked after by relatives, but the oldest one never did settle, got into trouble and ended up in a young offenders' centre. Just before he was coming up for release, he got into a fight or something. I don't have the details of that but as he was over eighteen, he finished his time in an adult prison. There he met another young man, Ross Cahn. Cahn apparently made threats to kill someone and perhaps threatened Paul in some way, so he'd become involved. At least that's the gist of what he told his mother. Johanna Pearson wants to protect her son, so she did some digging, found out that Ross Cahn and Morgan Springfield crossed paths some eight years ago, when Springfield presented an award to Cahn and a group of other young people for community services."

He tapped the printout Johanna had given him and turned it so that Jude and Terry could see. "Mrs Pearson is now convinced that Cahn killed Morgan Springfield, so she paid me a visit to present her evidence."

He watched as Jude and Terry studied the printouts and Jude said, "I can see how she made the leap. It's the kind of leap you might make when you're scared and trying to make sense of things, but—"

"Eight years ago," Terry said thoughtfully. "Morgan Springfield hadn't been here for long at that point. It's interesting that he should have been chosen to present the awards. I wonder if he was involved in setting them up."

Mike sighed. "Add it to the stack. Monday, I promise we'll have extra bodies to help with the drudge work, even if I have to go to the canteen and volunteer someone."

* * *

Johanna stared out of the window of the bus and wondered what more she could do. She realised that she was hungry — she'd eaten a hasty breakfast of cereal she didn't really like and now it was almost two. She recalled that yesterday at around this time she had been back at the community house and David had made a sandwich for her. Johanna felt her body sag under the weight of so much loss.

She had one more thing to follow up from what Steven had told her and that was the address that Paul sometimes used, unbeknownst to his probation officer. It was in an area of Norwich unfamiliar to Johanna and according to the map it would be a two-bus journey to get there. Johanna wasn't sure she had the energy for that today. Driven by desperation she might be, but was also exhausted by the long years of worry and incarceration, and the idea that this might be another wild goose chase just about defeated her. Steven had said this was an address Paul sometimes used — not that it was where her son lived. She should have told Inspector Croft, perhaps, that this might be where he could find her son. She had held back because this was not where Paul was supposed to have been living.

As for the official line? He'd been allocated a tiny bed-sit at the top of a converted house according to Steven. It was, he said, small and cramped and Paul had sub-let it to someone else just to give him some extra cash. She could go there, she supposed. Presumably Paul must come back sometimes, if only to claim the rent. It didn't sound like the kind of arrangement that went through any sort of official channel. She was familiar enough with the post-prison process to know that the actual landlord was probably getting paid directly for the use of the flat and probably had no incentive to check on who was actually living there. Any money from the sub-let would be going straight into her son's pocket.

Expecting the unofficial tenants to tell her anything was a long shot, Johanna knew, but it was at least in walking distance from the hostel and it felt less daunting than crossing town again.

Johanna left the bus and walked the twenty minutes back to the hostel, pausing only to buy bread and cheese and ham and, because it was a long time since she'd eaten it, a jar of piccalilli. She didn't expect it to be a patch on the pickles they had made in the community kitchen but it would do. She had loved that time of year. Late summer into autumn, when jams and pickled preserves and cordials were laid down for winter. But, she told herself sternly, it didn't do to dwell on that now.

Once back at the hostel she retreated to her room, made tea and assembled her sandwich. She would eat and then rest for a little while and then head out for the flat later that evening. Perhaps she might strike lucky and the residents would know where her son might be found. She just prayed that he was safe from harm.

CHAPTER 17

By mid-afternoon Mike had finished with the financials for Springfield's work and personal papers, and had perused Sid's records. So far as he could tell there was nothing particular of note. Springfield's had a small trust set up that donated regularly to charitable causes. The amounts were small but Mike imagined must make a big difference. New toys for a playgroup, a computer for a scout group, a grant towards musical instruments for an after-school club. He had retrieved and flicked through the lists that Sid Patterson had brought in and found mention of these organisations and more, together with a handful of contacts. This active altruism, Mike guessed, had been Morgan's baby rather than his partner's, as Sid seemed only to know some of those individuals Morgan Springfield had dealt with in this concern.

Mike realised that he was still not sure what Sid's role in the company had been. Morgan seemed to have been very hands-on in the day-to-day running, liaising with customers, and, as an engineer by training, presumably understanding what happened on the factory floor. Sid was listed as an executive director, (financial), but what precisely did that involve? The man himself had been equally vague about it all. 'Jack-of-all-trades.' That's what he'd called himself, wasn't it?

Mike supposed that, in such a small company, both partners would have to pitch in with whatever needed doing, regardless of their official job title.

Terry came over and dropped Johanna Pearson's printouts on Mike's desk before pulling up a chair.

"I got curious," he said.

"A dangerous trait in a police officer."

Terry grinned at him. "I've made some calls," he said. "I managed to get hold of Fi Perkins — she was chair of the charity, the Loftus Project, that was behind the Montgomery Awards that year. Those were the awards that Morgan presented. I thought she might be able to give me some background and tell us why Morgan Springfield was chosen to present the prizes. It turns out she knew him from a couple of youth projects they'd both been involved in and a young entrepreneurs' club they were hoping to set up, in association with the University of East Anglia, so he seemed like an obvious choice. She was shocked to hear what happened to him. She said something interesting, though — she reckoned that back then, Mr Springfield was really hands-on with the various projects and genuinely interested in what happened to the young people afterwards. But that all changed after the Montgomery Awards. She reckoned he was still interested, but preferred to keep his distance and just to make donations after that.

"I asked her why she thought that had happened and she got a bit defensive, but she finally admitted that one of the award winners had 'let them down' and it was decided that the Loftus Project should, and I also quote, 'change its direction'. She thought Morgan Springfield had taken a similar position."

"So, Ross Cahn blotted everyone's copybook," Mike said.

"Certainly looks that way."

By the end of Saturday, Mike felt that he knew a little more about Morgan Springfield. As Sid had explained, he had returned to his home county just short of nine years previously, after a few years in London and a brief time in Edinburgh. He was forty-three when he died, attended the gym three times a week straight after work — one of those days typically being

Tuesday. He was active in his local community, supporting a variety of charitable causes, mostly to do with young people, and he spoke regularly at the entrepreneurs' club set up by a group of local sixth-form academies, but open to all over-sixteens who were interested in business. It seemed that the project with the university had not taken off and Mike wondered if that too was indirectly because of the Ross Cahn publicity.

He'd had two serious relationships, prior to Sid. One of his ex-partners still lived at the address Sid had provided in London. Mike had spoken with him and found the man had been deeply shocked by the news of Morgan's death. They had been very young when they'd got together and the eventual split had been amicable. Morgan had even been an usher at his wedding. The second had not ended well. Morgan Springfield had followed his then-partner to Scotland when he'd moved for work. For a while he had commuted between his new home there and his business back in England, but it had been a hard task keeping both ends of his life happy. Arguments had followed, the relationship had faltered and eventually died.

Jude had spoken to this ex and though he'd been shocked to hear the news, Jude had the impression that he'd been no more shocked than if he'd heard of a vague acquaintance suffering a violent death.

"He'll be dining out on that story for a while," was Jude's rather tart appraisal.

In the background for the past decade had been Sid. Sid was now thirty-nine and, as he had told Mike, they had met initially at university. Both Morgan and Sid had gone to university as mature students, Sid at twenty-five, after leaving the army, and Morgan at around the same age, though he'd been doing his MA when Sid had first encountered him and Sid been on the last year of his degree. The friendship had been instant, it seemed, and the business association had followed after a few years. They had been partners since starting up eight years before.

Still, all this digging into Morgan and Sid's backstory was getting them nowhere fast.

By the time the end-of-day briefing came round, Mike had precious little to report. "But we're no nearer coming up with a motive." He looked out at the blank faces of his team. "No one has a bad word to say about him. No unusual activity has been noted near the unit, on the wider industrial estate or close to Mr Springfield's home. CCTV has turned up nothing significant so far, but coverage isn't great. Anyone familiar with the area or for that matter anyone taking the time to scope out where the cameras are, would soon realise that. There are, so far as we can tell at this stage, no financial irregularities and whoever committed the murder was forensically savvy. No prints, no trace evidence so far, and the briefcase and laptop are still missing. So, essentially, apart from knowing more about the victim, we are no further forward than we were on Wednesday morning."

He could see from their faces that everyone felt as frustrated by that as Mike himself.

When the rest of his team had gone, Mike sat down with the three boxes relating to the Gary Gibson murder. He'd been through the evidence, as had Jude, but nothing had leaped out at him, apart from those photographs of the crime scene. Was he imagining a connection? He didn't think so and neither did anyone else who had seen the images.

But no other deaths had turned up that were in any way similar in the intervening years. Which, for Mike's money, suggested that the killer had been prevented from further actions. And most likely had been in prison.

Jude had requested lists of recently released prisoners, refining her request on the assumption that they would have been inside for at least the past decade and so would have been convicted of more violent crimes. She had begun with those known to have returned to the area, because you had to start somewhere, but that didn't necessarily mean that the killer was a local man. He could have travelled in from anywhere, killed Morgan Springfield and left again.

Mike looked once again at the photograph of the crime scene, the oddly positioned pen that had nagged at him in the first place, and tried to tell himself that he was overcomplicating matters.

No, he thought. *I'm not. There's a link. I'm certain of it.*

* * *

By the end of Saturday evening, Johanna knew for certain that her son Paul would come to no good end if he continued to mix with the likes of the couple who were living in his flat. His official flat, that was — the one registered with the probation service, not the address that Steven mentioned as a place Paul sometimes used to crash. She had still not summoned the energy to cross town in order to get to that one.

The bedsit was right at the top of the house, a three-storey with a basement about a twenty-minute fast walk from where Johanna was housed. The main front door had been wedged open and cold air had flooded into the hallway alongside dead leaves and mud from wet feet. The house stank of damp and a smell Johanna identified as skunk. There had been a time when she'd known nothing about drugs, but the past years had educated her. No one challenged her as she made her way upstairs. The carpets were worn and the walls felt deeply chilled. Old, textured wallpaper had been painted over so many times that the pattern had become almost sculptural. The lights on the stairs were low wattage and triggered by her movement — they shut off automatically only seconds after she had passed. The whole lent the staircase a surreal air, as though she was ascending into a space that was not quite real. She passed landings and numbered doors, music leaking out of one, raised voices from another, a third oddly silent. Finally, she had reached the top of the house.

Johanna knocked on the final door.

Then knocked again.

From inside she could hear movement.

This time she hammered on the panelled wood and finally the door cracked open. A young woman peered through the gap.

The room stank of skunk and sweat and, Johanna thought, sheets unwashed for far too long. "I'm looking for my son," Johanna said.

The puzzlement on the young woman's face cleared slightly when Johanna told her she was looking for Paul.

"Oh, him. No, he don't live here. We do. He said it was all right. We pay him."

She seemed about to close the door, so Johanna reached out and pushed it back. The young woman staggered slightly. Johanna could smell alcohol on her breath. "Do you know where I can find him?"

"How the fuck should I know?" The girl — Johanna had revised her initial assessment of her age — turned and spoke to a man sitting on the bed. "She wants Paul."

"So?"

"I want to find my son." Johanna squared her shoulders and took a single step into the room.

"He's not here."

"I can see that. So where will I find him?"

"The fuck I know?" The man got up and moved towards her. He had a knife in his hand and waved it in Johanna's direction, but if he expected Johanna to quail or flee then he was disappointed. She had met with worse than him.

"What arrangements do you have with regard to paying rent?" she asked, noting the confusion in the young man's eyes both, she guessed, at her question and at the manner of its asking.

"What arrangements . . . what the fuck does that mean?"

"It means, does he come and collect it or do you take it to him?"

"We take it to him," the girl said. The man hissed his disapproval.

"And you take it where?"

"Wherever he tells us to meet him. He texts."

"And is this a regular thing? A weekly or a monthly meeting?"

The girl shook her head.

"And do you always have the money, when he wants paying? If these meetings are so irregular?"

For the first time, the girl looked truly uneasy. "We pay," she said. "Always. He's not—"

"Shut it," the man told her, his tone sharp, but Johanna also detected anxiety.

"Are you afraid of my son?" she asked, bristling slightly at the thought.

The man advanced further, practically nose to nose with Johanna now though, she noted, the knife was not in involved, merely clasped at his side. Was it her manner or was it the fact that she was Paul's mother that had put him on the back foot? He might be putting on a good front, but she could see in his eyes that he was far from as confident as he wanted to appear. She looked at his hands and exposed wrists, noting the crude tattoos.

"I take it you met my son in prison," she said. "Is that where you learned to be afraid of him?"

She stepped back before he had time to answer, knowing that she'd pushed her luck far enough. The door was slammed in her face.

Johanna went downstairs, pausing on the first landing where she had heard the music playing. She knocked on the door. The music paused and the door was opened by another young man, this one neat and clean, wearing jeans and what she guessed was a band T-shirt. It mentioned a tour and what she assumed was the name of the band and the album they were touring. His feet were bare.

He must have been expecting someone because there'd been a welcoming smile on his face when he opened the door. This had now been replaced by confusion. Johanna decided to be direct.

"The people upstairs, in the top-floor flat. Do you know their names?"

"What?"

"My son was supposed to be living there. I'm trying to find him."

He still looked bemused. Johanna glanced over his shoulder. The room was untidy, she noted, but not dirty, and there were books on the desk and a laptop on the bed. "You should keep your door firmly locked," she said. "And don't leave valuables in there. That pair are not to be trusted."

"Her name's Emmie. I think his might be Josh. That's all I know. I don't have anything to do with them."

"Keep it that way," Johanna told him sharply. "My son's name is Paul. He's about as tall as you and has dark hair and blue eyes. He's thin. Too thin. Have you seen him?"

He shook his head. "I don't take much notice of who comes and goes up there," he said, his tone somewhere between defensive and apologetic.

"Best keep it that way," Johanna said again.

The sound of footsteps and voices drifted up from the hallway and the young man looked relieved. Johanna guessed this was who he had been expecting when she had knocked on his door. She turned to go, wondering if it was worth asking the newcomers, two girls and a boy, all student types, she thought, if they had seen Paul.

She decided against. That if they were regular visitors then they too would have decided to remain ignorant of what went on in that attic room or who went up there. Instead, she marched down the stairs and out into the street and only then did she allow herself to think about what had happened. He had threatened her with a knife, that man in Paul's flat. He could have done her serious harm.

And then another thought hard on its heels. Once he had realised who she was, once she'd invoked her son's name, she'd seen the fear in his eyes and in those of the girl. They might be living in Paul's flat but they were doing so because it suited him and it suited him because they were paying him, and Johanna had got the distinct impression that whatever else that couple neglected to pay, it would not be what they owed in rent.

They had reason to be afraid of Paul.

CHAPTER 18

If Emmie and Josh were afraid of Paul Pearson, then Paul in his turn had reason to be fearful of Ross Cahn. Cahn, he thought, was a complete nutcase and someone that, had he been able to make a choice, Paul would not just have crossed the road to avoid but moved to another city.

For the last few weeks of jail time, Paul's life had been dominated by Cahn. The man had kept at him, day and night, about how when he got out he'd got a job to do and Paul was going to help him do it. Paul hadn't laid eyes on the man until the day he'd been moved into his cell and he fervently wished that had continued to be the case.

Once he'd got out, he'd toyed with the idea of going to speak to David and accepting the offer of returning to the community, albeit asking if he could be moved north to York or Scotland. Maybe that would be far enough away. But the idea had lost some of its shine when he'd realised that he really wasn't suited to returning. That it would feel like confinement, that he was no longer sure he could toe the line. Sure, he knew he'd be welcomed, his siblings were happy there, but Paul had never been, not as a teenager. Returning to the community immediately after their mother had killed his father and realising he had to remain there for as long as she was incarcerated . . . it had felt like being smothered. He hadn't wanted to be loved, hadn't wanted to be pitied, hadn't wanted the careful looks and even more careful words as the extended family watched to see how the children settled back into their old home; the quiet discussion about how their adults could help them cope. Then there had been the departures of those Paul had known in childhood, for the other communities in the north, so that their mother's actions and their father's guilt should not reflect badly on the lives of the young and those just starting out in marriage and childrearing.

Soon, the only ones remaining had been close kin to the Pearsons or had been older members of the community well used to weathering storms. Paul had been terribly aware that he and his siblings had been in some ways hived off from the greater community, were almost in isolation from them as though they were infectious and the Children of Solomon wanted to limit the contamination. The unfairness of that ate at him and, worse than that, he had felt that as the eldest child he must take on the role of responsible adult. Be strong and firm and reassuring and not admit to all of these roiling, bitter emotions that threatened to swamp him.

He had told everyone that he was just fine, that he didn't need to talk and, no, he definitely didn't need counselling. That there was nothing to say. He had recognised the anxious glances between the elders and the gentle acts of persuasion from his aunt and cousins, and the collective held breath when the social workers had come, in case his control broke and all of the hard work everyone had been putting in to ensure the children could stay with their families might come to nothing.

In his more logical moments Paul knew that even had he acted out, had misbehaved in front of the women from fostering and adoption, yelling and screaming like he'd wanted to, the outcome would have been the same. His siblings were evidently safe and loved and as happy as three traumatised kids could be expected to be. It was obvious that their friends and relatives would be the best caretakers. But he had enjoyed that illusion of control for the moments it had lasted. Had relished the idea that he, Paul, might be the one with the power who could yell and scream and fling false accusations at their guardians and cast suspicion on them all. After all, the stupid little ornament with the film negatives hidden inside that had caused all the trouble, hadn't that been at the house until that damned fool, Cousin Sam, had brought it over?

Didn't that prove that someone else was guilty? Not Eric or not just Eric? That Eric's brother, Paul's uncle, that he might be guilty too?

But even in Paul's wildest moments he could not keep up the pretence for long. No one in the community would have done anything like that to a child. Apart from anything else, with everyone living cheek by jowl, what opportunity would they have had? It was the fact that Eric had worked and studied elsewhere that would have given him opportunity. Had Eric been guilty.

In his lowest moments Paul had to acknowledge his father's guilt but, somehow, even then, he also held him to be innocent and the whole thing just a set-up. It was an idea he had to hang on to, if only to keep his sense of injustice burning, if only to feed his anger and sometimes, Paul felt, that was all he really had left.

He was sitting on the sagging old sofa at Cahn's place, waiting for him to come back from . . . wherever. With Ross Cahn you didn't ask and hoped he didn't tell, going over the events of the Friday morning in the probation officer's crowded little room. He was angry with his mother for dragging him into all this, angry with Steven for talking to her and most of all angry with himself for, in a moment of weakness, telling first Steven and then his mother that he was afraid of what Cahn was going to do.

OK, so two moments of weakness, he supposed. God, that was pathetic. What was he? A three-year-old that had to tell Mummy he was scared?

And he was scared, that was the long and the short of it. He was bloody terrified.

But he should not have confided in Johanna, not even in a moment of weakness. He should have remembered what she was like, like a terrier with a rat once she got hold of an idea — she'd shake it till all signs of fight were gone, not settle for anything less than the whole, bloody truth. He certainly didn't want her confronting Ross Cahn and not just because it would make Paul look such a fool, telling his mummy he was scared. Cahn was dangerous and had even more dangerous associates — Johanna could find herself in real trouble if she got too close.

Restlessly he got up and went over to the window. He'd not drawn the curtains, not wanted to shut out the light from the town, the noise of cars and people in the street, of life and normality. The flat was above a shop in a street that was all flats and shops. Rundown and tatty, the area was still vibrant and alive with people coming and going, off to work, off to the convenience store that stayed open all hours, off to the pub. In the morning he'd be woken by the sound of kids on their way to the local primary school, parents and buggies and toddlers in tow as they walked the school-age children along the busy road. Ironically, it was the school at which Eric had taught for a while, where he had met the kids who had made those accusations against him. On one occasion, when Paul had walked past the school, he had paused on the other side of the road and looked through the gates. The school was red-brick Victorian, the yard enclosed by high walls and the tarmac playground painted with hopscotch squares and a long-tailed snake with numbers on it for some game he did not recognise. He had wondered, as he stood there, what had happened to the kids Eric had taught.

Occasionally, he felt sorry for them. More often, when all the memories and fears threatened to overwhelm him, Paul knew that he would happily have destroyed them all.

The sound of the street door opening and footsteps on uncarpeted stairs announced the return of Ross Cahn. Paul sighed, turning from the window as the flat door opened and Cahn came inside. He was taller than Paul and more powerfully built. Good-looking, Paul supposed, never seeming to have any trouble attracting the women. None of them hung around for long though — what might seem attractively feral at first glance soon revealed itself to be downright dangerous and most made a quick exit. Often, Paul noted, before the second drink. Far from annoying Cahn, this amused him — reinforced his sense of being the man no one messed with. Not if they wanted to keep all of their limbs.

His dark hair needed cutting, Paul noted, falling forward over his eyes. Cahn pushed it back.

"You ready then?" he said.

Paul nodded. The option of a negative response was simply not there.

"Well, off we go then." Cahn grinned at him but there was no humour in it and his eyes were shark-like. Paul also sensed the uncertainty there. The fear of the man he was going to see. He realised that Ross, for all his outward confidence, did not want to go and see Brian Hedgecock alone. It also crossed his mind that Brian Hedgecock might have told Cahn to bring him along. Ross had been blunt about their disappointment that Paul had not gone along with whatever they'd had in mind, even for the offer of a great deal of cash. He had given him Hedgecock's number, urged him to make contact, make an apology, create some kind of excuse. He had been vehement about the need for Paul to do this, but so far Paul had resisted and been grateful for the fact that Ross did not seem to have given the big man his mobile number.

So far.

Paul was trying hard not to think about what he suspected they had done. He sensed that Ross had been on the verge of telling him on a couple of occasions but so far had thought better of it. His mood had vacillated between fidgety anxiety and a sort of triumphant agitation these past days.

"Pay day." Cahn nodded emphatically as though to reassure himself. "After which I can go anywhere I fucking well like." Paul plucked his jacket from the arm of the sofa and followed Cahn out of the flat. He knew who was meant to be doing the paying and Paul also knew it was no use at all telling Ross that he'd be better off catching the next bus or train out of town, heading anywhere right now, rather than trust this man to keep his word. This, he predicted, was not going to end well.

* * *

Later, much later, and Paul was running for his life. He dodged between parked cars, under the flyover opposite Anglia Square, his running footsteps echoing all too loudly beneath the concrete of the bridge above. He jinked right and down the footpath and cycle track that led to Magdalen Street, disoriented now and not even sure where he was. This was not a part of town he'd come to before, familiar only with the brutalist architecture of the flyover when he travelled by car or bus.

Dimly he took in the mix of rundown shops and smarter cafés and stumbled across the road in front of cars that had to swerve or brake hard to avoid him.

The man following him didn't care about being seen. A woman shouted — a man yelled that he was calling the police. But would he? Paul wondered as his feet almost went from beneath him as he slid on black ice. It had rained before he and Cahn had left the flat and later the cloud cover had cleared and the temperature plummeted. His breath plumed and his chest tightened as he gasped in the frigid air. He knew he was almost done for, strength gone and legs burning with fatigue.

Maybe he should just stop, give into the inevitable, maybe that would be easier in the end.

Desperate now, he stumbled into a gap between two shops and found himself in a yard with a low wall at the back. He scrambled over the wall and slid down on the other side between bins and other detritus. There was a pile of cardboard beside a recycling bin that was already overflowing, the lid half open, the boxes and cut-up card stacked in a corner between the bin and the wall. Paul squirreled his way beneath it, pulling the loose stack around himself and then lying very still, trying desperately to control his breathing.

He heard footsteps, booted feet running into the short alley and then, miraculously, the sound of sirens in the distance. He heard the man pull himself up onto the wall and could almost feel his gaze as he scanned the yard. Paul closed his eyes and held his breath, certain that the end had come. It wouldn't take long for his pursuer to figure out he must have gone over the wall. He just prayed he'd assume he'd then gone out through the gate at the other end of the yard.

The sound of police sirens was closer now, and Paul heard the man swear, the fury in the tone chilling him to the core. Then the sound of him dropping from the wall on Paul's side, kicking out at the bins in his rage and knocking one to the floor with a bang.

He's going to find me, Paul thought. He curled more tightly in his nest of card and boxes. *He's going to find me.* But instead he heard the noise of sirens very close and the sound of cars screeching to a halt. Booted feet crossing the yard and dragging the gate open, letting it close with a crash as he left.

A light came on from somewhere above Paul and a window opened. Someone shouted, demanding to know what was going on. Paul lay still — he didn't think the man would come down to investigate. On the whole people felt safer shouting from upstairs windows than they did coming down to the source of strange noises in the dead of night, especially as they too must have heard the police sirens.

He could hear voices from the upper storey, from the room beyond where the man's voice had shouted. A woman, a child, then the man again, and then the sound of the window closing. The light went out.

Paul lay still in the darkness, shivering with exertion and now with cold. But he couldn't move, not yet. He dared not move. Not yet.

Instead, he managed to reposition himself so that he had layers of the cardboard beneath him, protecting him somewhat from the damp and freezing slabs in the yard. He curled between two boxes that had been protected from the earlier rain by the layers above and there he lay, shivering and exhausted until finally he must have fallen asleep, because the next thing he was aware of was that the rain had started again and the grey light of a November dawn was creeping into his refuge.

CHAPTER 19

Brian Hedgecock was not a happy man, but then, unhappy seemed to have been his default state for most of his adult life. Those who had known them both speculated that it was a condition inherited from his stepfather, perhaps by some strange process of osmosis, he also being marked by a mood of constant dissatisfaction. No one was able to state that Brian had inherited anything from his mother — she had left when Brian was no more than four or five and any influence she might have had was most definitely eroded over the intervening years. Fortunately for Brian, his stepfather and Deidre, his long-term housekeeper, had taken over his care and Brian certainly had no complaint about either of them.

Right now, Brian Hedgecock was a man looking for answers and was definitely not getting the kind of answers he wanted.

His first port of call had been the flat where Paul Pearson had been holed up with Ross Cahn. He had been prepared to give young Ross the benefit of the doubt, seeing as how he could make himself useful, seeing as how their needs seemed to be aligned. But he'd always had his doubts about Cahn's fitness for the task in hand and never had any illusions about his loyalty. It would only be a matter of time before Ross

141

Cahn was mouthing off to someone about what they'd done, just like he had when they'd both been inside. Ross Cahn was a complainer, yapping about how bad life had treated him instead of stepping up and doing something about it. Weak, that's what he was and Brian despised weakness. Once you declared your intention to do something, you should carry it through.

Hedgecock turned his attention back to the matter at hand. The time had come to deal with Ross Cahn, and that other little tick who'd not even bothered to step up and help his friend, even after he'd made a promise that he would. That, in Brian's book, was reprehensible. You start allowing people to get away with the small stuff, they'd think they could get away with anything. The world would slide into chaos — and Brian wasn't having that. Brian wasn't having that at all.

It was four in the morning, the shops closed and the adjacent flats dark and quiet. It took little more than a push to break the flimsy lock on the door at the back of the shop, the separate entrance to the flat. The outer door opened with a bang but he did not wait to see if the sound attracted attention. This was not the sort of area where people investigated sudden noises and the back of the shop wasn't directly overlooked. Not that he cared anyway. He could deal with anyone unwise enough to poke their nose into his concerns.

The stairs creaked under his weight. The flat door gave way when he shoved it hard. It might, he thought, have a label on it that designated it as a fire door, but he doubted its validity.

The main area of the flat was open-plan. A kitchen area, small dining table, sofa, television and a bathroom and two bedrooms led off — all small. The two bedrooms accommodated a bed and bedside table and not much else. Clothes were hung on pegs at the back of the door and in what he guessed was Cahn's room, strewn untidily across the bed. The sheets smelt unwashed, the whole flat stinking of stale food and lack of ventilation. Brian Hedgecock was oddly sensitive to such things. He liked to be clean and for the space he occupied to be fresh-smelling and essentially tidy. It was one of his little quirks, he supposed, one he'd almost certainly adopted from his stepdad who had been an oddly fastidious man, in everything but the more extreme of his business dealings. Though, Brian thought, he had also been particular in that regard, never dealing out a punishment that wasn't deserved or carefully tailored to whatever the recipient was deemed to have done.

Searching the flat took all of ten minutes and that was only because he tossed it twice just to be sure. There was some cash in a drawer in Cahn's room, which he pocketed, and some bits of paperwork from the probation services. Brian was inclined to dismiss this as irrelevant until he read the letters more carefully. So, this was in fact Ross Cahn's designated address but the other lad, well, he was meant to be living somewhere else.

Brian left the flat and began to walk. It took him a half hour to reach Paul Pearson's official address. He stood under the security light, examining names on the buzzers in the porch, and decided that the one without a name was likely the one he wanted. Brian leaned heavily on the front door. It yielded with a crack as the wood broke around the lock but, just as before, he wasn't worried about the noise. He knew from experience that one look at him — should anyone be unwise enough to investigate — would be enough to send them scurrying back into their little rabbit holes. He made his way upstairs, booted feet heavy on the thin carpet. He was aware that someone behind the door on the first landing peered at him through the spyhole and then softly drew a bolt across. He passed by, amused. *That's right, stay inside, nothing to see.*

The flat on the top floor that was meant to be occupied by Paul Pearson was, he guessed, a converted attic. The stairs on the last flight were narrower and the ceiling lower when he reached the final landing. Servants' quarters back when this had been a house and not grubby little flats, he thought.

The old attics were freezing cold in winter and baking hot in summer with little more than roof tiles and a bit of plaster lath between the occupants and the outside world.

He didn't bother to knock.

The occupants of the flat were rudely awakened by the crash as the door flew open and hit the wall. A girl squealed and a male voice demanded to know what the fuck was going on.

I am, Brian thought. *I'm what's going on.* He stood in their bedroom doorway, filling the space as the girl tried to cover herself with a sheet and the boy first shouted then quailed and declared that they didn't want any trouble.

"I'm looking for Paul Pearson."

"Paul? What? He doesn't live here. We rent from him, see, we pay him to live here."

"And where will I find him?"

"We don't know. He don't tell us anything. Just gets in touch when he wants his rent. We take it to him, wherever he says."

This was not the answer Brian Hedgecock had been looking for. "What friends does he have? Where might he be?"

He watched as they exchanged a look. It was obvious to Brian that they wanted to tell him something — most people did, even when he wasn't asking specific questions — but that they were at a loss.

"He mentioned someone called Ross," the girl said. "I think he was staying with someone called Ross. Oh, and his mum came looking for him."

"His mum." Brian could not keep the surprise and an edge of disbelief from his voice.

"She came here yesterday, wanting to know where he was."

"And did she leave an address? A phone number?" He saw her shoulders sag as she realised that she knew nothing more. Had no way to contact Paul's mum.

Then the boy remembered a detail and his face lit up. "He said she'd been inside, got out only a few weeks ago.

He said she'd killed her old man. Paul's dad," he added, as though his meaning might not be clear.

So that was something. She might be staying in one of the hostels. Brian's eyes narrowed as he regarded the two young people whose room he had invaded. He doubted they were even out of their teens. They looked grubby and thin and the bedroom stank of sweat and sex and stale cannabis. The rest of the flat didn't look or smell much better.

"I'm going to give you some advice," he said. "Some free advice. Get yourselves cleaned up, get your bags packed and go back to wherever you came from. Your parents'll give you hell for a bit, but they'll get over it. Get back to school, make something of yourselves. Believe me, you don't want to end up like Ross Cahn or like Paul Pearson, when I get my hands on him, and that's the way you're headed. So go now, while you still got a chance."

He could see by their faces that this was not what they had expected from him. The girl was staring at him, the boy nodding fiercely as though he'd never heard such profound words of wisdom.

Brian Hedgecock sighed and turned away, made his way back downstairs and let himself out of the back door, through the gate in the yard and over the next-door wall. He guessed someone would have called the police, probably whoever was on the first-floor landing and the sound of sirens split the early morning quiet as he found his way down an entry way between two houses and into a parallel street.

So, Paul had a mother who was looking for him. A mother who had served time and for murder, if the kids were to be believed. He made his way back to where he was staying. It had been a B&B in his stepfather's time, basic but clean. Deidre, who had been his stepfather's housekeeper all those years before and who had practically raised Brian, had bought it and taken it over when his stepfather had died. She was now old and frail and long retired, but he had ensured she had been able to keep the house. Once he'd got out of prison it had been inevitable that he went to be with her.

145

He had his own kettle and hob and a microwave if he wanted to shift for himself, though most evenings he rustled up a meal for them both and kept her company for a while, watching nonsense on the telly and talking about old times. She was happy to have him there, he thought, even though she did fall asleep in the chair most evenings. He'd taken to ordering groceries online and making sure she ate better too and encouraged her to get out and about using her walker.

Brian Hedgecock knew that he was a contradiction. His world was divided into two kinds of people. Those he wanted to protect and those he wanted to kill — and right now Paul Pearson was topping that second list.

CHAPTER 20

Sunday

There was only one place that Paul could think of that might be safe, though he wasn't sure what kind of welcome he might get. He'd have to get out of the city; he daren't go back to the flat. He had the clothes he stood up in and he had about twenty quid in his pocket and no immediate means of getting more.

His whole body ached and he was shivering almost uncontrollably as he wormed his way from his cardboard sanctuary and back over the wall, jumping at every sound and certain that the man who had chased him the night before would be lying in wait.

Out on Magdalen Street, two uniformed police officers and a PCSO were asking questions of the early commuters. Paul turned in the opposite direction. He was aware of how dishevelled he must appear, and he checked himself carefully, suddenly afraid that he might have blood on him. But no, he'd not been close enough to Ross to get his blood on him. He'd been outside the yard, standing close to the gate. Still too close, as it happened. When Ross had told him to stay put at the corner of the road, he should have listened. No, he should have taken the chance to walk away. Run away. Just get the hell out. Not let that bastard catch sight of him. The memory of what he'd done to Ross set his stomach churning and he leaned against a shop window, suddenly afraid that he might throw up.

He had to get away.

Steadily and purposefully, Paul began to walk. He kept to the main roads and increasingly busy streets, finding solace in the crowds, afraid of suddenly finding himself alone, knowing that he was far from safe, images of what had happened to Ross Cahn refusing to leave his head. He'd hated Cahn in the end, but he wouldn't have wished that on anyone. Worse still, he knew that if that bastard got his hands on him then Paul was done for.

He spent a little of his remaining cash, catching a bus that he knew would take him to the outskirts of town. And then began to walk again. He was hungry and thirsty but felt a little safer now he was out on country roads. He was going home and he would ask for help. He just hoped and prayed that David and the others would not turn him away.

* * *

Maria had dropped him off that morning and now collected him from work. Mike had long since learned the value of taking breaks and he made sure to schedule time off for his team, even when they were in the midst of an investigation. True, when things were really busy, this might only be a couple of hours to go home, have a shower and a proper meal, see family, but he knew how essential it was to get away from the intensity of the work, even if only for a short time.

He suspected he had been less good at this before meeting Maria. Being in a relationship with a psychologist, one who had initially specialised in work-related stress, probably influenced his thinking somewhat.

He was not surprised that John Tynan was with Maria, though for a moment he felt disappointment. He'd wanted a few hours alone with her. But he soon got over his mild pique.

The journey passed in idle chat. Maria and John picked up the conversation they'd been having before Mike had joined them and he drifted in and out of the debate on what they would both be growing next year, half-formed plans for Christmas, only a few weeks away and not a present bought, and what rubbish they were watching on the telly.

Mike joined in occasionally, but mostly he just gazed out of the window, comforted by the voices of these two people he loved and the soft classical music on the radio. He recognised Vaughan Williams but got no further than that. Maria could have told him what it was and John probably quoted chapter and verse on when and where it was written, but for the moment Mike didn't care. His mind wandered and he allowed himself to enjoy this moment of contentment.

They drove out to the coast, even though the sky was leaden and early afternoon already dusky. This, he knew, was for his benefit. He did most of his best thinking near the sea, even when it was blowing a hoolie.

Maria had wellingtons in the car, her own and Mike's. John was wearing his favourite walking boots, the old leather gleaming with years of polish. They had survived many such treks along the beach. Theirs was the only car in the car park.

Mike glanced back along the track, towards the village. The disappearance of a child from this village had been his first major case when he'd returned to his home county as an inspector. Talk about being dropped into the deep end. This was where he had met John Tynan and the investigation had brought him into contact with Maria. The rest was history. The two holiday lets on the clifftop, close to the children's playground, were occupied. He could see a television set flickering in the living room of one and caught sight of a man sitting at a table by the window in the second. Not so long ago all the holiday places would have been closed up by October, but winter breaks and Christmas specials now seemed to be a thing. He wondered if these late visitors were really prepared for the frigid wind blowing off the sea and the vicious suddenness of the storms.

They descended the steps onto the beach, the wind slicing across the water catching at their breath as it always did this time of year. Maria pulled her hat down over her ears and Mike turned up the collar of his coat. John Tynan had a new flat cap, he noticed, as John and Maria ambled on ahead and left Mike to his thoughts.

He loved this part of the world, even though there were times when everything about it felt insecure and off kilter. Each winter a little more of the land would be devoured by the ocean. The great black breakwaters, looming out of the flat grey of the day, did indeed break the water as it crashed up the beach, but not enough to rob it of its full force. Jude had once called all of this borrowed land and she had a point. He sometimes thought that the deep cuts of the Norfolk Broads were in some way a compromise or a sacrifice to the gods of earth and water — *here, you have that and let us keep this.* It was a bargain that may have counted inland but it meant nothing on the coast. Walking on the beach, where the cliff erosion was so obvious and so devastating, it was enough to make a person wonder if another and bigger sacrifice might be coming due.

And yet, he reminded himself, this was also a place of ancient market towns and deep-rooted settlements. Norwich had been the second most important city in England in medieval times and one whose merchant citizenry had looked outward towards Europe, doing their deals with the low countries and the Mediterranean and even as far as Russia and Turkey. Remote it might be in some ways, but this part of England had always been outward-looking, seeing itself as part of the wider world and recognising its worth.

There was, he reminded himself, solid ground here, even if the pockets of poverty were as deep as ever and the wealth as unequally divided as it always had been. Perhaps more so than it had ever been. No surprise really that this was also the county of the nonconformist, the political radical like

Robert Kett who in 1549 had, along with sixteen hundred others, gathered on Mousehold Heath outside Norwich and threatened outright rebellion. Somehow this had always been a county of the independently minded, including those who bought a little bit of land and used it to gain a modicum of autonomy.

He found that he was thinking about Johanna Pearson and her children. Not Eric — somehow he found it very hard to care about Eric Pearson. He reminded himself that Johanna was a murderer, no less than whoever had killed Morgan Springfield or Gary Gibson. She had made the decision to take a life and she had done so and the fact that she had not cared about being punished for it did not make it better, or different, or more justified — she had still taken a life.

Mike sighed. He could tell himself that till he was blue in the face, but, despite the logic of the argument, he still viewed Johanna's actions as more worthy of forgiveness. Who, if they were honest with themselves, could not conceive of feeling such rage and betrayal that they might lash out at the guilty party? Most violent deaths happened precisely as a result of such emotions — a momentary lack of control and it was all over.

And that brought him back to Morgan Springfield.

Mike gazed out to sea, towards the horizon now only just distinguishable from the bank of heavy cloud that would soon bring rain. He looked down at the sand, poking his toes at a belemnite fossil, freeing it from the wet sand before picking it up and slipping it into his pocket. He turned and regarded John and Maria, deep in conversation and a little ahead of him along the beach, John's head slightly bent as he too looked for shells and fossils, a habit he had inherited from his beloved wife, now long gone in all but memory. Mike imagined driving a spike into the exposed neck of his friend, hitting it hard with a hammer, killing him stone dead. And then using the claw to withdraw the spike, the marks left on the neck as the hammer bruised.

No, he thought. However quick the killer was, he could not have done that alone. Even had Morgan Springfield been bending down in a way that exposed the neck, his instinct would have intervened, had the man come up behind him. He would have turned. Had Mike come up behind John, and John heard him or sensed him as of course he would, John would have shifted his weight and his attention towards the presence behind him, even if he knew that presence to be his friend. Mike was certain of this now — someone else had held Morgan Springfield in position long enough for the killer to drive the spike, the nail, the . . . whatever it was . . . home and to have held the body still as it was removed. They were not looking for one man working alone, but for two and that, Mike thought, changed everything.

He felt his phone vibrating in his coat pocket and sighed. Taking it out he saw that Jude was calling.

Mike turned his back to the wind, lifting a shoulder in an attempt to shelter the phone enough to hear what Jude was telling him. He had only been vaguely aware until then just how loud the rising wind and the crashing waves had been, but now he had to strain to hear her voice.

"Who's dead?" Mike asked again. "Okay, I'll be with you in . . ." He glanced at his watch and reminded himself that they still had to walk back to the car. "It will probably be about an hour."

Maria and John had paused and were now looking back in his direction.

"I'm guessing we're cutting our walk short," Maria said as Mike pocketed the phone.

"I'm afraid so. We've got another body. Ross Cahn was found early this afternoon, stabbed to death. Jude is already there. I'm sorry."

Maria nodded. "Best head back then," she said. "Just as well we decided to have lunch before we came out here. At least you got the chance to eat."

"So is this connected to the Springfield murder?" John asked.

Mike recalled his meeting with Johanna, the woman's insistence that Cahn had been involved in Morgan Springfield's death. That Cahn had tried to involve her son, Paul.

"Your guess is as good as mine, but it's one hell of a coincidence if not," Mike told him.

CHAPTER 21

Ross Cahn lay on his back staring up at the scudding clouds, rain falling on his face as the team of CSIs tried to erect a tent to cover the scene. The wind had got up as Mike, Maria and John had left the beach and chased them back to Norwich, carrying with it a sharp edge of driving rain. Mike stood beside Jude, sheltering under a golf umbrella that was somehow managing to stay right side out. The concrete edge of the Magdalen Street flyover was visible above the red brick of the pub, the sound of traffic a steady buzz against the beat of the rain.

"Estimated time of death is somewhere between midnight and five this morning. It rained after five and the ground beneath the body is drier than that surrounding it. We know he wasn't here before midnight because the landlord of the pub came out then to stack some empties." She indicated the stacks of crates beside the back door. "It's unlikely he'd have missed a body lying in the middle of his yard."

"Does he live on the premises?"

"No, he was gone by around half past midnight. He's sure he bolted the rear gate but frankly, that wouldn't have been much of an obstacle. He found the body when he came to stack more crates after the lunchtime opening."

Mike nodded, peering out from under the umbrella, taking in the scene. "Not really overlooked from anywhere," he said. "What about security lights?"

"Working when he left last night, now smashed."

The CSI had finally wrangled the tent into place and the crime scene manager beckoned Mike inside. Ross Cahn looked older than the photograph of him that Mike had seen. But then, he was older, Mike thought, and he had been in prison and that could age even a young man. His dark hair was plastered to his head and spread wetly across the bricks of the yard. He looked shocked. One hand lay at his side, the other was across his belly, palm flat as though he had tried to stop the bleeding from the jagged wound in his abdomen. Was that being fanciful?

A second stab wound, again jagged and open, exposed a lower rib. "What was he stabbed with?" Mike asked. "It doesn't look like a wound from a knife blade."

"No, I agree, but what the weapon was I don't know. It made a right mess, though."

Mike nodded. "I'll get out of your way," he said and went back out into the now pouring rain.

* * *

Rain had turned to sleet and then snow before Paul reached the community house. He was soaked to the skin, hair dripping and water running down his neck. He was shaking with cold and, he was beginning to realise, with shock. He had almost died back there. Ross Cahn had died. The man who had chased him, the man who had killed Ross, wasn't about to forget about him. He needed sanctuary and, he supposed dimly, he was going to have to talk to the police.

He rang the bell a second time, suddenly afraid that there was no one home. How could that be? It was rare indeed for the whole community to be absent. Despairing, Paul slumped down on the step, head in his hands, and that was how Evelyn found him a moment later when she opened the door.

"Paul? Paul, what the?" She turned then and ran back into the house. "David, Steven, it's Paul and he's hurt."

Was he hurt? Paul wondered. He felt so ill that he could not be sure.

Hands on his arms, lifting him to his feet, helping him inside. "God, you're soaked through," someone said.

"Let's get him to the guest room." David's voice now, calm and authoritative. Vaguely, Paul recalled that the guest room was on the ground floor, just off the main hall. He was grateful he wouldn't have to climb the stairs.

"Evie, make some hot-water bottles and a hot drink. Come on, son, let's get you warm and dry."

Afterwards, Paul wasn't sure who'd stood him in the guest bathroom and stripped him of his clothes, though he thought it might have been his brother. They dressed him in old, washed-soft pyjamas and helped him into bed. Hot-water bottles at his feet and against his back, warm blankets, a warm drink. Paul realised that he was crying like a little child.

"What happened to you?" Evie asked him, but Paul couldn't find the answer.

"Let him rest," David told her gently. "You can sit with him."

And then Evie took his hand and Paul settled under the blankets, and fell into a deep sleep.

* * *

"There was a disturbance in and around Magdalen Street," Jude told Mike as they drove away. "A younger man being chased by an older man carrying a knife, according to some reports, or a lump of metal pipe according to another. We've got a bit of mobile-phone footage, apparently. Several calls to the nines and a handful of witness statements."

"What time was this?"

"Around two fifteen this morning. The man didn't directly threaten anyone else, but then the few folk out at that time of the night had the sense to keep out of his way.

156

I've arranged for everything to be sent over to us, should be there by the time we get back. Two mobile units were deployed and got there pretty sharpish but by that time both men had vanished. Frankly, they were lucky the witnesses were still around."

Mike nodded. "You think it's a stretch to link the murders of Morgan Springfield and Ross Cahn and last night's incident?" he said. "We know Springfield and Cahn were known to one another. It's not beyond the realms of possibility that some connection was maintained. Morgan Springfield might at least have been interested in how the kids that got the awards turned out."

"He might, but just because he presented them with their prizes doesn't mean he followed their careers. I got several awards at school, but didn't know the people presenting them from Adam and they certainly didn't know me. It was all a quick handshake, a fake smile and that was that."

"Prizes for what?" Mike asked. Then, "No, you're probably right. Johanna Pearson's insistence on a connection's probably just rubbed off on me."

"It's still a coincidence though and worth keeping in mind. This isn't exactly a crime-ridden city, not compared to some. Volume crime is up, and that's distressing for the people whose houses are burgled and cars are stolen, but we're behind the national curve even for that. Murder is certainly not the norm."

She took a breath. And when she spoke again, her voice was different. "Unless you're looking at domestic violence, of course. The stuff that goes on behind closed doors. It's often much easier to get an arrest and a conviction too, so it doesn't grab the headlines or the public imagination. It happens, it's dealt with, it's gone from the public consciousness, and it's left to the family to deal with the fallout."

She sounded bitter, he thought, as well she might. He knew that her last long-term relationship had ended badly. He knew she'd come to work once, just before it ended, with bruises on her arms and face and if something like that could happen to a woman as capable and self-possessed as Jude . . . He'd wanted to help but Jude had said she could handle it and others, it turned out, had been better placed to step in. He'd heard that Terry Gleeson and his wife had been instrumental in helping Jude get out of the situation, but he'd been careful not to ask too many questions. He suspected that Terry would not have been too subtle in his problem-solving.

He'd heard rumours that she and Seth Harding were now an item. He hoped so, Seth was a good man — gentle, kind, and often Mike thought, rather lonely.

"So, then we have last night's incident," Jude said as they pulled into the car park. "We'll be able to plot the direction of pursuit from the witness statements but from the sound of things the two incidents are definitely connected and whoever killed Ross Cahn then chased another man who maybe witnessed the killing. Maybe," she qualified. "It's all speculation until it isn't."

Isn't that the truth, Mike thought.

"Officers went round to Cahn's flat, but the place had been trashed. There was some evidence of another person living there but there was such a mess CSI are still sifting through."

Her phone was ringing and Mike went ahead of her while she answered it. He had made coffee by the time she came into the incident room, and he could see from her face that the phone call had been significant. She took the mug and sat down.

"Now this is interesting. There was a third incident, happened a couple of hours after the chase down Magdalen Street. A man answering the same description burst into a house on Rose Street and terrorised the occupants of the top flat. I'm having the statements sent over but it seems whoever he was, he was looking for Paul Pearson."

"Paul Pearson? Why? Now that's just too heavy on the coincidence."

"Isn't it though. And I made a call to the officer on scene at Cahn's flat. The CSI have turned up some bits of paperwork that suggest who might have been living with Ross Cahn."

"Pearson?"

"Exactly. Maybe we need to talk to Johanna Pearson again."

"I think that's a given." Mike grimaced. "She's not going to let us off lightly, is she."

"I wouldn't think so."

DS Terry Gleeson arrived then and told them that the recordings of the chase were now available. Mike made him coffee while he set up the computer and whiteboard. Others were drifting in, the team assembling itself to accommodate these new developments. Jude brought everyone up to speed. Then Terry set the film show in motion.

First time through they watched in silence. Terry ran the sequence again, this time pausing when anyone had a comment or an observation.

"He's bloody fast for a big man," Jude said.

"He's certainly a big bugger," Terry said.

Mike nodded. Gleeson was built like a brick outhouse and this man, picked up on CCTV as he pursued a much smaller, slighter and fortunately for him, much faster man, made Terry look small. "He's going to be in the system," Mike said. Hopefully that would mean a quick arrest.

"I can't quite make out what he's carrying," Jude said. "It looks like a bit of broken pipe."

Mike froze the image and then stepped through the frames trying to get a better impression. They had footage from several CCTV cameras and a couple of mobile phones. Mike guessed that there'd be more out there — it wasn't often you'd see a giant carrying a length of pipe, chasing another man through the streets of Norwich at two in the morning, and now everyone was a citizen journalist. "Looks like a length of pipe that's been broken at a jagged angle," he said. "That would seem to fit with the wound profile on Ross Cahn's body."

He brought up on the screen a picture of the two stab wounds. Then let the film run on. The big man briefly faced the CCTV camera and then turned away as he raced along past a line of shops. He turned his attention to the smaller, skinnier man running for his life. The images of him were not so clear. He had his head down and though he was clearly reaching exhaustion, his arms and legs were pumping hard as he fought to stay ahead. Was it Paul Pearson? Given all the circumstances, it seemed likely. They had called up Pearson's record and compared his picture to that of the running man, but it was impossible to be absolutely certain.

Jude pointed at the time code. "That's when the three nines calls started," she said. "We got four in total, all reporting a big man with a weapon chasing a smaller man. One person thought he had a knife, but the others just said a weapon of some sort. The patrols turn up about two minutes later; fortunately they were only a few streets away."

Mike was flipping through images trying to get a better fix on the man being pursued but he couldn't get a good enough angle on the face. "We need to get Johanna Pearson in to view the footage," he said. "She'd recognise her son, if it is him."

"Looks like he turns down between those two buildings," Terry said. They watched the film run on, the larger man lumbered up the road in pursuit and then also made the turn.

"I suppose the alleyway's been checked for bodies," Mike said.

Terry laughed. "Apparently it has."

The patrol cars screeched to a halt a moment later and two officers took off down the alleyway, prompted by the pointing fingers of two of the witnesses who had called the incident in. They returned more slowly, moments later, and Mike made a mental note that he must walk the scene later, see how the two men might have disappeared.

"I'll get some images of both men circulated," Jude said. "The pursuer is pretty distinctive so hopefully only a matter of time before he surfaces again. The other man isn't as clear, but someone will know him. It's worth putting out appeals for more footage too."

Mike nodded. "And get someone round to the flat, show his picture to the witnesses. I'd make a bet on it being the same man, but best to get some confirmation."

Hopefully, Jude was right and the man would surface quickly. The level of violence wrought upon Ross Cahn had been severe and Mike doubted the man being chased would have survived had he been caught. He also doubted that his would-be assailant would give up, just because he'd got away that time.

CHAPTER 22

Johanna was told she had a visitor. She found her second eldest, Steven, standing in the hallway, hopping from foot to foot in impatience.

"Mum, it's Paul, you've got to come." She hurried back upstairs and collected her bag and coat, informed the hostel manager that she was going to visit her family and climbed into Steven's old car.

"What happened?"

"We're not sure. He turned up at the community house a couple of hours ago. He was soaked through and freezing cold and something had scared him. I mean really terrified him. We got him into bed and a hot drink into him and got Doc Jonas to take a look."

"Hasn't he retired?"

"Two years ago, but have you tried getting a home visit lately?"

"Well, hardly," Johanna reminded him. "What did the doctor say?"

"That he was on the verge of hypothermia but he'd be all right. He reckons Paul is in shock. I mean, it didn't take a genius to work that out, but as far as we can tell he walked all the way from the city and the weather's been filthy. Soon as the doctor had taken a look, David sent me to get you. We weren't sure if we'd have to take him to the hospital. If we had, I'd have taken you straight there. Mum, he looked so bad. He was white. Even his lips were blue."

It was, Johanna realised, the second time he had referred to her as his mother. Up until now, it had just been Johanna. She could have cried. Instead, she reached across and gripped her son's arm. "He's young and strong and he'll be all right," she told him.

He nodded, a slight release of tension in his expression telling Johanna that even after all this time, after all that had happened, what his mother said still mattered. This time the tears did come. She turned to look out of the window at the lightly falling snow and surreptitiously wiped her eyes.

By the time they reached the community house, the snow was falling fast and hard. David opened the door as they pulled up and hustled Johanna into the guest room. Her two youngest children, Daniel and Evie, sat on either side of their brother's bed. Evie was holding Paul's hand. She got up and hugged her mother, took her coat and seated Johanna in the chair she had occupied.

"He's so cold," Johanna said as she took Paul's hand.

"He's looking better than he did. Dr Jonas is calling back later. Paul's had warm drinks and he's a bit more coherent when he does wake up. The doc says the sleeping isn't because of the cold. He thinks Paul's kind of trying to get away from something bad. He keeps talking about being chased."

"Chased?"

Evie shrugged. Daniel had got up and come round the bed to give Johanna a hug. "I'll go and make everyone some tea," he said. "Evie, you sit in my chair."

Johanna could see his relief in having an excuse to get away. "He's a bit young for sick-room duty." She smiled at her daughter.

"Oh, Daniel's just not very good at sitting still." Evie laughed. "Actually, he's been great. He was really scared when Paul arrived — he looked half dead — but he did his best to help out. He's a good kid."

"I'm very proud of all of you," Johanna said softly. "And I'm so sorry I let you down."

For a moment Evie said nothing and Johanna worried that she'd overstepped some invisible line. Then she said, "Mum, you did what you thought was right. It wasn't, it was stupid and impulsive and if any of us had acted on even a fraction of that impulse, we'd have been grounded for life."

Johanna laughed, unable to help herself. "Put like that, it sounds—"

"It sounds exactly like it was," Evie said gently. "It was a stupid thing to do and we all paid the price. But I'm not mad at you. Neither is Steven, not really. And Daniel's got so little memory of all that. He thinks of Gordon and Esther as his mum and dad, and you really can't blame him for that."

"I don't," Johanna told her. "I'm just relieved you were all looked after."

"And we were. Couldn't have been better taken care of. And we talked about you a lot and why you did what you did. They let us get angry and they let us cry and they let us ask questions and do whatever we needed to come to terms with it all. As much as you can. Mum, what you did was so damned stupid, does it make sense if I say I can forgive you and love you and want a relationship with you, but I'm still mad as hell with you? Sorry, got to use strong language for strong feelings, so you'll have to let that pass."

Johanna flinched, but nodded. As Paul had reminded her, she had no right to correct any of them. "It makes sense," she said softly. "Thank you, Evie."

The door opened and Daniel came in, followed by David. They carried trays with hot drinks and toasted sandwiches and set them down on the chest of drawers.

"Eat," David said. "And see if you can rouse him enough to get a hot drink into him. I have to say he's looking a hundred times better than he did. I almost called an ambulance, but in this weather I didn't know how long it would take and Doc Jonas is literally two minutes down the lane."

Johanna nodded. "He's a good man." The sandwiches smelled good as did the hot chocolate. When was the last time she'd had proper hot chocolate? Johanna could not remember.

Suddenly the tears began to flow again. David patted her gently on the shoulder and then left with Daniel. Evie came over and hugged her mother close, then busied herself with drinks and food. Paul stirred. Johanna leaned over him. "Paul, wake up, darling. Here, let me lift you up." She rearranged his pillows so he could sit. He seemed disconnected, unable to focus, puzzled at where he was and how he'd got there.

"You're safe," Johanna told him. "You're home." And for a blessed moment she dared to hope that she was too.

* * *

From being a source of mild annoyance that could be dealt with at some future date, Paul Pearson had upgraded himself to an immediate and acute irritation. It riled Brian that he'd had the chance to kill two birds with one stone — or at any rate, one long length of broken pipe — and he had fluffed it, as Deidre would have said. His stepdad, far less restrained in his language, would have called it an almighty cockup and made a joke about Brian's name. They would then have sat down and figured out a way to set things right — Brian and his stepfather, Jimmy, that was, Deidre never got involved in any of the heavy stuff. Neither Brian nor his stepfather would have considered that proper.

Brian Hedgecock liked technology and was rather in love with the internet. The revelation that Paul Pearson's mother had been looking for him and that she had also done a spell in prison had given him a place to start. He didn't know her first name, so he had begun with the search words

Pearson and *murder* and it hadn't taken long for him to find reports of Eric Pearson's death and Johanna's arrest.

She certainly had a sense of style, he thought, putting her old man down in front of police witnesses. He knew she had been released recently and guessed she might have been staying in one of the halfway houses that served as temporary accommodation while jobs and benefits and more permanent accommodation could be sorted out. Pearson would not have found sanctuary there. It was possible he'd persuaded a friend to shelter him but from what Cahn had said, Pearson didn't have that many friends or even acquaintances. He was a bit of a loner, not encouraging any kind of social contact in which Pearson didn't have the upper hand.

A bit more searching brought up stories of the family's adventures after Eric Pearson had been accused of taking pictures of a bunch of kids and had then set about accusing other people. And that led Brian Hedgecock to references to the Children of Solomon. Some kind of cult? he wondered.

He did a search for them and lo and behold they had a website. On the homepage, children and adults posed outside a big house. They looked happy and well-scrubbed and not what he'd have thought of as a religious community but then, what the hell did a cult actually look like? Reading on, he found a history of the community and discovered that they were organic and regenerative farmers, with a market garden and a farm shop, and they also ran courses and summer schools for anyone with an interest in more natural methods of growing. *Well, good for them*, Brian Hedgecock thought. *Time someone tried to un-fuck the planet. Would Pearson have run to them?*

It seemed like a good place to start.

CHAPTER 23

Monday

Mike and Jude had driven for two hours to talk to Ross Cahn's mother and now they had arrived, Jude wasn't sure she was even going to let them in. Mrs Cahn stood on the doorstep with the door half closed behind her and her arms folded across her body as though she was holding herself together. She must be cold, Jude thought, dressed in faded blue jeans that clung to a tiny waist and almost non-existent hips, and a plain white T-shirt. Her feet were bare.

"Mrs Cahn, thank you for agreeing to see us," Jude said. The local police had taken care of the death notification and had been helpful in setting up this meeting. The question now was whether or not Theresa Cahn had changed her mind about talking to them.

She was a tall, thin woman — not slim or slender, Jude thought, just thin. Her hair was blonde, cut into a jaw-length bob, and her eyes a pale, washed-out blue. Her lipstick seemed too bright for such a pale face. It was as though the woman wanted to add a touch of vibrancy to her look but somehow it just accentuated the pallor.

"May we come in?" Jude asked. She held out her hand. "DS Jude Burnett, and this is my boss, DI Mike Croft."

Theresa Cahn eyed the hand but made no move to take it.

"It's cold out," Jude said, noting the goosebumps rising on Theresa Cahn's arms. "Why don't we go inside?"

"Sorry, yes, of course." The woman turned and headed into the house. Jude raised an eyebrow at Mike and then they followed her in.

Theresa Cahn filled the kettle and motioned for them to sit down at the kitchen table. The house was small, semi-detached and built in the 1930s, Jude guessed, with a small bay window at the front and such a highly polished wooden floor in the hall that she wondered if they should have removed their shoes.

"We're very sorry for your loss," Mike said and Jude saw the woman's shoulders stiffen.

"He was difficult," Theresa Cahn said. "We thought he might get back on track at one point, but it didn't take."

The kettle boiled and she made three mugs of instant coffee — a supermarket's own brand, Jude noted, wondering if perhaps Theresa Cahn was struggling now she was on her own.

Theresa placed the drinks on the table on small flowery coasters. She paused, before adding a sugar bowl and pouring milk into a jug. "Help yourselves," she told them, clicking sweeteners into her own drink. It came as no surprise to Jude that she drank her coffee black.

"Look," Theresa said, and Jude could see how uncomfortable she was even talking about her son. "I get that Ross is dead. That some bastard killed him. That . . . but what are you doing here? What do you want me to say? I've not laid eyes on him since he went inside. Barely saw him before that, truth be told. We couldn't cope with it, not anymore. That boy was trouble from the day he was born. His sister? Never any bother, couldn't have asked for a sunnier child, but Ross. He was just . . ."

Jude glanced at Mike and they let the silence settle for a time. Finally, Mike asked, "When did he start getting into trouble?"

"Don't you have his record?"

"We do, but trouble often starts before the police get involved. Was that true of Ross?"

She sighed and slumped back into her chair. "It started in school," she said, "when he was just a little thing. He'd lash out at the other kids. No warning, no reason half the time. We thought maybe he was being bullied but in the end we had to admit that Ross was the bully. He couldn't seem to help himself.

"We got counselling for him, paid a small fortune getting him to see psychiatrists and psychologists and anyone else that might have helped. He got a diagnosis in the end, for all the good it did. Borderline personality disorder, they thought, but then someone else said different and, oh, I don't know, what good did any of it do."

"But there was a point at which he seemed to turn things around," Jude said.

Mrs Cahn nodded. "He was seventeen. It was like a light had been switched on. Almost two years of normal." She sniffed. "Couldn't last though, could it? Back to his old ways soon enough. Violent, argumentative, downright impossible to live with. It was only a matter of time before he did something that got him put away. And by then he was too old to be put in a young offenders' centre, so he got put away in an adult prison. Like that was going to help him! He was just nineteen."

"Did you visit him?" Jude asked.

The woman shook her head. "No. I told him, he got in trouble again, went back to the way he was, I'd wash my hands of him. I couldn't cope with it anymore. It broke my marriage and it broke me."

"Did you know any of his friends?" Jude asked.

Theresa Cahn shook her head. "Far as I know he didn't have any left, not from when he lived at home. We moved, four years ago, thought it might make a difference, fresh start, fresh place. Six months later our marriage was over. He found someone else, someone with a couple of kids. They seem happy enough. We came to an agreement. I wouldn't chase him for maintenance if he signed the house over to me, so he did and well, here I am."

"That's an unusual arrangement," Jude said.

Theresa Cahn sighed. "I earn twice what he does. And I know he tried his best. What's the point in punishing someone for what they couldn't help. Isn't it best for one of us to make a fresh start?"

Jude made no comment. This was the guilt speaking, she thought. Guilt that Theresa Cahn could not change her son. That she had expended all of her energies and time trying to do so, probably to the exclusion of other family members. She wondered if the daughter had really been so angelic or if she'd just been good at keeping out of the way.

"Could you make us a list of friends anyway?" Jude asked. "Just in case they can shed any light?"

Theresa Cahn sighed but nodded agreement. "Though what good it'll do you, I don't know."

"Have you ever met either of these two men?" Mike showed her photographs of Paul Pearson and the unnamed man.

She shook her head.

"The younger man is Paul Pearson — did Ross ever mention him?"

Again, the shake of the head.

"When your son was released from prison he wanted to go back to Norfolk, even though you'd moved and, as you say, he'd lost contact with his friends. Do you know why that would be?"

She gave him a blank look.

"What did he think was there for him?" Jude said. "Would it have not been more sensible to have stayed in Bristol? Or moved closer to you?"

She was sure she saw the woman flinch.

"You didn't want him closer?"

"I told you, I've not set eyes on him since he went inside. He wrote a few times, called once or twice and I wrote back, spoke to him on the phone, but I made it clear he'd made his bed and I wasn't going to be taken in again. He was on his own."

"And he never mentioned going back to Norwich or why he might want to do that?"

She shrugged. "He liked it there. He said it was the one place he'd actually been someone. The one place he'd got things right."

"The award he received," Mike said.

"For a while we thought that was it. He'd changed. He could actually do something with his life. He helped set up that project to help those kids and he worked his backside off. It was like he had something to prove." She paused. "Well, I suppose he did. We were stupid enough to think he'd turned a corner."

"What did the project involve?" Mike asked.

"It was all about kids helping kids, going into school and talking about the mistakes they'd made and what helped them get back on track. Setting up support groups for kids that were at risk. There was always an adult in charge, but they encouraged young people to talk to one another, to listen, to open up about their difficulties and stuff. It was supposed to be teaching kids that it was okay to have mental-health problems and to talk about them."

She sniffed. "Fat lot of good it did Ross. And I can't think he set much of an example for the others, not with what he did afterwards."

"What got him involved in the first place?" Jude asked.

Mrs Cahn shrugged. "I never knew. He just came home one day and said he'd got involved in this project and, well, I thought, that won't last, will it. I had to sign the consent form for him to do some training or something. Look, it was a long time ago — what difference does it make?"

"Did you go to watch when he got the award?" Mike asked and Jude watched the woman's reaction with interest.

For a brief moment her expression softened and she seemed to shed some of the stress and pain.

"Proudest moment I ever had where Ross was concerned," she said. "Didn't last though, did it. Next thing we know, he's put that girl in a coma."

"Did you know his victim, Priscilla Eames?" Jude asked.

"No. Never heard of her until that happened. Couldn't believe it, could we. Not after, not after all we'd hoped for. I couldn't cope after that."

"Did he keep in touch with any of the other volunteers, or with any of the kids he'd helped?" Jude asked.

"Not that I know of. You know, something upset him, something set him off again. It was after he'd got that award. There was a trophy thing and there was some money. Not a lot — but a lot when you're a teenager. He was happy. I'd never seen him so happy. Then one night he came home and he trashed the place. I called the police. I thought he was going to kill me, I really did. He said everyone was lying to him. That no one ever told him the truth. That everyone cheated him. That everything was just a waste of time."

"Did he explain what he meant?"

Theresa Cahn shook her head. "The police took him away. I refused to let him back home. He sofa-surfed for a while till even his friends were sick of him. Then he beat that girl, put her in a coma, ended up inside." She hesitated and then said, "I was relieved. I didn't have to deal with the fallout or the temper or not knowing what was going to happen next. I'm only sorry they let him out again."

They left half an hour later with a short list of names, friends that Theresa Cahn recalled from when her son had been younger and she had still held out some hope for him.

"I don't believe she's that sanguine." Jude started the car, with a shake of her head. "After everything she's been through with her son. And her husband just walking out on them like that. She can't really be okay with it all. She's just got used to telling herself so."

"She's a very unhappy woman," Mike agreed. "But who can blame her. So, next step, we need to talk to Johanna Pearson — bring her in so she can look at the video. Get someone tracking down this list of possible contacts. Check in with Sid Patterson and assure him that Morgan Springfield hasn't been forgotten, see if he's noticed our big man hanging about, and it's worth canvassing the industrial estate again, now there's someone specific we're looking for." He paused. What else?

"We need to contact the other prize winners and whoever organised the awards. That's already in hand but I don't know what progress has been made. The PM results on Ross Cahn's body should be in by the time we get back and Terry was chasing up some other possible witnesses to the chase."

Mike nodded. He had spoken to the team earlier about his thoughts on there being a second man involved in the killing of Morgan Springfield and that morning he had spoken to Seth Harding. The consensus was that it made sense. Mike's phone rang. It was Amit Jacobs. The big man had been identified. And unsurprisingly, he had a record. Mike fished his notebook from his pocket and made quick notes as Amit filled him in.

"So," he told Jude when Amit had done. "Our man is Brian Hedgecock. He was released three weeks ago and went AWOL within a few days. His probation officer hasn't seen hide nor hair of him since day three after his release."

"What was he in for?"

"He killed a man called Charlie Fairford. Ambushed him as he came out of a pub, bashed him over the head. It took six officers to bring him in, two were injured in the process. According to Amit, he refused to give any reason for his actions when he was charged, and he didn't seem inclined to explain it to the psychiatric service or anyone else for the first ten years of his sentence, so he didn't have a shot at parole until two years ago."

"And what happened then?" Jude asked.

"We're still waiting on details, but something must have done. The board rejected him first time round but second time he must have got his script right. But the final part of his sentence was served in the same category B prison as our Mr Ross Cahn. Paul Pearson was also there, though only for a few weeks. He finished his sentence in a cat D, preparing for release. Pearson seems to have kept his head down throughout his sentence, apart from that one incident that saw him do extra time."

"And the journalist he attacked, Tom Andrews, spoke up for the Pearson boy," Jude mused. "I like Tom."

"Have a chat with him. Tom's been around the block more than a few times — get him to tell you what didn't make our records or the press. Then see if you can catch up with anyone on that list of friends Theresa Cahn gave us. I'm going to get Terry onto the prize winners, see if they knew Cahn or if they only met him at the award ceremony and follow up with the organisers, see what background we can fill in. Cahn was obviously a troubled young man, but something about that project seems to have settled him for a time. I'm going to have another chat with Sid Patterson." He paused, frowning. "So far we've got a lot of disconnected threads. We've got the Springfield murder and Morgan Springfield had a tenuous connection to Ross Cahn. Now Cahn is dead and this Brian Hedgecock is most likely his killer. He's now looking for Paul Pearson, who's gone to ground somewhere. Johanna Pearson may well have been right about there being a more substantial link between Cahn and Morgan Springfield, but as yet that's still up in the air. And there may be a link of some kind between the murder of Morgan Springfield and the killing of Gary Gibson eighteen years ago."

"*May* be?" Jude raised her eyebrows. They had reached the main road and she was waiting for a break in the traffic. It was snowing — wet, slushy, unpleasant snow. Mike had the sudden desire to be walking on the beach. It would be freezing cold, the wind off the sea hurling slush-laden rain in his face, but it would still be wonderful.

"I think," Jude said, "we should work on the assumption that the connection is definitely there. If we're wrong, no harm done. If we ignore that possibility and there is a link, then . . ."

"Agreed, but if it's the same killer, why the long gap? Maybe he was inside, maybe he changed his MO."

"Or maybe no one crossed him in the interim. But, no, it is a big gap. Could be a copycat?"

"In which case someone would have to have known about the posing of the body in the Gibson case and, frankly, I think I was the only one on the team who thought there was anything unusual going on. I was told I had too much imagination and should be applying myself to the facts."

Jude grinned at him and pulled out into a gap, accelerating hard to keep ahead of a Mercedes barrelling up behind them. "You have imagination?" she asked. "Who'd have thunked it. Add to that, half the Gibson evidence is missing, misfiled or AWOL, which doesn't help just now. I'll get onto Alison, see if she's had a chance to look for anything else, but have you seen the size of that archive? If something's been misplaced, it could be anywhere." She paused. "You think Hedgecock killed Morgan Springfield?"

"That would mean he also killed Gary Gibson. Those killings have a very different MO to the murder of Charlie Fairford. From what Amit said, he simply beat the man to death in the pub car park."

"But it's possible," Jude said.

Mike nodded, his mind quietly tugging on the threads to see what felt loose, what could be unravelled. The connections would be there, he was sure of it, something that pulled Morgan Springfield, Gary Gibson, Paul Pearson and Ross Cahn into the same frame with Charlie Fairford and Brian Hedgecock.

And in the meantime, he hoped Paul Pearson was safe.

CHAPTER 24

Brian Hedgecock had been stealing cars since he was four-teen years old. The technology had moved on since then and after more than a decade inside he wasn't about to start exper-imenting with anything that might be computer controlled or keyless ignition. First thing on Monday morning, he went out in search of something that his old skills could deal with and his out-of-date brain relate to. Fortunately, he thought, as he trudged through the bitter cold of the morning, slushy pave-ments and hurrying commuters, there were still a lot of people around who bought older cars. In a side street he spotted a man parking a Vauxhall Astra that looked to be about his era. He watched as the man slammed his door, clicked the lock and hurried away. He entered a building at the end of the street. Brian waited until he was sure the man would not re-emerge and then he set to work. Five minutes later he was in the car and driving away, following the satnav route on his phone out of the city and on towards the community house. He had no plan in mind once he got there but that did not trouble him unduly. Brian Hedgecock was a man who reacted to circum-stance, and he wasn't about to change that habit now.

* * *

Jude and Mike arrived back at police headquarters in time to grab a late lunch before the briefing Mike had arranged for 3 p.m. Usually this would have taken place at the end of the day but new officers had joined the team that morning, others had been out canvassing and interviewing and still others running background searches — it seemed best to get everyone together earlier in the day. It meant the newcomers could be brought up to speed, tasks could be assigned, arising from the morning's enquiries — such as the list of contacts that Theresa Cahn had given to them — and the remainder of the afternoon could be usefully taken up with those tasks. That way, Mike thought, no newcomer would be twiddling their thumbs and the Tuesday morning briefing might well report new leads.

Mike was aware that events were overtaking them. Last week they'd had one murder and very little to go on apart from the brutality of the killing. No forensics to speak of, no witnesses, no reports of strangers hanging about. Now, five days later, they had two bodies and a very public pursuit to deal with. And an obviously dangerous man on the loose who had quite probably killed Ross Cahn. So, had he also murdered Morgan Springfield? And what, if anything, did this have to do with the death of Gary Gibson, all those years before?

At the briefing, Mike made no bones about the fact that they were still groping about looking for connections.

"All we can currently be certain of is that we have two dead and one, believed to be Paul Pearson, under threat. A statement is going out to all local media this afternoon and should make the national news this evening, that the public should be on the lookout for Brian Hedgecock. Hopefully we'll get some idea of where he's been and who's been sheltering him. We've no intelligence on any contacts in this area and until last night, and his very public pursuit of the man we believe to be Pearson, we had no sense of where he'd been for the past three weeks since his release. We know that Pearson was living with Cahn and that he had illegally sub-let his registered flat. Cahn's place had been tossed before our officers got there and as a neighbour saw a man fitting Hedgecock's description in the street at around four this morning, probably by him. Was he looking for something?"

A telephone rang. Terry Gleeson picked it up and it was obvious from his change of expression that something important was being said. He put the phone down.

"A report just came in of a disturbance at the community house. The, er, Children of Solomon, their place. A man matching Hedgecock's description turned up and he's looking for Paul Pearson and is threatening to break down the door. Officers are en route along with an armed incident team."

"Right, Terry, you're with me. Jude, finish up here and assign tasks."

And then he was leaving, a nagging at the back of his mind telling him that he should have listened more closely to Johanna Pearson.

* * *

The community house was almost two hundred years old. The front and back doors were solid oak and heavy locks and bolts secured them to a hefty oak frame. The downstairs windows were still equipped with their original shutter, usually kept folded back in their side recesses but used in winter when the drafts found their way in through the mullioned windows. CCTV cameras had been fitted a decade before when the community had been worried about fallout from the Eric Pearson accusation. They were active, but rarely used, David having left them in place at the suggestion of the local police constable who dropped in for the occasional chat about rural crime and security. It could be an effective deterrent, he had said, and David was relieved now that he had taken the advice.

The banging on the front door brought Evie out into the hall. David was coming down the stairs.

"Don't open the door," he told her. "Not until we know who it is."

"I wasn't planning on it," she told him. Whoever was out there was a clear and present threat and he was shouting her brother's name.

David shot the remaining bolts, large and ancient rods of steel that were original to the house and penetrated several inches into the frame. "Go and check the back door," he told Evie. She ran to do so.

The man outside was still shouting and ranting and now he thudded against the door. Others had come into the hall, summoned by the noise. They looked puzzled and scared. Johanna joined them.

"What's going on?"

"I don't know, but it's not good. Alex, call the police. Johanna, Daniel, pull the shutters across the window." He headed for the tiny room off the hallway that housed the feed from the cameras. The man outside seemed aware that he was being observed. He was carrying a long metal bar and his size and demeanour did nothing to reassure David that he'd back off any time soon. Alex came to the doorway and observing the camera feed as he spoke to the emergency services, he described the man hammering on their door. The dispatcher could obviously hear him shouting and David could make out the renewed tension in her voice as she assured Alex that help was on the way.

David returned to the hall and picked up the landline, called those members of the community that were not in the house but in their own cottages or the farm shop further down the lane. He hoped the man would keep his focus on the house and not seek out an easier target.

Johanna returned. "We've fixed the shutters and drawn the curtains. If he decides to break the windows he shouldn't be able to get any further."

He nodded. The panes were held in stone mullions, the individual sections quite narrow. He doubted even a child could have got through, never mind this giant of a man. The

179

shutters were held in place by a flat metal bar that dropped down into U-shaped recesses. They should hold well enough.

"What does he want with my son?" A thought suddenly dawned on her. "Is this the man who chased him? No wonder he was terrified."

Evie returned, accompanied by a woman who had been working in the kitchen. "Back's all locked up tight. Are the police coming?"

"They are, now let's get everyone upstairs and into the big meeting room. Evie, help your mother with Paul. Try to keep him calm."

He saw her flinch at the sudden sound of shattering glass. This must be bringing back such bad memories for her.

She gathered herself, went into the guest room and returned a moment later with Paul and her mother. Her brother was swathed in a too-large dressing gown but he was able to stand and walk with help even though his legs were shaking. He heard the big man shout again, calling out his name. "Paul Pearson, I know you're fucking well in there."

David saw Paul's eyes widen in fear. "He's come for me. Oh God, I'm so sorry."

"No time for that. Get yourselves upstairs. The police will soon be here."

More smashing glass. David found himself wondering if the insurance company would consider attack by rampaging madman as an act of God or riot or civil disobedience.

Daniel, he realised, was still standing in the hall. The kid was white-faced and shaking. He'd been such a little thing when all the trouble had happened, but the memories would still be in his head and this was supposed to be a place of safety. A place where he could forget all that.

"Come on, up the stairs," David said gently and shepherded the boy ahead.

Alex appeared on the landing. "Police are three minutes away," he said.

"You see," David told Daniel. "It's all going to be fine."

They joined the others in the big meeting room. It was at the front of the house, a large table at its centre, comfortable chairs and small sofas set around the edges. This was a place where the community met to make decisions and sometimes where they held their seminars and summer schools, and in summer it was flooded with light from the large windows overlooking the drive. Paul was standing by the window, looking down.

"He wants me," Paul said and there was such despair in his voice that it almost broke David's heart.

"He's out there and you're safe in here. The police are coming."

Paul didn't look reassured.

"Who is he?"

Paul shook his head. "I don't know, but he killed Ross and then he spotted me. I ran. I've never run so fast. I've never been so scared. I managed to hide and then I came here. I'm sorry, I never thought he'd know about the community house."

David patted the young man on the shoulder. "Where else would you run to," he said. "Of course you came here. No one blames you for that, Paul."

He looked down at the man who was now pounding at the door with his metal pipe and hurling abuse at the world in general. The door would hold, David thought, but his relief was profound as, in the distance, the police sirens could be heard and from the sound of it several were now screaming towards them.

The man stepped back, looked up at the window. David instinctively stepped aside. "We're not done here," the big man yelled, then drew his arm back and sent the pole hurtling upwards. It crashed through the window and skidded across the room, catching David's arm as it did so.

If he hadn't moved . . .

He put the thought aside. The man was running now and David heard a car engine start and glimpsed the outline of a car through gaps in the winter hedge. Moments later the police cars skidded into the drive, scattering gravel as they pulled up in front of the house. Three cars and then a fourth. David leaned out of the window and shouted down. "He drove off a moment ago. Grey estate car, I think, turned left." Seconds later, two of the cars took off in pursuit.

David went down to let the remaining officers inside. He stood on the step, surveying the damage. It could have been worse — broken windows could be mended, no one had been hurt though the door was now gouged and scarred, and he doubted those marks could ever be erased.

"As a parting gesture, he threw a length of piping through the upstairs window." David pointed upwards. "It was one hell of a throw," he added, feeling that the mild curse word was justified under the circumstances. His arm was now starting to throb and when he pushed back his sleeve, black bruises had already formed.

"It hit you?"

"Caught me on the arm. Thankfully, I'd moved out of the way in time."

Looking at his arm, remembering how the pole had shattered the window and still had force enough to bruise his arm and then slide across the floor, he felt suddenly shaken. He lifted a hand to wipe his face, aware that his cheeks felt wet and that there was pain there as well, now he had time to register it. The police officer stopped him, gently taking hold of his arm.

"I wouldn't touch your face, sir; in fact, I think we should call an ambulance for you. I think you might need stitching up and someone will need to remove the glass."

"The what?" The pain intensified now, and he did touch his face, albeit more gently. His fingers came away bloody. Of course, the window had shattered and he'd been standing there when it had.

He was aware of others now standing on the doorstep and of hands reaching and leading him inside, of being told that the front of the house and the big meeting room were now crime scenes, of being settled at the kitchen table and Evie cleaning his face and calling Dr Jonas. Better a friendly face to deal with his cuts than calling an ambulance and having to deal with the hospital. Later he would remember that he had wept — not because of the pain — perhaps because of the shock — but mostly because of the violation of their home.

How must Johanna and the children have felt, enduring all those months of broken windows and hatred. He had felt sorry for them of course, but not really understood until now what it meant to have no place that could be described as sanctuary. No space in which to feel safe.

* * *

By the time DI Mike Croft and DS Terry Gleeson arrived at the community house, Dr Jonas was patching up David Laughton and had removed several fragments of window glass from his scalp. Laughton looked pale and shocked, his wounds held together with paper sutures, and Mike suggested that he ought to be checked out at the hospital.

"I'm fine. I had a tetanus shot only a year ago. Doc Jonas here is capable of sorting me out and I'm needed here. I can be of more use staying put than I can hanging around in some hospital waiting room for the next four hours just so someone can insert a few stitches."

Mike looked at the doctor, who shrugged. "Man knows his own mind," he said. "I've cleaned the wounds and the edges are neat enough to knit well, given time. Personally, I think he just wants to show off his scars."

David Laughton had the grace to laugh, though clearly it hurt.

The officers attending had already filled Mike in on what had happened and Terry had shown the witnesses the picture of Brian Hedgecock. There could be no doubt in anyone's mind — this was their man. Mike went upstairs to the large meeting room and studied the length of pipe. He stood in the doorway so as not to interrupt the photographer and marvelled at the damage done. It had been a disturbingly impressive throw — if Laughton hadn't moved, only seconds before, Mike could have had a third death on his hands.

"Could you take a picture of the end of the pipe and send it to my phone?" Mike asked the CSI.

"It's a nasty bit of kit, and it looks like there's blood and tissue on the end. Give me your number and you can see for yourself. Best make sure Mr Laughton's had a tetanus jab recently and maybe suggest he has some blood tests done, just in case."

Mike nodded. He stared at the pipe. It looked as though it had been broken off a larger piece. It was rusted and jagged, probably partly rotted through before Hedgecock had wrenched it free of whatever it had been attached to. The end had a vicious point and then a rough and barbed profile that Mike thought would definitely match the damage done to Cahn. He might have balked at the idea of a man being able to drive this weapon home, deep enough to have practically pierced through the body, and then wrenching it out again. But having seen Hedgecock in motion on the CCTV cameras, both from his pursuit of Paul and also here, and seen just how powerful the man was, hurling this weapon through the upstairs window, he had no such doubts.

He went back down the stairs to talk to Paul Pearson. Terry was already in the guest room, taking down Paul's initial statement. Johanna Pearson was not in evidence and Mike felt guiltily relieved. He would have to speak with her but was happy to delay the encounter. A young woman who introduced herself as Evie sat beside her brother's bed and Mike guessed that she could be as stubborn as her mother should the occasion demand. She had Paul's hand clasped in her own and her expression dared Mike to suggest she leave. He had no intention of doing so. The young man was clearly at the end of his tether and seemed to be holding himself together by sheer force of his sister's will.

Mike sat down and listened as Paul continued with his story, not wanting to interrupt the flow.

"So," Terry had glanced at Mike as he walked in and now seemed to be backtracking a little. "Let me just check I have this right. Your friend, Ross Cahn, he believed that he was going to get paid for something he had done for this man we now know to be Brian Hedgecock?"

Paul nodded. "Ross was excited, nervy, I don't know, kind of . . . He said he'd get his money and then he'd be off. He could go anywhere. It was like he thought something was finally over. He was scared and relieved and, I don't know, just glad it was finished."

Glad what was finished? Mike wanted to ask, but Terry clearly thought he needed to creep up on the issue, not force an early confrontation with it, and Mike was happy to allow him the lead. Terry had good instincts when it came to how people were going to react and was often right about such things.

Terry nodded. "So, you and Ross Cahn went to the meeting in the pub yard. Had he told you who he was going to meet?"

Paul nodded. "He was supposed to go on his own, I think, but like I say he was nervous and excited and . . . I've never seen him like that. Most of the time he seemed to be in control. He scared me, if I'm honest. But this time *he* seemed scared. He'd have denied it, but I think he really was."

Paul licked his lips and Evie handed him some water. He drank thirstily and then shivered. He was sitting up in bed, wearing the thick, too-large dressing gown Mike had seen him in earlier and with blankets and quilts covering him, but still he seemed chilled. Mike knew well that some kinds of cold just didn't respond to any kind of heat or comfort. He felt for the young man. Life had not given him the best of starts but then, neither had he made the best decisions.

"And you say you know who he was meeting?"

"Brian Hedgecock. He was meeting him."

And this was the man who was chasing you? Mike wanted to ask, but again he remained silent, leaving Terry to do his work.

"What happened when you got there?" Terry asked.

"At the corner of the street, Ross stopped walking. He said he'd changed his mind and he should go and meet Brian on his own. That he wouldn't like it if I was there."

"But he'd been insistent before?"

"Yeah, but now he seemed to have lost his nerve. Like he'd got really scared. So I said okay and that I'd see him back at the flat."

"But you didn't go back to the flat."

Paul shook his head. "I was worried about Ross and I guess I was curious too. I waited until he'd got to the gate and gone into the yard and then I followed." He swallowed nervously. "I heard voices. Ross was asking about getting paid for the job and the other man said something like there was still someone on his list. And Ross said something about he'd never agreed to do anything else. He sounded really panicky and then I moved so I could see through the gap in the gate and . . ."

"Go on," Terry said gently. "Take it slowly."

"I saw Ross. He didn't scream or cry out or anything, it was like he was too shocked. He was on the ground and the man was standing over him and there was like this metal rod sticking out of his chest, and while I watched the man wrenched it out and stabbed him with it again."

"And then he realised you were watching him."

Paul nodded. "I must have made a noise or moved and he realised I was there. I ran. God, did I run. I was so scared."

"We've got the pursuit on CCTV," Terry told him. "You were both shifting. He didn't seem to care who saw him."

Paul shrugged. "I'd seen him kill someone."

"And a whole bunch of witnesses saw him try to chase you down. If he'd caught you, you'd have been as dead as your friend. Suddenly he didn't seem too bothered about that."

Mike could see Paul's puzzled look and wondered what Terry was getting at.

"Ross said the man he was meeting, he'd be all right most of the time, but he'd get these rages and he'd not think about anything after that. He'd just want to lash out, hurt people. There weren't many people about, not until we reached Magdalen Street. I dodged down a gap between shops and went over a wall. I knew I couldn't keep running so I hid and hoped someone would have called the police. There was a load of cardboard next to a recycling bin and I got underneath it and just hoped for the best. I heard him coming down the alley. He was wearing these heavy boots. Then I heard the sirens and I thought thank God, they'll get him. Then he came over the wall and I was shitting bricks, I swear. But he just crossed the yard and went out the gate and I just stayed put and I daren't move in case he came back. Soon as it was light, I decided to come here. I got a bus and then walked. I was half dead by the time I got here."

"And then he came here," Terry said. "Again, he doesn't seem bothered about witnesses. Any idea how he found you?"

Paul shook his head. "I never meant to bring trouble here."

"Hush, we know that," Evie told him. "No one blames you."

"I could have got people killed."

"But no one was." She turned to Mike. "Do you think he'll come back?"

"I doubt it, but I think we should get your brother away from here. Find him somewhere safe."

Evie nodded.

"What else do you know about this man?" Terry asked. "What had Ross Cahn done for him that he expected to be paid for?"

Paul hesitated. "I know they met in prison. I only knew Ross for a few weeks, just before I was released. Then he turned up here. I thought he'd forget about me when I left. I thought he was all mouth. He said he'd met someone inside that was up for release just after him and that he was going to help him do something important, that he needed backup, in case things went wrong. I told him I didn't want to know. I told him it wasn't my problem but then he turned up here and—"

"And you were scared of him?"

Paul nodded. "I'd seen what he could be like. He never did anything that . . . well, no one ever grassed on him because they knew what he was like. But I saw what he did when someone crossed him. I was just trying to stay on the right side of him and trying to stay out of trouble. But it was like he wanted to draw me in, like he couldn't bear the idea that once he'd told someone what they were going to do that they might not. You don't walk away from people like him."

"And he met Brian Hedgecock in prison. But you never did."

"No, Ross was transferred a few weeks before release and I got to know him then. I was due out before him. He must have met this man before he got transferred. He told Ross he'd got to come back here. That he needed his help with something here. Ross said he wanted me too. Ross said they needed a third person. I told him no, but he said . . . he said Brian Hedgecock didn't like people saying no to him. I said I'd think about it and last week . . . last week he said this was it. That I had to help him. I . . . I made sure I was somewhere else. Ross was mad as hell when I got back to the flat, told me I'd let him down and I'd have to make up for it."

"And what happened then?"

Paul hesitated. "He came at me with a knife and we fought. I thumped him, hard. Then all of a sudden it was like the air had gone out of him. He just collapsed crying like a baby. Said Hedgecock was mad as hell because I'd not turned up to help him. That we'd both suffer for it."

"And when was this?"

Paul shrugged. "I was supposed to meet them both on the Tuesday night. I went back to the flat Wednesday morning."

"Why did you go back?" Terry asked.

Paul seemed baffled by the question. "Where else was there to go?" he said at last. Then, "I was scared what he might do. I wanted to talk to him, tell him it was nothing to do with anyone else. That *I'd* decided I wasn't going to help him. That if he wanted to take it out on someone then it should be me. No one else. I had to tell him. I had to go back."

Looking at the young man, the shame and confusion in his eyes, Mike understood that he'd found himself between the proverbial rock and hard place. That he could see no way out. *You could have talked to your probation officer,* he thought. *Properly opened up to your brother or your mother. Pushed that little bit harder to get to talk to the police . . .*

But could he have done? Any of those options would have involved others, brought them into the sphere of Ross Cahn and Brian Hedgecock, brought consequences down on their heads. He understood that Paul didn't feel he could risk any of that.

"You were afraid he might threaten your family," Terry said.

Evie gasped. Paul nodded.

"We could have protected you — if only you'd let us know the danger you were in," Mike said. He was shocked by the sudden surge of anger in Paul's eyes.

"Like you protected us before?" he demanded. "Like you protected us for all those weeks and months when we were just little kids and—"

"Paul, Eric was the one started all that," Evie said quietly. "Like it or not, he was the one who started it all. For it to stop, *he* had to be the one to finish it."

Paul looked thunderstruck and for a moment Mike thought they had lost Paul; that his anger and pain would make him clam up and he berated himself for the interruption, but Terry still had things under control.

"And do you know what Ross Cahn and Brian Hedgecock planned to do?" he asked, his tone as level and calm as though there had been no interruption in their conversation.

Reluctantly, Paul nodded. "I didn't really believe him at first but it turns out Ross knew the man that this man, Hedgecock, was after. That he reckoned Ross could get close to him without ringing any alarm bells. You've seen the size of that bloke — anyone sees him coming they'd barricade the doors just to be sure."

Which, Mike thought, was exactly what David Laughton had done.

"And what did he plan to do to this man?" Terry asked.

"He said he'd done something to someone this Brian Hedgecock knew. He said he wanted him to pay for what he'd done. I think — no, I know — that he wanted to kill him."

And that's what they'd done. There was one more thing Mike had to ask. "Did you know the identity of the man they were after?"

"You think if I'd known I'd have just let it happen? I'd have done something. Told someone." His tone was furious, but Mike could see in his eyes that the boy believed, on some level, that he had just let it happen. Morgan Springfield was dead — Paul would have to live with that.

* * *

"Do you believe him, that he doesn't know the reason Hedgecock was planning a murder?" Mike asked.

"I'm inclined to believe he didn't want to ask," Terry Gleeson said as he manoeuvred their car past the remaining police cars in the drive.

The two cars they'd sent in pursuit of Brian Hedgecock had reported back. They had been unable to find him. There was a crossroads less than a mile away and he could have taken any route.

"You think the victim was Morgan Springfield?"

"In the absence of any other bodies, yes. And the fact that Ross Cahn apparently knew the victim and so might be able to approach him."

"Unless the murder hasn't happened yet."

"Let's hope that's not the case. The overtime budget will never handle it."

"So, where to now?" Terry asked.

Mike paused. Weighing the options. It all hinged on Hedgecock's whereabouts. *My guess is he'll have headed back to town. But until he surfaces and someone spots him, we'll never find him there . . .*

If only he'd listened more closely to what Johanna had to say. But it was too late for that.

At last, he made up his mind. "To see Sid Patterson, talk to him about Ross Cahn and Brian Hedgecock. Then try to sort out some accommodation for Paul Pearson."

CHAPTER 25

Jude had spent the last couple of hours looking at the victims. There was Morgan Springfield, of course, but her list also included Tom Andrews, the journalist that Paul Pearson had attacked. Gary Gibson, Mike's cold case from years ago. Then there was the young woman, Priscilla Eames, whom Ross Cahn had hit so hard she'd been in a coma for weeks, and the man Brian Hedgecock had attacked and killed in the pub car park.

In her notebook she drew up a timeline. Gary Gibson was first. December, eighteen years before. Fifty-five at time of death, he had been an accountant for a major building firm and had been killed at his desk. He was divorced and had two children from whom he was estranged. Hedgecock's victim, Charlie Fairford, sixty-seven years old, had been retired, married but with no children. Oddly, he had also been an accountant, self-employed and specialising in sole traders and small businesses.

Ross Cahn's victim had been only nineteen years old. Priscilla Eames had been walking home from a night out with friends. She had known Cahn and there was some suggestion that they had been an item at one time, though her family had been vehement that this was not the case and Theresa Cahn had denied knowing the girl. And of course

Cahn himself was now dead so no one could ask him. She presumed someone must have done but could find no record of that in the casefile, only the denial from the parents that their daughter could ever be involved with someone like him.

Someone like him, Jude thought. Odd that the timing coincided with the one episode in Cahn's life that had actually been quiet and calm and useful. That eighteen months or so when his mother had hoped he was turning his life around. Had the Eames family known Ross Cahn before and been mistrustful of the change?

Priscilla Eames had survived the attack and apparently made a good recovery but frustratingly Jude could find no current address or contact details for her. There was a victim impact statement in the file that had been recorded just before Ross Cahn's trial and when Priscilla Eames had still been in hospital. It spoke of her shock and pain and that her life had been ruined by Cahn's actions, but nothing of use from Jude's point of view. She also got the odd impression that someone else had written the statement — or at least tidied it up. The phrases used were too trite and generic for her to get any real sense of the young woman and the consequences she had suffered.

But there had been another survivor in all this — Tom Andrews. Paul Pearson had attacked but not harmed him — though through ineptness rather than lack of intent. And Tom Andrews had been a local journalist, according to Mike, since he'd been in short trousers. Her boss liked the man — he didn't exploit people or take the piss, like some Jude could name, and he was possessed of a genuine concern for local causes.

Jude picked up her phone and found his number. "Tom, it's DS Jude Burnett here. I wondered if you'd be free for a drink this evening."

* * *

It was Luce that opened the door to them and invited them inside.

"I'll stick the kettle on," she said. "And tell Sid you're here. He's been trying to get some work done, but I don't know how successful he's been."

"It must be very hard." Terry Gleeson kept his tone sympathetic. "But I suppose if you've got a business to run, there's only so many jobs you can delegate."

Mike noted that Luce studied Terry as though looking for meaning or accusation behind the words. "I'll tell him you're here," she said.

Sid came down a few minutes later. Luce had left them in the small front room Mike had occupied before and they could hear Luce clattering about in the kitchen. Neither had spoken though Terry had mooched about the room, much as Mike had done the first time, examining books and photographs, though he seemed more taken with Sid's record collection. Mike hadn't spotted this the first time. It was housed in a cupboard on the opposite side of the room, the door of which had been left ajar.

"Eclectic," Terry commented as Mike heard Sid's footsteps on the stairs. He glanced around. "I don't see the deck anywhere. A collection like this deserves something decent."

"I have a vintage Garrard in the other room," Sid told him as he entered. "The collection outgrew the space I had in there, so I just take a few through at a time. I had the speakers matched to the acoustics. I'm happy to show you later, if you're interested."

Terry reached into the cupboard and withdrew an album, his expression that of a small child pleading for a treat. Sid could not help but laugh and Mike felt he caught a glimpse of the man he had been before grief threatened to wipe that man away.

"You like Nick Drake?" Sid asked.

"I do, but I can never quite get my head around the production on the second album. *Five Leaves Left* is simpler, more stripped down somehow."

Luce came in with a tray of coffee and biscuits, and Terry slipped the album back in position. "I told them you were working," Luce said as she set the tray down and then settled on the small sofa by the window. "How's it going?"

"Slow, but I've delegated what I can and I'm just dealing with stuff that needs personal attention. Fortunately everyone is being patient."

"Is the business yours now?" Mike asked. "You've no one else to help shoulder the responsibility?"

"I have really good staff. Cath, our PA, she deals with most of the day-to-day admin. Raj, over at the manufacturing side, he handles the practicalities better than I ever could, deals with the customers and has assembled a first-rate team of toolmakers. Mostly it was Morgan's job to drum up new business and I dealt with the financial side. When we first started we did most of everything ourselves. Morgan was a brilliant engineer and I'd say I wasn't bad. We built our team slowly. Raj outshines both of us on that side of things, so we let him do the hiring. We've three, full-time, permanent toolmakers and others we can call on for more specialist stuff."

"So, you make tooling for CNC machines and the like?" Terry asked.

"Yes, and lathes. We make the tools that make the tools that make, well, I don't know what a lot of the time. Our customers are corporations, defence contractors, the aerospace industry, universities . . . but we have customers depending on us and I have employees who need to keep their jobs. So, I have to get back to it."

Mike nodded. He took his coffee and sipped, realising how tired he felt. It was now almost five and it had been a busy and eventful day. "Mr Patterson, does the name Brian Hedgecock mean anything to you?"

He saw Sid about to shake his head and then suddenly frown.

"That sounds familiar," Luce said. "But I can't think from where."

Sid nodded.

Terry handed him photographs of Paul Pearson and Ross Cahn and the frame grab from the CCTV camera that showed Hedgecock most clearly, alongside his prison photo ID.

Sid went through them and handed the images to Luce. "None of them seem familiar," he said.

Luce was staring hard at one of the pictures. She turned it around so Mike could see. "This one came to the club," she said. "He made quite a scene."

"Ross Cahn," Mike told her. "Mr Springfield awarded him a prize at the Montgomery Awards when Cahn was just seventeen. For a youth work project he'd helped to set up."

"I remember that," Sid said. "We'd not been here long; from what I remember Morgan had chucked a bit of cash into the prize pot and he knew the then-chair of the board, Fiona somebody. She asked him to come and give one of the prizes. I remember him joking that he was the board's nod to diversity and widening participation. It was a very white, very middle-class board back then."

"And you say Ross Cahn came to the club?" Mike asked Luce.

"Yes. These things happen, you know? People have too much to drink and make a scene . . . I'm sorry. I should have thought of it earlier, but it seemed like just one of those random incidents, you know?"

"And you're certain it was this man who was involved?" Mike asked.

Luce studied the photograph again. "Pretty sure."

Mike nodded. "What happened?"

"He came into the club one night. It must have been a Tuesday because Morgan was on his own. That was Sid's night to see family. Tuesday is a quiet night so the club gives it over to open-mic sessions and does vouchers with money off drinks. It's always good to encourage new talent and nice to get a younger crowd in. I generally do a closing set around ten thirty; we don't have an extension to the license that early in the week, but we leave earlier slots for young musicians and singers. Like I said, it's generally a younger crowd on Tuesdays and Wednesdays, coming in before they go off somewhere else. It wasn't unusual for Morgan to come in for the last hour, and this particular night, must have been about a month ago, he'd come in just before ten and he'd just sat down when this young man approached him. This Ross Cahn."

"And what did he want?"

"Well, I don't know. He was drunk and abusive, effing and blinding and spilling his beer on the floor, mad as hell about something. Morgan kept saying that he didn't know him, that he must have mistaken him for someone else. Anyway, Security threw him out on his ear and by the time we left there was no sign of him. Morgan left with me, so that would have been about half eleven, maybe a bit later if I'd helped with the clean-up, which I do if they're short-staffed. Colin Bateman, the owner of the Cold Moon, is an old friend — we've known each other since we were both kids. The Moon is like a second home."

Mike nodded. "And did you ask Mr Springfield about the confrontation?"

"I asked him, but he said it was nothing important. I could tell he was shaken, though. But to be honest, he didn't seem to want to talk about it, the subject didn't come up again, this Ross Cahn didn't reappear, so I put it down to being just one of those things."

"Except I think he must have seen him again." Sid spoke hesitantly. "Luce, do you remember me telling you that Morgan came in late one day, all flustered and annoyed, reckoned he'd run into someone he used to know and didn't want to see and they'd tried to talk to him. I asked him who it was and he just said it was some scrounger, always wanting a handout or a favour. The sort that just pisses it against the wall, no matter what you do to help. It wasn't like Morgan to get so angry or to talk about anyone like that. Morgan was kind. He'd help people again and again, even when he could see it wasn't doing any good. It seemed odd at the time but, well, by lunchtime he seemed to have forgotten all about it and I suppose I just let it go."

"It could have been this Ross Cahn," Luce said.

"And Cahn was alone that night in the club?"

Luce shrugged. "I'm not sure. I'd not really noticed him until he went up to Morgan and started swearing."

"Can you recall anything that was said, apart from the swearing?" Terry asked.

Luce thought carefully and Mike could see the gears clicking as she sought the memory and examined it.

"Morgan had just sat down. He'd gone to the bar and got a drink, then sat down at the table in the corner. The place was busy, but that table's often free because it's really cramped, it's wedged into a corner between the bar and a kind of alcove, so it's okay for one or even two, but it's not a really sociable spot. This young man went straight up to him and stood in front of the table, so Morgan had nowhere to go. He couldn't get past him. He slammed his fists down on the table and he yelled in Morgan's face. He said something like, 'Everyone thinks you're so fucking perfect, but you're just another fucking liar.' And that Morgan owed him, big time. Morgan said he didn't even know him and to get out of his face. That he's mistaking him for someone else and the kid said yes, he'd mistaken him for someone who gave a fuck, but then Riley, one of the bouncers, grabbed the kid and chucked him out. I went over to see if Morgan was all right and he tried to play the whole thing down. The kid was pissed, Morgan seemed disinclined to let it spoil the rest of his evening and so I let it go."

"Do you think he killed Morgan?" Sid asked. "Have you arrested him?"

"Ross Cahn was murdered last night," Mike told him gently. "By this man." He tapped the photograph of Brian Hedgecock. "We're now trying to find him and also trying to establish if he had any link to Mr Springfield."

Sid had grown even paler. Luce left her seat and went to him.

"Hedgecock was caught on CCTV chasing this man, Paul Pearson. Luckily for Pearson, he didn't catch him. You're sure

Morgan didn't cross paths with this man or you didn't see him hanging about near your office or either of your homes?"

Sid shook his head.

"He'd be hard to miss," Luce said wryly.

"The two deaths, Ross Cahn's and Mr Springfield's, may be totally unconnected," Mike said. "But we're looking into all possibilities. And if either of you think of anything, please don't hesitate to get in touch."

Mike stood. "I'll leave the photographs of Cahn and Hedgecock with you. Show them to friends, family, people at the club. These images are going to be all over the news this evening anyway, but it's possible someone in your circle might have seen Cahn or Hedgecock."

"What about the other one? The Pearson boy," Sid asked.

"We're not sure how he fits into the picture yet, or even if he does," Mike told him. "It could simply have been a case of wrong place, wrong time."

He was aware that he had left them feeling more nervous and insecure and upset than they had been before, but he felt it was best for them both to be on the alert. Just in case. Brian Hedgecock was unpredictable and dangerous, and if he had been involved in Morgan Springfield's death, then did that make him a threat to Springfield's friends and associates? Mike didn't know.

"What I don't understand is why he's after Paul Pearson," Terry commented as they got into the car. "It can't be just that the Pearson kid witnessed him killing Cahn. If he was that bothered about witnesses, he wouldn't have chased him through the middle of town, or tried to break into the community house. It has the feel of a grudge, if you ask me."

Mike nodded. Terry was right, the witness angle simply didn't make sense. Brian Hedgecock seemed positively cavalier when it came to allowing others to witness his actions. Although, "Okay, so I'm playing devil's advocate here, but if you look at the witness statements, all they tell us is that they saw a big man chasing a smaller man. That the big man had a weapon of some kind and was dressed in either dark clothing or army fatigues or blue jeans and a dark jacket. None of the witnesses are consistent with each other because they were focusing on getting out of the way. True, a couple of them did film the fracas on their mobile phones and there's a bit of decent footage there. More, obviously, from the street cameras, but that's down more to luck than anything else. Most of the mobile-phone images are of the back of said big man, when he was safely past them. Yes, they'd probably recognise him if they saw him again, or rather they'd recognise his size and mass, but more than that? I'm not so sure. I think our man knows what impression he makes and knows that nine times out of ten, people will be suddenly uncertain that it's him they saw, because they're more afraid of the repercussions, should they ID him, than they are of being vague with the police. No doubt it's a lesson he learned inside, if not before. He scares people, they therefore tend not to witness what he does. But Pearson, presumably he knows him, so—"

"So do we, now," Terry said. "Though what you've just said doesn't hold for the folks at the community house. David Laughton and his people got a good look and recorded him on CCTV. You ask me why he doesn't care about being seen because he doesn't care about what might happen. And what's the worst we can do? Catch him? Put him back inside? He's killed at least once and none of us think Ross Cahn is his only victim so, getting hung for a sheep or a lamb, what difference does it make?" He paused for a moment and then said, "Though with the likes of Brian Hedgecock it could just be that Paul Pearson pissed him off."

Mike laughed grimly. "It's an interesting thought and if it's true, probably makes him even more dangerous. Whatever the truth of the matter, we've still got to find him. Someone's protecting him. Someone who is either too scared or too loyal, for whatever reason, to turn him in."

"You think Pearson might know?"

"I think he's our best shot at the moment." Tomorrow they would talk to Paul Pearson again. In the meantime, Mike had to get him somewhere safe, somewhere Brian Hedgecock would not think to look for him.

CHAPTER 26

Brian Hedgecock was indeed being protected, but Mike would never have suspected he was being looked after by anyone like Deidre Jones. She'd been a distant relative of his stepfather and Brian's memory of her was that she had always been kind, had treated him more like a son or favourite nephew than the stepchild of her employer. Treated him better than his mother ever had.

Brian had never known his real father. His stepfather had been his dad as far as he was concerned and even after his mother had left to go and pursue her dreams elsewhere, he and Brian had remained close. He'd been a little kid when his mother left. Years later she had contacted him to say she was coming back for him, but he'd been sixteen by then and told her not to bother. He was happy where he was, thank you very much.

Later — much later, when his stepfather was gone and Brian was in prison — Deidre had bought a little B&B and made a tidy living offering cheap but clean and welcoming accommodation to visitors, some of whom came back year after year to visit Auntie D.

Brian kept a discreet eye on her, even while he'd been away, and sent her the occasional carefully worded letter. It amused Brian to send these care of the local vicar, Brian's stepfather having been a semi-regular churchgoer. Deidre, despite her previous associations, had never been charged with anything and over time she had simply dropped off everyone's radar.

She was old and increasingly frail now. The B&B had long since closed its doors, but even so . . . the house was not really suited to a lady who could no longer climb the stairs. It had seemed obvious to Brian, once they'd let him out of prison, that he should come and stay with her while he dealt with business, though of course this was not the address he'd given to his probation officer. After that, he'd make sure she was properly looked after and had a more suitable place to live.

While still inside, he'd arranged with old associates that they sort out Deidre's house, moving her bedroom downstairs and creating a wet room in the old scullery. Brian's stepfather was long gone, but his financials had been in good order at the time of his death and so, by extension, were Brian's. Not that either the law or the Inland Revenue would be aware of that.

She was making tea when he got back. He'd messaged her to say he was on his way and would be picking up fish and chips for supper. She liked hers with mushy peas and curry sauce.

Brian had long since learned that he couldn't help but stand out in a crowd, but there were ways and means of standing out. He kept a decent jacket, smart and tailored in heavy wool, in his car — not the vehicle he had stolen for the purposes of pursuing Paul Pearson, which had been dumped on the outskirts of town. He combed his hair and set his smile in place, no longer the vicious, slavering monster who had chased Paul Pearson through the town or killed Ross Cahn just hours before. He was Bri, who had moved in with his elderly relative to look after her. Bri, tall and well built, and, so it was rumoured, ex-army. Possibly ex-regiment. Affable and polite — though you probably wouldn't want to cross him. Though for most who encountered him regularly and casually, that added a frisson of excitement to the acquaintance, rather than out-and-out terror. Brian had decided way back that if you didn't look guilty, then the vast majority of people would assume that you couldn't be. His stepfather had once told him that he was brazen and Brian rather liked the description.

Sooner or later, of course, someone would make the connection, as the police and media reports seeped into the public imagination and the police put a name to the face. Then he would have to move on. The knowledge that this would be sooner rather than later was on his mind as he opened the front door. He would have to talk to Deidre, tell her he was going away on business for a bit. She wouldn't question it or even ask for an explanation. She'd worked for his dad for far too long to do that. What she didn't know she couldn't tell, and he knew Deidre had always been happier that way.

"Hello, love, how have you been today?" he asked as he set the parcel of fish and chips on the table and then went to hang his coat in the hall.

"Not so bad, though you must be all a-dudder, being out in that cold. Did you find the man you were looking for?"

"I'm warm enough. No, he wasn't at the address I'd been given. I'll try a few other places tomorrow, but I reckon my contacts were wrong and he's probably skipped off somewhere else."

"That's a shame. I've warmed the plates."

"I'll get them. You sit yourself down. Tea ready for pouring, is it?" He picked up the oven gloves and fished the plates out of the oven. There was already a plate of bread and butter on the table and place mats and cutlery. She set two mugs down, next to the milk jug and sugar bowl, the salt and vinegar, and the tartare sauce. Deidre used a wheeled walking frame, both around the house and when going out. She had written to Brian in prison and told him about the nice lady from the Red Cross who had come and measured up, so they could make a slightly narrower, bespoke frame for her, as the hall from the kitchen to the new wet room was narrow. It helped keep her steady on her feet and she'd become adept at steering it with one hand and using the other to move stuff around. He'd also provided her with perching stools so she could prepare food and the kitchen had been refitted with an oven that was at a level she could reach easily. He still worried about her though, wondered how long she would be able to maintain her independence.

He unwrapped the fish and chips and divided their supper onto the plates.

The radio was on, tuned to a station that played mostly forties and fifties music that reminded Deidre of her younger days. There would still be news on it, he supposed, but he doubted it would be local. Had she watched the telly today? Had she seen him?

Brian had no worries that she might betray him — that just wouldn't happen. But he didn't want her upset, not until it was absolutely necessary.

"I'm going to be leaving for a little while," he said, reaching for the jar of tartare sauce.

She nodded. "I knew you'd not be stopping," she said. Then added softly, "You always were a troubled kid. Many ways you were just like him."

"I know." He reached out and clasped her hand. It was trembling slightly and it felt so fragile, all skin and bone and impossibly soft skin. She meant his stepfather, he knew. He had no argument with the comparison.

"You should go tonight," she said quietly.

"I thought I'd wait a day or so."

She shook her head. "I watch the news, you know. I know what's going on. Or some of it, at least, and, no, you don't tell me no more."

"I won't and if you think it's right then I'll go after I've done the washing up." He poured her more tea and topped up his own cup. Helped himself to a piece of bread and butter and carefully layered his chips over one half before folding it over.

"I've nearly done here, anyway. I'll get myself set up somewhere else and then I'll come and fetch you. Or if I can't, I'll get you brought to me."

She nodded, smiled at him.

His mother, Brian reflected, had made a similar promise to him when she'd left, but unlike his mother it was a promise he would keep and Deidre knew that. Brian always kept his promises.

CHAPTER 27

"I wouldn't ask if I didn't think it was urgent," Mike said. "No one will think of him being with you and it will only be for a day or two, just until I can get something else sorted out."

John laughed. "I've heard that one before. Look, Mike, I'll take the boy for a couple of days, but I've got to admit I'm not happy about getting involved with the Pearsons again. And, yes, I know I agreed to meet with Johanna but to be honest I was glad when she stormed off and I didn't have to get in any deeper."

"And I really wouldn't ask—"

"I know. Are they expecting me?"

"Yes. There's a couple of officers still there, just in case Hedgecock decides to come back. Though I can't keep them there much longer, just until the shift change. After that—"

"So, I'd better get a wiggle on then," John told him.

Truthfully, John felt somewhat irritated. Not so much with Mike and not even with Paul Pearson. He'd not turn anyone away if they were truly in difficulties. It was more that, for him the Pearsons just spelt trouble, the sort of trouble that just expanded to fit the space available.

It was dark, and a mix of rain and snow that didn't quite manage to be organised enough to describe as sleet fell on the car windscreen. He turned the heater up full, turned on the radio and wondered if he had enough food in the house for an extra person over the next few days.

Paul Pearson looked nervous, John thought. No wonder about that. In fact, he looked very different from the rather angry and somewhat arrogant young man John had encountered at the probation office the week before. He'd definitely had the wind knocked out of his sails. The community had managed to put clothes and toiletries together for him, Paul having turned up with nothing but the clothes he was wearing, and Paul clutched at the holdall as though it were some kind of life raft that he might have to scrabble into at a moment's notice.

There was also a carrier bag full of groceries and fresh veg, handed to John by Evie who introduced herself as Paul's sister. "It's short notice," she said. "We wanted to make sure you had some extra bits and pieces."

John thanked her. "We're going to take a bit of a circuitous route back," he said. "Just to make sure we're not being followed. Paul will text you as soon as we're at my place. Are you all going to be all right here? Mike tells me the patrol car will have to leave soon."

"We'll be fine," Evie assured him. "The doors are solid and we've closed all the shutters on the windows. The families with kids have gone to stay in the community up in York. They let us know they'd arrived about twenty minutes ago. Everyone else is in here and we'll call the police at the first sign of trouble."

She paused. "Daniel, my younger brother — he went with the others. This has upset him a lot. I didn't think he remembered anything about what happened before, but this seems to have brought it all back."

"And you?"

"I think I'm all right," she said. "But if not, I've got people I can talk to, so I'll be fine. I'm pretty worried about Paul though." She glanced over at her brother, perched on a hall chair, the holdall on his lap.

"I'll take good care of him." John realised that despite his reservations and, yes, his resentment, he meant that.

* * *

In the end, DS Jude Burnett and Tom Andrews had settled on the Adam and Eve pub on Bishopsgate for their meeting. This had given Jude the opportunity to go home and shower and change first, and to make herself a sandwich. Her route home had taken her over the Magdalen Street flyover, a universally hated structure — Jude had never heard a good word said about it — cutting through one of the most historic parts of the city as it did, carving through medieval with 1960s architectural brutality. Driving through the slush and rain in a stream of traffic, she wondered how many of the motorists were aware of the drama that had been enacted beneath them. She supposed that most must be — were they straining to see through their side windows, vainly hoping to catch a glimpse of something beyond the concrete parapets that edged the elevated road?

Seth had called, wanting to meet, but was unfazed when she put him off. Both were in the habit of putting work first and he knew she was deeply involved in both the Morgan Springfield case and these latest developments. She found herself hoping he wouldn't get a sudden desire to go to the same pub and told herself she should not have given Seth the impression that she'd still be at the office. It made her feel oddly guilty and also oddly discomfited. How seriously were they taking this relationship? Was that going to be enough?

The Adam and Eve was a medieval inn, reputed to be the oldest in Norwich. The top bar, the original pub, was small, and the tables between the tall settles usually occupied. Tom had texted to say he was down in the lower bar, her least favourite part of the pub, created from the old cellar but far less atmospheric than the original space upstairs. Still, she told herself, she wasn't here for the atmosphere.

Tom was sitting at a table tucked into the corner and already had a beer and a glass of red wine in front of him.

Jude wasn't surprised that he'd remembered. She was usually wary of reporters, but Mike had introduced her to Tom just after she had joined his team and told her that Tom Andrews was one of the good guys. She had gathered that Mike and Tom's friendship went back quite a way and that Tom and John Tynan had known one another since Tom first started at the *Courier*.

"So," he said, pushing the wine across the table. "What brings you out on this dark and stormy night? Our old friend, Brian Hedgecock, or is it Johanna Pearson and her kin?"

Jude raised an eyebrow, wondering at the 'old friend' comment. She reminded herself that the chase through the middle of Norwich had been all over the news and that Hedgecock and Paul Pearson's pictures, as recorded on the CCTV cameras, had both been shown. "So, you recognised Paul Pearson," she said. "Despite the fact he had his head down."

Tom nodded. "After what happened, I felt concerned about him. I kind of kept in touch with how he was doing. David Laughton, the elder at the Children of Solomon community, was kind enough to keep me updated."

"He seems like a decent bloke," Jude said.

"For a cult leader." Tom couldn't help but tease.

"OK, so for a cult leader. I've got to admit, though, they're not what I expected. They seem . . . well, they seem kind of ordinary."

"Get David going on the benefits of organic and regenerative farming and you'll witness someone dead set on conversion, but apart from that I think they just want to be left alone to do their own thing. Even when I've dropped in unexpectedly, I have to say I've always been made welcome. I honestly don't think they've got a hidden agenda. I'm not of a religious turn of mind, but it doesn't seem to be doing them any harm."

"The Pearson problem," she hesitated, "I'm not sure what else to call it. That must have hit them hard."

"It did, but they weathered it. And if Johanna had simply reported what she'd found, then she and the kids could have gone home and settled down and life for all concerned would have been so much better. But she's a fearsome woman and I don't think she trusted the wheels of justice to crush Eric as completely as she felt he deserved."

"You mentioned Brian Hedgecock being an old friend. Does that imply that you've run across him before?"

Tom laughed. "Oh, yes, and where Brian went, trouble always followed. Not surprising, considering his upbringing though." Tom drained his glass. Jude had scarcely started on her wine but she supposed he'd had a head start on her. She picked up his glass. "What are you drinking?" She looked curiously at the bottle that advertised Fat Cat bitter.

When she returned from the bar, he had a notebook and a sheaf of printouts on the table top. She saw that most were press clippings.

"I've brought these for you to look through. There's another notebook somewhere, but I'll have to have a root around to find that. They all date from around twelve, thirteen years ago, and the notebook from before that, but all from prior to Hedgecock finally doing something that got him banged up. Though we all reckoned, those of us following his career, that he was good for the Gary Gibson murder."

"What?"

"I thought that would grab your attention. No proof, of course, and my recollection may not be as accurate as I'd like. I've made arrangements to see an old friend later this evening, who may be able to fill in some of the gaps. If so, I'll get back to you and I'll certainly look out the other notebook."

"What was Hedgecock's connection to Gibson?"

"Nothing direct, but Gibson's wife left him about a year before he died. No one seems to know where she took herself off to, though the smart money's on a little villa in Spain. Somewhere she could play her part in a money-laundering scheme, run on behalf of her brother. You know who he was?"

She nodded. "Jimmy Hargreaves, though I've not had time to find out much about him."

"Well, one of the things you probably don't know, is that Brian Hedgecock was Hargreaves' stepson."

"You're joking."

"I jest not. The rumours were that Brian, being built like a tank even then, was useful to his stepdad, especially when someone failed to pay their debts on time, or when he wanted someone out of the way on a permanent basis. Now Jimmy wasn't given to violence, not as these things go. He had a reputation for self-restraint, would go out of his way to reach an accommodation that suited everyone but mostly that suited Jimmy. His thinking seemed to be that if you maimed or killed someone because they'd failed to cough up what they owed, then you were diminishing their ability to pay their debt at some future point and, compound interest being what it is, if instead you reached an accommodation, they'd likely go on paying until they were in their box and six feet under. Then Jimmy might let the family off the rest or he might not, depending on his mood."

"I see," Jude said. "Tom, how far back are we going? I've been here five years and I know nothing of this Hargreaves."

"Not surprising. His star was burning out by the time of the Gibson murder and after that his business went downhill, fast. It didn't help that Brian Hedgecock, his main enforcer, had been put inside for killing Charlie Fairford."

"Who was a retired accountant," Jude said.

"Who was also a semi-retired bookmaker and not the kind you'd find in the high street."

"I didn't find any reference to that in the files."

"No, you wouldn't. On the face of it he was scrubbed and shiny, but it was well known in, shall we say, less official circles. It's interesting — gambling was one of the few pies Hedgecock's stepfather didn't have a finger in. That particular business was run by the type of people even Jimmy Hargreaves wouldn't have gone up against. But I've a feeling there was another connection. I just need to check it out."

"With your old friend. I don't suppose he has a name?"

Tom just smiled at her and she let it pass. If Tom's speculation proved to have foundation, she knew he'd give her chapter and verse later. She sipped her wine and thought for a moment. "So, what do you know about Ross Cahn and Paul Pearson," she said.

"Collectively or separately?"

"Was there a collectively? I thought they met in prison."

"Well. They might have renewed their acquaintance in prison, but I'm pretty sure they knew one another before. When Johanna went to prison, her former community did all they could to look after her children, but Paul was a very angry kid and became an even angrier teenager. He was forever running off somewhere and getting into trouble. It started small, as I'm sure you know."

"Shoplifting, petty theft, then later he got into drugs and housebreaking."

"And ran with the same crowd — they weren't really organised enough to be called a gang — as Ross Cahn. Now Cahn was a bit older than Paul and seemed to have had bigger ideas. He was heading for a major fall whereas Paul was still paddling around in the shallows. They'd both managed to avoid getting into big trouble, I think more by luck than judgement, but they were known to the police and social services and classed as vulnerable and at risk. I know from what David Laughton told me that the community was worried that Paul's actions would jeopardise their position as guardians of his siblings, and they were looking at the possibility of him going to live in one of the other communities in the hope that would get him away from bad influences. Anyway, Paul's actions eventually took those decisions out of his hands."

"When Paul attacked you."

Tom nodded. "David and the elders had approved the article I wrote before it was published. I wanted it to have a positive spin. The kids were thriving, they were maintaining contact with their mother, the love and affection they had received from their foster parents was healing some of

212

the pain . . . but I guess even after all my years in the job, I can still suffer from moments of naivety. I should have left well alone. All I did was scrape open old wounds. Paul wasn't alone in thinking I was betraying them in some way. There were victims of the paedophiles that had come to trial around the time of the Pearson business, who seemed to feel that I should have been concentrating on them and not the children of a guilty party. And Paul, well, he was furious. He had no trust in authority figures of any kind. He felt that the police, social services and the media had all let his family down and that I'd been chief among them. I can see his point, I suppose — I wrote extensively about the scandals in the children's homes and then I wrote extensively about Pearson and his accusations, some of which, as you know, proved to be accurate and true. And it didn't help that one of the officers heading up the investigation into the alleged paedophile ring turned out to be involved up to his neck."

"Jacques," Jude said. It had left deep scars on the force and especially on Mike, who had initially trusted the senior officer.

"So, what actually happened the day he came to your house? I've read the official account and the various media accounts and heard what David Laughton had to say, but—"

"But you want it from the horse's mouth." Tom Andrews nodded. "Right, well, first let me tell you that I have never been that frightened at any other time in my life. Second, let me say that recognising just how scared I was made me think of those children, holed up in that house with an insane father and a mother at the end of her tether, while their home was attacked. Just how scared they must have been."

"Which is why you spoke out for him."

"It is. Though it took me a few days to calm down first, I'll admit to that."

Jude nodded. "So, talk me through it. What happened on the day?"

"Well. It was a Friday evening and I was a little late home so I knew Brid would be looking out for me. We were due to go over to her sister's for dinner and she hates to be late for anything. I pulled up in front of the house, started to get out of the car. The driver's door opened onto the road side. I saw a movement out of the corner of my eye and I turned and he was there with this bottle in his hand and a lit rag poking out of the top. I backed off and he pulled another one from his pocket and lit the fuse on that one too. Then he chucked a bottle into the car and threw the second one at me. By now I was running but I felt it hit my leg and the flame caught my trousers. The first bottle he'd thrown into the car — that had broken and petrol spread all over the footwell. By the time I got inside, the floor mats and the seats were on fire. The second had hit me as I went through the front gate and it must have bounced off my leg because it didn't break, it just caught my trouser leg and spilled accelerant all over the path.

"Brid had seen what was happening and had the front door open. I remember her slamming the door and the relief I felt and then I heard her talking on the phone and realised she'd called the police."

"He didn't run away."

"No, he just stood there, shouting abuse, and I was worried in case he had more of his petrol bombs and that he might chuck something through the window. I realised then that my leg was hurting and that at some point, while she was still on the phone, Brid had beaten out the flames with the door mat."

He laughed at that but the sound was tense and hollow.

"Good for Brid," Jude said. She had met Tom's wife on a few occasions and recalled a slim, blonde woman with a ready smile and a way of putting people at their ease. She could well imagine her taking control of the situation.

"Anyway, the police arrived very quickly. I remember him being arrested. I remember that he was laughing, can you imagine that? And I remember thinking in that moment that he was completely off his head. The police insisted I got checked out at the hospital but the burns were superficial and I came out of it very lightly.

"Most of all I remember driving back home with Brid and realising that I was just shaking, shivering like I'd been dunked in freezing water. I got home, she wrapped me in a blanket, made tea and poured what looked like half a bottle of brandy into the mug. Anyway, when I woke up the next morning I'd had the worst dreams, but at least I'd stopped shaking."

"And you decided to speak up for him."

"Not then. A few days later. David Laughton heard what happened and phoned me. I'm afraid he got the full broadside, but after I calmed down, I realised that if *I'd* been that scared, what must those kids have gone through?"

"So, your victim impact statement asked for leniency."

"It asked for the past circumstances to be taken into account. Problem was, he already had a record, had escaped being put in a young offenders' centre by the skin of his teeth, so whatever I said he was going to get a custodial sentence. It was just a question of how long. He'd have been out in a couple of years if he'd behaved himself but . . . as it was, he served five and the final year was in an adult prison. That can't have done him any good."

"You still feel sorry for him." She could hear the surprise in her own voice.

"I suppose I do. His siblings have grown into remarkable young people. I'm sorry that he didn't seem to find a way through."

Jude went to fetch more drinks. Ginger beer for herself and another pint for Tom. He'd assured her that he'd be getting a taxi home.

"So, what do you know about Ross Cahn?" she asked.

"Let me return the question."

"Well, that he had a history of petty offending from around thirteen, then things got serious from around fifteen when drugs came into the picture. He was dealing a couple of years later, then suddenly all of that stopped. I spoke to his mother and she said it was like a miracle. They'd hoped he'd turned his life around. He got involved in community projects for the Loftus Project and even won a Montgomery award."

"Which poor Morgan Springfield presented to him."

"You knew Mr Springfield?"

"Yes, in his own way he was a prominent member of the business community and also backed a number of local charities. I got to know him when Brid got him involved in a charity fundraiser."

Brid, Jude recalled, worked as an administrator for a local hospice.

"We became friends. So of course I know Sid too. The poor man is in bits, isn't he."

"He is. A friend is staying with him. Lucille Connolly?"

"Luce, yes. Magnificent voice. But you're asking about Ross Cahn."

"I'm asking for anything you know. I've read everything I can lay hands on in the official records and I've scanned the media reports, but you and I both know how much gets left out."

"So, Ross Cahn. I knew nothing about him until Morgan got involved. The Loftus Project was designed to encourage young people who were in danger of serious offending to find another path. Kids were referred through police channels and social services. All the kids on the scheme had been in trouble and the Loftus Project gave them opportunities for community service, with the possibility of training and apprenticeships at the end of it, if they were seen to have made sufficient progress. From memory, roughly a third went on to find work or training after the scheme. Ross Cahn must have believed he'd be one of them, especially after winning that award."

"That's a good rate," Jude said. "But it didn't happen for Cahn?"

"No. As I understand it, Morgan had arranged for Cahn to do a six-month stint of work experience with his company. Then if Cahn took to it, he'd help him find a college place with the eventual aim of studying engineering at university.

Ross Cahn was far from stupid — in fact that was probably half the problem. He'd get bored, he'd get disruptive."

"But this didn't happen? Tom, Sid thinks Morgan had a run-in with Cahn shortly after he left prison. He's not certain it was with him, but said that Morgan came into work one day clearly upset. He said he'd met an old acquaintance who thought Morgan owed him something. Mr Springfield was very shaken up."

"I imagine Ross Cahn was very upset when what he saw as his right was taken away from him."

"And why was that? I've got to admit, I hadn't realised there was more than a trophy and a cash prize at stake. DS Gleeson spoke to the chairwoman from back then but the Loftus charity and the prize fund no longer exist and she couldn't tell us much. I spoke to a couple of the prize winners but none of them really knew Cahn and I didn't think to ask about awards other than what they received at the prize giving."

Tom laughed at her tone, and she realised how pissed off with herself she sounded. "Don't beat yourself up," he said. "It was an unusual set-up. No, unfortunately Loftus folded the following year. There were accusations of mis-management of funds. Nothing was found but the damage was done. The accusations were anonymous, I believe, but seemed specific enough that they had to be investigated. I always wondered if Cahn was at the back of that."

"So why did Morgan Springfield pull his offer?"

"Because he caught Ross Cahn stealing from him. He took money from the petty-cash box in the office and stole two cheques from the company cheque book. Tried to cash them at the local bank, but they were business cheques — the counter clerk queried the transaction and the manager rang Morgan, who went to the bank and viewed the CCTV. They'd already realised the cash was gone, so—"

"So, he withdrew the offer of work."

"And only a few weeks later Cahn is arrested for assaulting Priscilla Eames. You know she was in a coma for weeks after."

Jude nodded. "I've not been able to get a current address for her. Neighbours say the family moved about five years ago, they think to be closer to their daughter during her rehab, but they don't know where they went."

"You know she and Cahn were an item for a while."

"I know that's the rumour. He denied it, her family insisted they barely knew one another."

"They were together for at least a couple of months. She came to the awards dinner as Cahn's plus one. They were still together when Ross Cahn stole the cash because she was also on the CCTV. There was no suggestion she knew what he was up to, in fact she seems to have broken it off as a direct result. It's possible the attack was a response to her rejection of him. Another reason for Cahn to resent Morgan."

"Tom, do you think he's responsible for Mr Springfield's murder?"

"I think he may have been involved. But certainly not alone. Cahn was a streak of piss. Morgan was built like a rugby prop. Of course, if Brian Hedgecock was involved?"

"Now you're sounding like a reporter," she told him.

"Of course I am. But it's got to be a possibility, doesn't it."

"And what motive would Hedgecock have for helping Cahn kill Morgan Springfield?" She narrowed her eyes and studied him suspiciously. "You know something?"

"No," he told her. "Not know, as I said I have a vague tickle of memory about something. When I leave you, I'm going to see my friend, see if he can help me ferret it out. If he can, you'll be the first to know."

"Or your editor will."

"Okay, so you'll be the second to know. Seriously though, it might be nothing. Either way I'll give you a call in the morning."

And with that, Jude had to be satisfied.

CHAPTER 28

Fred Donner was long retired but Tom had kept in touch with the one-time DS and they'd meet up every so often to reminisce and set the world to rights. Fred not being in the best of health these past years, now preferred to meet at his home rather than one of the local pubs they had used to frequent. Tom always arrived with a liquid tribute, especially when he had particular questions to ask. Fred, like many in his profession, had a memory like an elephant and was still possessed of a mind like a steel trap. Tom had been asking him about the Gibson case, sipping his own beer and observing as Fred Donner gulped his like a man who has thirsted for too long. Some things never changed.

"The SIO on that was DI Foston," Tom said, already anticipating the reaction.

Fred laughed. "Stupid bugger couldn't find his own arse with both hands and a guide book."

"He had a good track record," Tom said.

"Because he was good at delegating and then taking the credit. Didn't get him far in the Gibson case though. Largely because he was looking in the wrong place."

"Oh." Tom watched as his old colleague drained his glass and then sat back expectantly. Fred reached for another beer. Tom had a preference for real ale but his old friend was not so particular. He preferred anything that came in a six-pack.

"So, where should he have been looking?" he asked. "I heard a rumour about the wife and her lover."

"The wife had left him long since. Emptied the bank account, left him with the house and the bills, disappeared into the wide blue yonder. Or that was the story anyway."

"You going to tell me he'd buried her under the patio?" He looked at his friend's expression and then said, "Really?"

"Maybe not the patio, but they'd been fighting like cat and dog for years and I don't just mean verbals. The pair of them beat seven shades out of one another. A neighbour told me she broke his jaw then took him to A and E and didn't even try to hide what she'd done. Another time he broke three of her ribs. The kids left just as soon as they could, though there was never any suggestion either parent so much as slapped them. This was purely between Gibson and his wife."

"Then why stay together?"

"Why indeed. But we all reckoned she'd finally had enough and decided to do a proper job. But there might have been more to it than that. You know who her brother was?"

Tom shook his head. He remembered very well, having furnished Jude with the information not an hour before, but he knew the best way to get information out of Fred was to claim ignorance and let him talk.

"You remember Jimmy Hargreaves?"

"You're kidding."

"Half-brother, he was. Or maybe stepbrother, I don't remember the finer points, but thick as thieves the pair of them. Word was Jimmy was using Gibson's accountancy skills to his advantage, but that Gibson was skimming off the top and in Jimmy's world, that would never do. She gets to hear about it, tells the brother, and, bingo, no more Gary Gibson."

"And this was never looked at by Foston's team?"

"Rumour was Foston was taking backhanders from old Jimmy."

"More than rumour?"

Fred shrugged. "Who knows. But it's interesting that he took early retirement with a full pension when the Gibson case went cold."

Definitely interesting, Tom thought, but not conclusive. "What happened to Mrs Gibson?"

"As I said, disappeared into the wide blue yonder, with or without her mythical lover. Even her kids didn't go looking for her."

"And she never turned up?"

"Not so far as I know. To be fair she wasn't the sort of woman anyone seemed to have missed and no one reported her missing, not officially anyway. I always figured she'd been party to what her husband had done, that she told her brother so he'd get rid of an encumbrance and she just took the money and left."

"I can't help thinking that divorce would have been simpler. You reckon she really hated her husband so much she wanted him killed? Why not just walk?"

"Ours not to reason why, my son. For a while she was chief suspect, but our dear leader, DI Foston, was right about one thing, it would have taken strength to kill Gary Gibson that way. I figure a woman like Lizzie Gibson could have done it, but more likely it was a man. And someone Gibson knew, to have got that up close and personal."

Tom nodded. He wondered about Morgan Springfield's death. The police reports all described his death as being the result of a stab wound to the neck but, talking to Sid, Tom had discovered the truth. He had no intention of telling Fred Donner what he knew as Fred had a loose tongue in his head, always had. And he understood why the police were withholding the exact details — for one thing they were pretty horrific but in investigative terms they were also details known only to the killer. Or killers. Gibson had been a small man and Brian Hedgecock would have had no trouble with him. Morgan had been anything but. Even someone built like Hedgecock might have wanted a bit of assistance. That's if he'd done it of course, though Tom had no real doubts in his mind on that score. And of course, with Ross Cahn also having a grudge, Hedgecock might have found himself a willing accomplice.

"You ever run across Brian Hedgecock?" he asked.

"Hedgecock? Sure. Thick with Jimmy Hargreaves, wasn't he? Did his dirty work for him."

"Did he come up in relation to the Gibson murder?"

"He was interviewed. Alibied. Not that it meant much, seeing as he was alibied, if I remember correctly, by Jimmy himself."

"And what did you reckon?"

"That it was possible he'd done it. That it was possible Jimmy had taken it on himself to settle the score. That it might have been the wife. It were one or the other, that much was sure, but nothing stuck."

He shrugged. "I hear Hedgecock is back on the scene. I saw him on the news. He was a big bugger back then, but he's twice the size now. He can still shift, though, for a big lad."

Tom agreed that he could. He poured Fred another beer — Fred had never liked to drink out of the can — and allowed the conversation to drift to other things while he thought.

Eventually he said, "The man that Hedgecock was put inside for — what was the story there, do you reckon? I covered the trial, but he never did give an explanation."

"Charlie Fairford? Well, I don't know what the official thinking might have been, I'd transferred to another division by then, but I always reckoned it had something to do with the Ellison business. Gifford was a witness, maybe more than that. And that was the beginning of the end for Jimmy Hargreaves."

"Remind me," Tom said, still sipping at his first pint now grown warm and insipid. And Fred did remind him and by the time he had done so, Tom was beginning to wonder if he would indeed have something useful to tell Jude.

CHAPTER 29

Paul had not appeared until nearly noon on the Tuesday. He had been too exhausted, John had realised, to do anything but collapse into bed and go to sleep.

John hadn't allowed the presence of another person to interrupt his day. He'd had breakfast at his usual time, pottered in the garden until the rain set in, late morning, and then when he heard the sound of the shower, he set a pan of bacon and sausage cooking on the stove. By the time the young man made it downstairs, John was cooking eggs and had made fresh coffee.

"Food is almost done," he said as the toast popped in the toaster. "If you can grab that toast, the butter's in that blue dish, knives are in the drawer next to you. I'm sure you must be hungry by now."

Paul looked momentarily startled and then obediently set to buttering toast. There was a small television in the kitchen and John switched it on, found the lunchtime news.

He brought the pan of bacon and sausage and then the eggs to the table, set them down on cork mats, then reached for the warmed plates. "I'm not standing on ceremony," he said. "You help yourself." John set an example by doing just that and after a moment Paul followed suit.

"Thanks," he said.

John was unsurprised to find that the hunt for Hedgecock had made the national news. He watched his friend, DI Mike Croft, in deeply serious mode, advise the public that Brian Hedgecock was a dangerous man and should on no account be approached. If seen, then the police should be notified immediately.

They would be getting false reports from John o'Groats to Land's End, John thought.

"They won't find him." Paul had paused with a piece of sausage, dripping egg, hovering above his plate.

"Oh, and why is that?" John helped himself to a piece of toast.

Paul, seeming to remember his sausage, chewed thoughtfully before responding. "Could I get some more coffee?"

"Of course, help yourself and if you wouldn't mind topping mine up while you're there." He was glad he'd made a large pot. It was very good coffee.

Paul brought coffee over to the table and then sat down. "I know he looks like he'd stand out like a sore thumb," he said. "But he doesn't. He kind of disappears into the background any time he wants. It's like he chooses not to be noticed and so people don't notice him."

John nodded. "I've met people like that. Though I admit Brian Hedgecock is larger than most. You know, I think the trick is that most people still have that instinct for predators that our ancestors needed just to survive. You become aware of something you know is dangerous, you get away from it as fast as you can. But in this day and age, we can't get away with sticking the dangerous thing with a spear or even running like hell, so instead we pretend it's not there and hope it will do us the same courtesy."

Paul laughed. "That's your theory, is it?"

"Indeed, it is and it's not half bad, if I do say so myself."

They cleared the table in an almost companionable silence. John guessed that the young man was as surprised as he was that they were getting along. After all, John had brought him nothing but trouble in the past, albeit without intent. It had been the accusation Paul had made when they had met at the probation officer's.

"How long do I stay here?" Paul asked as he dried plates with almost exaggerated care and attention.

"Probably a few days. It really depends how fast they find Hedgecock." He paused, wondering how far he could push this entente cordiale. "Paul, do you have any idea where he might have gone? Or even any idea why he wanted to kill you?"

The plate went down with a clatter. "Sorry."

"No harm done. Okay, lad, I've no official right to ask you questions. My job is just to offer safe haven until this mess is sorted out. You don't want to talk about this, then I'm not going to try to force you."

Paul took a deep breath and picked up another plate, dried it with the same level of attention. *He's so scared he can hardly hold it together,* John thought. *But at least he managed to eat. At least he's clinging on to normal and ordinary. That's got to be a good thing.*

He wondered about suggesting the boy talk to Maria, but thrust the idea aside almost as soon as it occurred.

"Now," he said. "What do you want to do with the rest of the day? I could drive you to the beach and we could have a walk or you could watch the telly. Don't worry." He gestured at the small, ageing set on the shelf above the kitchen counter. "I've got a better one in the living room and a collection of DVDs and there's Netflix. Or if you need to sleep some more, you can do that."

"What are you going to do?"

"Well, now the rain has stopped I'm going to do a bit more gardening. I've a veg bed I'm going to sow with a cover crop and a few other little jobs to do."

"You're a bit late with that," Paul said.

"I am, but it should still get going over winter. It's a clover mix so it'll be slow, but still do the job. You like to garden?"

"At the house it was all about growing stuff. If you don't mind, I think I want to sleep some more."

John finished tidying up in the kitchen. He heard Paul go up the stairs and into the bathroom and then into the spare bedroom. The slight creak as he flopped down onto the bed. Yes, he was holding on to normal, John thought, but he was doing so by the very tips of his fingernails. The break point would happen, sooner or later, and he would lose his grip and then a very scared, very angry young man would burst forth. John found himself hoping Paul would be gone before then.

* * *

"Right, so are you ready for a history lesson?" Tom Andrews asked.

"I am, I've got you on speaker. Mike isn't here but Amit and Terry are — you know both of them, don't you."

"Of course. Amit, Jude, you won't recall the Ellison case, but, Terry, you'd have been around, though I think not yet have been a police officer. It didn't make a big splash as there was nothing particularly glamorous about it, but it was the beginning of the end for Jimmy Hargreaves and in fact for a good few others of his ilk. It started with a VAT audit on the company Gary Gibson was working for and by the time it got to court, about a dozen companies were caught up in a fraud investigation. Now fraud cases, unless they involve big names or public-sector companies, don't get a lot of press coverage, mainly because they are boring and complicated to report. This one made a bit of a splash, but faded from public interest precisely because it was so complicated and boring. The most exciting part of it was Gary Gibson getting killed, but public interest seemed to focus on the wife and her possible lover, and only very briefly on the possibility there may be a connection to the Ellison business."

He paused and Jude heard him take a sip of something.

"Ellison's was a parent company for a small financial advisory network, mainly dealing in short-term, high-yield investments. Ellison's was the parent company, but the group traded under a variety of different names. You'd have to think of it as a franchise agency, I suppose. However, Gary Gibson was the chief accountant for the entire group and, it was suspected, also kept track of the finances for the likes of Jimmy Hargreaves. That was all well and good so long as he kept his business interests separate, but the trouble was that Gibson came up with the bright idea that he could launder the dodgy money alongside that of legitimate investors and none would be the wiser. After all, this was a business that involved the movement of funds in and out of investment accounts all the time. So long as none of the individual amounts were more than ten thousand pounds, which, as you know, triggers closer interest from the banks and the authorities, he was free and clear. Unfortunately, our Mr Gibson was perhaps less than careful when it came to accounting for those additional funds with the VAT office. You with me so far?"

They were, though Jude was beginning to wonder where all this was leading and what it had to do with recent events.

"Anyway, the rumour was that this, plus the probably true allegation that Gibson was skimming, is what got Gibson killed. Most likely, anyway. Jimmy Hargreaves didn't take kindly to having his assets frozen, which was effectively what happened during the investigation. Gibson had tied up a big chunk of Hargreaves' cash flow because, of course, he'd been filtering it through these other accounts. Hargreaves not only lost cash but he lost face and that was far more important in the long term.

"Gibson was killed, the investigation failed to make a prosecution for the murder, the Ellison case rumbled on and Hargreaves, most likely, squirreled away what was left of his resources and went to ground."

"Gibson's wife was Hargreaves' sister, wasn't she?" Jude said. "And she disappeared around the same time that he was killed."

"That's right. Now, what's the likelihood that she went and set up a place for her brother to join her? Whatever the truth of the matter, a few months after Gibson's death, while the Ellison case was still taking up court time and Jimmy's business was falling apart, both he and his sister were gone and so was Brian Hedgecock. He resurfaced a few years later and the result of that was the death of the unfortunate Charlie Fairford, retired accountant and, as I told you last night, semi-retired bookmaker."

"And he had a connection to the Ellison business," Amit hazarded. "Did he work for them?"

"Yes, he did, as one of the financial advisers running an investment franchise. Though Gifford's had closed its doors and Charlie retired by the time Hedgecock came back on the scene. However, there's a distinct possibility, according to my contact, that he may have been the one that reported the tax irregularities and that subsequently led to the whole house of cards falling down."

"And your contact is?" Jude asked.

"Well, most of what I'm telling you will be in the Ellison files and the rumours may have found their way in there too. I'm just giving you a catch-up lesson, saving you time." His tone, Jude noted, had a teasing edge to it. Tom Andrews was enjoying himself.

"Your contact has to have been a serving officer," Terry Gleeson commented. "I'm guessing he'll be in the files too."

"No doubt he will, though not in the Ellison case. DS Fred Donner worked on the Gibson murder. Mike will no doubt remember him. He remembers Mike well enough. Anyway, Fred's happy to talk to you. It'll cost you time and a six-pack of lager, but it might be worth your while. For now, though, I'd search out the files — it might be quicker. Fred likes to take the scenic route when it comes to storytelling."

"And he reckons Hedgecock did for Gibson?" Terry asked.

"He does and I'm inclined to agree. In both cases, a spike or a nail was driven into the back of the neck. And, yes, I know that's been kept back, but remember, I know Sid Patterson. Sid insisted on knowing exactly how Morgan had died. He felt he had to face up to the worst of it. Fred Donner doesn't know and I didn't raise the Springfield murder with him, though he's seen the news and knows Hedgecock is on the loose, so he'll be wondering."

"So, there's a direct connection between Gibson and Hedgecock and Charlie Fairford, but what about Morgan Springfield?"

"Well, that's less clear cut," Tom admitted. "But there is a tenuous connection. Morgan would have been around twenty when the Ellison thing was happening and so far as I know had no connection with them. I asked Sid, but the name meant nothing to him. However, Morgan's dad was a gambler, and he's known to have worked with or for Charlie Gifford, after he lost his teaching job."

"Teaching job?" Jude asked.

"Now I really am piecing things together," Tom said. "I spoke to Sid this morning, which is why I'm a bit late contacting you. I needed a few details clearing up. But between Sid and Fred Donner, this is what I know.

"Morgan has always been reluctant to talk about his father. I knew he'd died when Morgan was in his early twenties, but Sid told me privately that his dad had committed suicide and Morgan was the one who found him hanging. He told me initially, I think, so I'd know to steer clear of the subject. I could understand why it would be painful, so I always respected that.

"Morgan did tell me that his dad was a science teacher, until he lost his job."

"Do you know what happened?" Jude asked.

"Not in detail, but I know he was a compulsive gambler. Sid did tell me that much when I spoke to him this morning. He also remembered Morgan telling him something about his father being very stressed because he had to appear as a witness in some court case or other. Like you, he knew nothing about the Ellison business, so I did a little digging in our morgue and Springfield senior was definitely due to give evidence, as a business associate of Charlie Fairford."

That, Jude thought, was interesting. It was a connection, of sorts, like another tumbler clicking into place. But . . . two questions came to mind.

Amit was ahead of her. "Are we sure he wasn't helped on his way?"

"There's nothing to suggest that."

"And what's the connection to Morgan Springfield? If his dad didn't even give evidence in the case, then he can't have done anything to interfere with Jimmy Hargreaves. So, what possible grudge could Hedgecock have against the son?"

"That I don't know," Tom said. "All I can think is that Hedgecock liked the idea of being biblical about it and was maybe also killing Morgan to please that little toe rag, Ross Cahn."

Jude could hear in Tom's voice and see on her colleague's faces that no one believed Hedgecock was doing anything for Cahn. As to being biblical — would even Hedgecock look to visit the perceived sins of the father on the son?

When Tom had ended the call, the three of them, Jude, Amit and Terry, were silent for a moment or two, then Jude said, "Well, I suppose now we contact the archives and get the Ellison stuff sent over. Terry, did we get the post-mortem report for Gary Gibson?"

"I'll check. You know Tom Andrews better than I do and I know the boss rates him. You reckon this is all kosher?"

Jude nodded. "Tom feels he's involved, maybe even guilty, because of the Pearsons. Okay, there might not be logic to that, but I think he feels he made some bad decisions, and he wants to make amends." She grinned suddenly. "You know who DS Donner is, don't you? He's the one who told the boss he'd got too much imagination, when he said he thought the Gibson killing had been staged. This is really going to amuse him."

CHAPTER 30

Tuesday evenings at the Cold Moon ended at eleven. There was no real profit in getting the drinks licence extended that early in the week — anyone intent on staying out really late, on a school night, could take themselves off to one of the student-friendly venues elsewhere. Tuesday was open-mic night and, as she had told Mike, Luce took over the last slot before closing. The length of that slot varied, depending on how many hopefuls had come in to test themselves in front of a — usually quite forgiving — live audience. It might be ten minutes, it might be longer, but it was rare for Luce to have to fill for the entire last half hour as she had that night.

It had been a slow night all round. Punters had arrived in groups, hardly anyone coming in alone, and the atmosphere had been nervy and febrile. About a half-dozen people had signed up to sing, but two of those had chickened out. There had, Luce felt, been a restless and edgy feel to the evening that as Colin, the owner-manager, had observed, could only have been due to a maniac running about the streets.

When she left at half past eleven, the street at the back of the club, where she parked her car, seemed unusually dark. Rain was falling now, washing away what was left of the snow, and the sky was heavy with cloud. At first, Luce thought that must account for the lack of illumination but then it occurred to her that the security light that was always on at the back door until everyone had left, had gone out.

Glass crunched beneath her foot. She glanced down and then looked up. The lamp was broken.

Almost, Luce turned to go back inside. She stood in the doorway and glanced both ways along the street. Her car was literally only a few feet away but the feeling that she was being watched was now intense. Luce made up her mind. If she went back inside, there was only Colin and young Alice, Ben, that night's doorman, having left at eleven as he usually did on a Tuesday. He had a second job elsewhere. Luce didn't reckon either Col or Alice would be good in a crisis. But what crisis? Was she letting her imagination run away with her?

She pulled the door closed with a slam, pressed the key fob to unlock her car door and ran. The sound of running feet echoed her own, though these were booted and heavy and closing fast. Luce dived into the car and locked it, turned the key in the ignition, praying it would catch first time. It did, just as a man's fist crashed against the side window with enough force to rock the car.

Instinctively, Luce revved the engine and then slammed the vehicle into reverse, mounting the pavement to get away from him. He turned; was now running alongside.

She shifted into first, swerved off the pavement and, because she could not think what else to do, drove straight at him, the engine screaming in protest at being over-revved.

For a split second she didn't think he'd move out of the way. She clipped some part of him as, at the last moment, he pivoted aside, but he'd not done with her yet. She sensed rather than saw him grab at the door handle. Luce floored the accelerator and she must have changed gear because the car surged forward and picked up speed. She heard the rear screen break as he hurled something after her, something that hit the glass and then bounced off the car, but Luce was breaking speed limits at that point, hurtling towards the main road.

Sid, what if he went after Sid. What if he had a car and was following her? What if he got to Sid first?

Some vestige of common sense told her that if he was after Sid then he'd have gone to his house rather than to the club. He knew about the club because Morgan came to the club. He knew about the club because the Cahn boy had confronted Morgan there and this man, this Brian Hedgecock, had killed Ross Cahn and chased the Pearson boy through town, trying to kill him too.

But what did he want with her?

A few minutes later she was fumbling with Sid's door key, then racing up the stairs.

"We've got to go — grab some things and then we've got to go."

"What?"

"Just do it."

It was testament to Sid's trust in her that by the time she had called the club to warn them what had happened and make sure they called the police, and she had called Mike on the mobile number he had left them, that Sid was ready to leave. They took his car, the damage wrought to Luce's horribly evident now she had the time to look.

"Where are you going?" Mike asked.

"A hotel. I'll let you know when we get there. Just make sure Colin and Alice are okay."

"What the hell is going on?" Sid demanded when she rang off.

"Brian Hedgecock, that's what's fucking well going on. He was waiting outside the club for me — he attacked my car."

"At least he didn't get to you. God, Luce, you could have been killed."

She had known this, of course, but having someone say it out loud was just too much. Luce, indomitable, reliable Luce, broke down and cried.

CHAPTER 31

Brian Hedgecock wasn't done yet. The woman at the jazz club had, he knew, been a friend of Morgan Springfield's and, if he was honest with himself, he hadn't expected her to know where Paul Pearson might be — she had just been another name on his mental list.

His next target, however, was much more likely to know where the police had stashed her son.

The hostel was equipped with a keycode entry system and security cameras, but Brian had already assured himself that everything was focused on the ground floor and the main entrance into the building. There was a single CCTV camera above the back door but nothing on the fire escape. This was not a secure unit, it was merely a hostel, a halfway house whose inhabitants were free to come and go as they pleased and with ageing sash windows that, above the ground floor, had no locks worth the name.

Johanna woke to find a man standing in her room, a man whose next action was to clamp a hand over her mouth and nose, and then drag her from her bed. His breath was hot on her face, he smelled of vinegar and grease and she was suddenly afraid she might be sick. That she would choke on her own vomit. She could hardly breathe, so tightly was he covering her mouth and her nose she was certain that he was going to kill her.

"I want your son," he said. "I've no quarrel with you, but him, I want. And believe me, woman, I'll not let anyone or anything stand in my way of getting to him. You understand?"

Numbly, Johanna managed to nod.

"So, I'm going to let you speak and you'll tell me where he is and I'll go away. You understand?"

Again, she nodded.

Suddenly she could breathe. He released his grip and Johanna gulped in air, light-headed with relief. "Now tell me where he is."

"I don't know where he is. The police came and took him away. They didn't tell me where they were going. I'd left by then. I have to get back here by a certain time. I'd gone and no one told me where they were taking him. Paul didn't want me to know."

The words had come out in a rush, and she could see by the expression on his face that he did not believe a word of it.

"You'll tell me," he said. She saw the fist raised and tried to lift her arms to protect herself, but he was much too powerful and much too fast. Johanna collapsed under the blow, stunned and almost fainting from the pain. She tried to crawl away, but he had grabbed her again, pulling her to her feet.

"I want to know where he is."

"And I don't know, the police took him away." This time she managed to cry out before he hit her again. As she fell, she crashed into the bedside table. Dimly she heard it thump as it hit the floor and the sound of breaking glass as her water glass hit the wall and the dull thud as the lamp bounced onto the rug.

"I don't know where they took him, I don't know." She could hear her own voice, thin and pained and muffled, as though she could not quite shape the words.

He grabbed her again. She could feel his hands on her but her head lolled back and she could not stand. If he hit her again, that would be it. She sensed it, knew it. She heard him laugh, actually laugh, and the sound chilled her.

"It doesn't matter anyway," he said. "He'll come to me now."

Johanna tried to raise a hand. If she clawed at his face, perhaps he would let her go. But the thought only half formed. The action not at all, and she slumped down as her legs gave way. He let go of her, leaving her to drop like a rag doll to the floor.

CHAPTER 32

The phone call came at a quarter past one and had John leaping from his bed and hammering on Paul's door.

"She's in a bad way," Mike told him. "Broken ribs, broken jaw and a suspected fractured skull. I've contacted the community house and David is bringing Evie and Steven to the hospital."

By two they were all sitting in the family room and waiting for news. Evie held Paul's hand. Steven paced as though trapped in too small a cage. John and David Laughton sat in near silence, not knowing what to say or do and, John suspected, Laughton too was feeling somehow as though he should not be there. That they were not family and the siblings wanted only one another.

John went and fetched coffee. David took a trip to the vending machine for chocolate. They all looked up every time footsteps approached the door — then looked guiltily away each time they passed by, as though being caught in the act of expectation was somehow wrong.

A constable John did not know dropped by, reassured them that a police presence would be maintained outside their mother's room and that she would be kept safe.

"What if that man guesses Paul might have come here?" Evie asked.

It was, John thought, a very good point.

The constable beckoned for her to come into the hallway and pointed at the two officers — two armed officers, John noted — standing at the end of the corridor.

"I promise, you're safe here," the constable said and John found himself wanting to tell the over-confident young man that there was no such thing as safe, not really, and that he should not make promises he could not personally hope to keep.

Eventually a doctor came and drew up a seat. He had a folder in his hands and showed them X-rays, explained as best he could what was going on. Mostly he said that they would have to wait, see how Johanna responded to treatment, hope the brain did not swell.

John could barely take it all in, so how were the kids coping? And suddenly, they were all children to him, even Paul who was supposedly a grown man and Steven who at nineteen was also a nominal adult. They clung to one another, all quarrels forgotten, just wanting their mum to survive and eventually, to John's profound relief, Paul broke down and wept, heartbreaking, gut-wrenching sobs that drained him dry and, John hoped, syphoned off a little of the anger and the rage.

"You want to go home?" David asked them.

No, they did not. Could not. In the end, David fetched a couple of blankets that he had in the car and John fetched the plaid rug he always kept in the boot in the winter and they settled the young people in the most comfortable chairs. By four, exhaustion had won and they had gone to sleep.

"You should go," David told him. "I can hold the fort here. You've done enough."

"I'll go down to the café, fetch you all some drinks and sandwiches," John told him. "They'll be hungry when they wake up."

David was right, John knew. There was nothing he could do, but he felt, quite unreasonably, that he was somehow being dismissed.

Before he left the hospital he called Maria, knowing she'd be up, despite the early hour. "Mike's gone into work, of course. I couldn't sleep. How is she?"

"From what the doctor said, it's a bit of a waiting game. Head injuries are unpredictable. I think it's bad, Maria."

"Mike said someone in the next room heard a commotion and got up to check she was okay. They saw a big man running down the fire escape at the back of the building. No prizes for guessing who that was."

"Well, they probably saved her life."

"Did you hear about Lucille? Sid Patterson's friend?"

"No, what happened?"

"Apparently, he was waiting for her when she came out of the club where she performs. She managed to get into her car and she got away but it was a close thing. They've got to find him, John. But I can't understand what this is all about. None of it seems to make any sense."

John agreed that it did not. "You want some company?" he asked. "I know I should be getting home to my bed, but I know I wouldn't sleep if I did. Are you working today?"

"Only ten till two. I shifted my hours to cover for someone. Come over. We'll wait to see if Mike calls, and we'll have some breakfast together. Then you may as well crash in the spare room for a few hours, as you'll be over for dinner tonight anyway."

Of course, it was Wednesday. Just over a week since Morgan Springfield had been killed. Somehow the events of the past few days had caused time to flow oddly, for the days to become hard to separate.

Collecting his car, he felt aware of every shadow, his neck prickling at each sound he could not immediately identify. Suddenly John felt old and tired and sick of the drama, glad it was someone else's responsibility these days and only sorry that it had fallen to his friend to sort out the mess.

CHAPTER 33

At six in the morning, Jude made her way into the Norfolk and Norwich University Hospital and was directed up to the waiting area. David Laughton was dozing in one of the chairs, a stack of sandwiches and soft drinks on the table beside him. The Pearson siblings slept, blankets tucked in around their sleeping forms, but even as Jude watched from the door it was clear that their sleep was restless. Paul twitched and roused as she came in, Evie murmured something and she could see tears on Steven's cheeks.

"Mr Laughton?"

David Laughton blinked awake and stared at her, his expression puzzled.

"DS Jude Burnett," she reminded him. "DI Croft wanted me to come and give you an update." And find out what Paul might know. When Mike had last called the hospital, it had been suggested that the siblings might be able to see their mother soon. She was in the ITU, but so far seemed stable and they had been asking since they first arrived when they'd be allowed to be with her. Mike hoped that the sight of Johanna's injuries might shake information out of young Paul. That the shock might do what questions had not. If not, Jude had been told to bring him in for formal

240

questioning, though she knew it bothered Mike that he'd be separating him from his family at a time that might be critical for Johanna. He had authorised Jude to use that as a lever, if she thought it might work.

The sound of a strange voice roused the sleepers and they looked at first hopeful and expectant, and then disappointed as they realised she was not a doctor. "I need the loo," Evie said and cast her blanket aside.

"Have you found him yet?" Steven demanded.

"No, not yet. We're hoping your brother can help us with that."

"I don't know where he is."

Jude sat down and David handed out drinks and sandwiches. "Eat," he said. "Paul, just tell the detective what she wants to know. This is a dangerous man — any small thing might help to catch him."

Paul looked mutinous and then sighed. "I know a few places he might hang out. I know a few names, but they don't mean anything to me, just names Ross mentioned when he was talking about him. Look, I just kept out of his way. He's totally mental! Look what he did to Ross."

"What did he do?" Evie had returned and now stood in the doorway. "Paul, you talked in your sleep when you came to us yesterday. You were half dead and you kept talking about him killing your friend. Now he's almost killed Johanna. She's still our mother, despite everything. We still love her! He killed your friend and he almost killed her, so tell the police what you know. If you don't, and someone else gets hurt, it'll be on your head and I won't forgive you."

Paul looked shocked. To be honest, so was Jude. Evie was small and slight and had the look of someone for whom gentleness and compassion were second nature, but she was blazingly angry now. Maybe, Jude thought, that was exactly what was needed.

She was about to add pressure in the form of Mike's ultimatum, that if Paul didn't furnish them informally with details relating to Brian Hedgecock, then she'd been told to take him in for questioning. She had a constable ready and waiting to assist, should that become necessary, but would be happier avoiding the fuss. She was pre-empted, however, by the arrival of a doctor with the news that they could go in and see Johanna.

"There'll be a lot of machines, a lot of tubes and wires," he warned them. "And your mum's face is very badly bruised."

"Will she be able to hear us?" Evie asked.

"You should talk to her," he told her, which, Jude noted, wasn't quite an answer.

She waited with David Laughton as the doctor escorted the siblings to the ITU. David helped himself to a drink and a sandwich, and offered the same to Jude. She shook her head.

"Courtesy of John Tynan," David said. "He's a nice man."

"He is. How are they coping? Is the younger boy not here?"

"We shipped Daniel off to stay with family up in York. The incident with Hedgecock upset him greatly. They'll be bringing him down this morning. Poor kid, he's going to need careful handling to get over this. As for the others, I think they're just shocked right now. They managed to sleep. I mean, what else is there to do? Places like this you wait and you sleep and you talk about nothing when, all the while, all you can think about is what might happen and you try to avoid saying it."

Jude looked quizzically at him.

"My wife. She died of cancer three years ago. Thankfully, we managed to take her home, which was what she wanted. The hospital staff were wonderful, but at least at home some-one could be with her all the time. The last two days I just sat and held her hand."

"I'm sorry," Jude said. "I think feeling helpless is almost the worst part."

David nodded. "So, what's happening with this Hedgecock?"

"Well, it seems he gained entry through the window. He climbed up the fire escape and then managed to get along to Johanna's window. It's not clear how he knew it was her room as there are two at the back on that floor, but Johanna's neighbour says she hadn't quite closed her curtains, so likely he looked through the gap, realised it must be the next room."

"How did he even know what floor she was on?"

Jude sighed. "There are pigeonholes for post in Reception with names and room numbers on. It's possible to see them through the glass door. The hostel plans to change that, apparently."

"It's a bit late! Anyway, go on."

"We picked him up on CCTV at several points after he left, then lost him near the Magdalen Street flyover, but we've got a team trying to pick up the trail. He seems to be carrying an injury. There was an earlier incident when he tried to attack a young woman. She drove her car at him and, we think, clipped his knee."

"Good for her. Is she all right?"

"Scared, angry, but, yes, unharmed. But Paul is our best lead. Anything he overheard or was mentioned to him or that Ross Cahn said, even if it doesn't seem relevant, might help us. Someone must be sheltering Hedgecock. We just need to know who."

"Do you know what this is all about?" David asked.

Jude nodded cautiously. "It seems to be about something that happened almost fifteen years ago."

"What?"

"Hedgecock has been in prison for the past twelve, almost thirteen. He was in prison for murder, but we now think he was responsible for another death."

"And now he's been let out and he's killing again. But why? That boy, Ross Cahn, he would only have been a child when he was locked up."

"We don't know why he killed Cahn," Jude admitted.

"But you're hoping Paul might be able to enlighten you."

The sound of running feet broke into their conversation. At first Jude assumed this must presage some medical

243

emergency, but when Evie and Steven burst into the room, she groaned, guessing what they were about to say.

"Paul's gone. He left. We were seeing Mum and he said he felt sick, so he went to the toilet and he didn't come back. We went to find him, but he's nowhere."

"How did he leave the hospital?" David asked. "There are police at the end of the corridor and someone guarding Johanna's room."

But Jude was already on the phone. He couldn't have gone far and he'd have been picked up on CCTV. There was more than one way he could have gone out of the hospital and the police officer guarding Johanna's room would not think to have stopped him going to the toilets. He was there to stop people going in, not coming out. And she knew that the ITU was along another corridor from the one the armed police were currently occupying, their brief to keep anyone from getting near the siblings. But if the Pearson kids had been with the doctor, further down the corridor, they would have been no use in intercepting Paul.

Mike was not best pleased. Jude winced at the tone as much as the language, but he calmed down almost immediately.

"Find him on CCTV. I'll get reinforcements. And call John, just on the off-chance Paul might try to make contact. Stupid little fool, he's going to get himself killed."

CHAPTER 34

They picked Paul up on CCTV cameras as he passed the Edith Cavell building and assumed he'd be heading down Colney Lane. Patrols dispatched saw no sign of him and Jude guessed he'd cut across the UEA playing fields. Her guess seemed wrong when they failed to pick him up again on CCTV anywhere near the university campus. He must have come back onto the road to cross the River Yare, she thought, but there was open parkland between the university campus and the University Village and Paul could have taken any route across.

He was on foot, Jude kept telling herself. He wouldn't be moving fast. But it was dark and raining and Paul was, it seemed, determined to avoid everyone who might persuade him to return to safety. Jude wished they still had bloodhound packs at their disposal, like the police did in Victorian-era movies.

Mike arrived at the hospital half an hour after Paul had gone missing and they studied maps, asking the hospital security team about likely routes — local knowledge being everything in a search like this. The buses would have started running by then and it was possible Paul would have hopped on a bus to get back to the city centre. Drivers were alerted but there seemed to be no sign.

It was only a little later, when David Laughton went to fetch something from his car, that they realised what Paul must have done. David's keys were gone. Paul had not returned to the family room after he'd been in to see Johanna; both David and Jude had been there and would have seen him.

"He planned this," Jude said. "He must have taken your keys sometime in the night. Maybe when you fell asleep or left your coat when you went to the vending machine or the toilet. He must have been planning to leave all along, go and confront Hedgecock."

"I never thought!" David was distraught.

"None of us did," Evie told him. "Steven and I assumed he'd decided to leave when he saw what that man had done to our mother. We thought it was just on impulse, because he was so shocked. And he was shocked, wasn't he?"

Steven nodded. "He was horrified. God, she looks half dead. Her face—"

"The doctor says she's stable and doing okay," Jude reminded him. "Your mum's tougher than she looks."

Mike had been spreading the news that they should be on the lookout for a car. An old-type Volvo estate that the community had owned for years. Dark green.

"Can he actually drive?" Mike asked. "I mean, well enough not to draw attention to himself."

"All the kids can drive," Steven said. "We learn to drive the farm vehicles and there's an old VW we learn basic skills on. There's enough land behind the house to get to grips with driving off-road. Then as soon as we're old enough, we start lessons. Paul had lessons before he got sent to the young offenders' centre. The day he attacked Tom Andrews, he'd driven to his place. He'd stolen one of the cars."

"Borrowed," Evie said. Then, "Okay, I suppose he took it without permission. But this means he could be anywhere."

"He'll get picked up on CCTV," Mike said. "Now we know what we're looking for. Look, are you stopping here for a bit longer or do you need transport to get back?"

"I think we'll be staying for a while. I can arrange for a lift later, don't worry about that. Just find him before he gets killed."

* * *

"I thought they were big on people being entitled to make their own decisions and living with the consequences," Jude commented as they got into Mike's car. Her own would have to stay in the hospital car park for a while. She decided she was damned well going to reclaim the parking charge from petty cash.

"I think this whole episode may have loosened that attitude a tad," Mike said. "Now, where the hell will the young idiot have gone?"

"I say head towards Magdalen Street and the flyover," Jude said. "Hedgecock seemed to know his way around there and that's where he arranged the meet with Cahn."

And that had ended badly.

En route they had two notified sightings, and these seemed to back up Jude's guess. Police units had been mobilised. There were many pairs of eyes searching for Paul Pearson and for Brian Hedgecock, the big man presumably now on the way to meet his quarry. But after those two sightings, Paul seemed to have disappeared.

They were almost at the flyover when the call came in that the car had been found, parked up under the flyover itself, but of Paul Pearson there was not a trace.

CHAPTER 35

Paul drove with his mobile resting on the passenger seat. Traffic was light, the sky only just starting to lighten, though that owed more to the city lights coming on in offices and homes than to dawn breaking. The light was yellow, artificial, dirty, and suddenly he longed to be anywhere but here. He could drive away, get out of town — his mother would not want him to go up against this man who could crush him down with a single blow. Paul was under no illusions about what would happen when he met with Hedgecock. Only that the man had now forced his hand. *I got to your mother*, he was saying. *I can get to other people you care about, and I won't give up*.

But as Paul was driving, he realised something else. That there might be a better way.

Paul drew up at the side of the road and picked up his mobile. There were missed calls from Evie and Steven, and a number he didn't know, which he guessed was the police. Hedgecock had responded to his call earlier, but not yet called back with details of where they should meet. Paul's instinct told him it would be somewhere close to where he had summoned and then killed Ross Cahn. It was a part of the city where Hedgecock seemed to feel at home — it was also a part of the city that to Paul was far less familiar.

He ignored the new call coming in from Evie, swiped to decline the call and then stared at his contacts list. He had another number in his phone, one given to him the day before. Yes, perhaps there was a better way.

Paul skimmed through his contacts once again and this time he called John Tynan.

CHAPTER 36

It was eight in the morning and rush-hour traffic had started to build, the sound of it echoing off the concrete of the fly-over, though it was already petering out as the emergency diversion began to take effect. The rest of the city centre would be gridlocked within the half hour. He was afraid that Brian Hedgecock would wonder at this, smell a rat.

Twice now, Paul had ignored Hedgecock's calls and three times read the texts that told him where to meet and threatened what Hedgecock would do to his siblings if he did not. He had not replied, just relayed that information to Jude, who had passed it on to the Gold Commander in charge of the team. The big man was growing impatient.

"Just hold your nerve until everyone is in position," John had told him and Paul wondered again why he should trust this man. But he found himself leaving the line open — having John's calm presence there to reassure him helped. They were now just a short distance from the rendezvous and Jude, the police officer who had come to the hospital and who had been with him for the past hour, was tucked out of sight behind a broken wall a few yards from the pub yard where Ross Cahn had been killed. From where they stood, they could see the cars parked beneath the flyover and a section of the footpath along which Paul had fled that night, with Hedgecock in pursuit.

Jude had bought him a pay-as-you-go phone from a twenty-four-hour convenience store nearby. He was using this to speak to John so that Hedgecock would not find the phone engaged when he rang. He jumped as Jude's own mobile chirped, even though the sound had been turned down to almost nothing. She looked at the text, then showed it to him. She must have noticed how twitchy he was because she switched her phone to vibrate and then slipped it in her pocket.

"So, we'll be ready to go in five." Her voice was barely above a whisper. "You can call him back and tell him you're a couple of minutes away."

The idea of meeting Brian Hedgecock close to where he had killed Ross horrified Paul, but he could see the sense in it from Hedgecock's point of view. He clearly knew this ground well. The area around what Paul learned was called Anglia Square seemed like it was open and there were good sight lines. Adjacent was a bit of empty space that didn't seem to lead anywhere, like the city planners had intended to do something that then hadn't happened. It would be easy to see anyone approaching the area, but it was also isolated from both traffic and pedestrians.

Thinking about it, though, Paul could also visualise all the places where the officers involved could hide, behind the pillars and the parked cars and all the high ground they could occupy in the derelict flats, and he supposed even the flyover itself, once the diversion was in place. The cordon, invisible but Jude assured him absolutely solid, would contain Brian Hedgecock and protect Paul. All he had to do was show up, draw Brian into the open and the police would do the rest. He could see their destination from where he stood, but of Hedgecock there was no sign.

"I can't seem to stop shaking," he said. His phone rang again. His phone, not the new one Jude had given him. "It's him."

"Then answer. You're going to be okay."

He could hear the fear in his voice as he responded to the call. He heard himself tell Brian that he'd changed his mind, that he didn't care what he'd done to Johanna. That she was a traitor who'd deserved all she'd got. He'd seen what Brian could do.

"You've got people you do care about, though, don't you? A little sister, two brothers, all those loonies in that cult you grew up in."

"It isn't a cult." The answer came automatically, and Brian Hedgecock laughed.

"No? And the moon is made of cheese. I can take any of them, you know that, do what I did to Springfield."

Paul's chest cramped — he knew Brian Hedgecock meant every word.

"And I can find you, don't think I can't. You're a slippery little bugger, I'll give you that, but I'll find you and then, because you've given me trouble, I might go and find that sister of yours anyway—"

"I'll meet you." Paul could listen no longer. "I'm on my way. I'm just down the road. But look, I'll go away, I didn't see nothing. I don't know what you did and I don't care."

Brian Hedgecock's laughter was loud enough to make the phone vibrate.

"You must think I'm really stupid," he said, and this time the voice came not from the phone but from close by. Brian Hedgecock stood and then stepped out from between two parked cars. He pocketed his phone. In his other hand was a long metal pole, the other half of the one he had used to kill Ross Cahn.

"Who's your friend?" Hedgecock said.

CHAPTER 37

Jude took an instinctive step back. She calculated — they were perhaps fifty metres from the rendezvous point, so where were the armed officers in relation to them? Other officers were in the building behind her, ready to make the arrest, but they were of little use to her now. Jude didn't know but hoped at least someone from the armed response unit would have them in their sights. She thought it was now too late for a conventional arrest. Frankly, she had always thought so. The cordon, hastily arranged though it had been, had been thrown around an extensive area beneath the flyover and she knew, from listening in to the call-backs as everyone took their positions, that she and Paul could presently be seen from at least some of the positions.

But that didn't prevent her from being scared.

"What's the second phone for?" Hedgecock asked. "So you can talk to the police, is it? Better chuck the both of them over here, then." He gestured towards Jude. "Yours too," he said. "Though on second thoughts, you'd better call your boss and tell them we're walking out of here. All three of us. And that I want a car."

Paul chucked both phones close to Hedgecock's feet. Hedgecock brought the metal pole down on first one and then the other, crushing both. "Well, go on," he said. "Make the call."

Jude shook her head. "What, and tell them a man with a pole wants a car. I don't think so."

Paul looked at her as though she'd gone mad. Even from where she stood she could see how much he was shaking and, truthfully, Jude could feel her own legs threatening to give way. She had to buy some time and she had to get him to move closer to the rendezvous site, when she could be certain he could be seen.

"So," she said. "How long have you been waiting for him to arrive? My guess is the past hour at least and of course him not answering the phone would have made you wonder and then when the traffic on the flyover stopped . . ." She shrugged. "So, we, clever buggers that we are, surrounded you and now you're stuck."

"Not stuck, girlie — I've got me a couple of hostages. I could still dispose of that little toad and still have you."

She shook her head, moved away from the shelter of the wall and out into the open, gesturing to Paul that he should do the same. She had worked it out now — they were at the edge of the cordon. A cordon that had been established to give clear sight lines at the rendezvous point. She had probably been invisible to the police sniper where she stood beside the wall, and Hedgecock, emerging from between the parked cars as he had done, was likely still not in any line of sight. He still stood in a position that was partly hidden from above by the flyover, and she and Paul, unless they moved, would likely be between the firearms officers in the flats beyond and Hedgecock himself.

She had been out of the way, but Paul, he would definitely be blocking the shot. She knew for certain now they had to lead Hedgecock closer to the original rendezvous point. She had to get him in position.

The original idea had been to arrest Hedgecock, for officers to move in as soon as Paul was in sight of the big man. The assumption had been that he would have to enter the cordon to get to the meeting and the cordon would close in behind him. The hurried plan had always been problematic, but Jude supposed it was the best they could have done at such short notice. That lack of flexibility had come back to bite them now.

She shivered and thrust her hands into her pockets to stop them trembling.

"Hands where I can see them."

"I'm just cold."

She could see that he was both annoyed and unsettled by her behaviour. Paul was shit-scared and that was what Hedgecock expected. To be truthful, so was she, but she was determined not to show it — she needed to keep the man off balance. Jude had seen the injuries inflicted on Ross Cahn. She had no doubt he could pin her to the ground, like a moth to a collector's card and with as little conscience. She moved further out into the open.

"You got one thing right," she said. "We're walking out of here."

"What?" Paul sounded terrified and awed in equal measure.

"Like hell you are."

Jude took Paul's arm and tugged him forward, away from the shelter of the wall and towards the cars parked beneath the underpass. She walked quickly, dragging the reluctant and bewildered young man beside her.

"Fuck you," Brian Hedgecock said, and drew his arm back, preparing to throw.

* * *

John had heard Hedgecock's voice through the still-open call and then moments later, the crunch as the first phone was demolished and then his own went dead. He called Mike. "What the hell's going on?"

"He was there all the time; he was waiting for them."

"No one swept the area first? Mike—"

"There was no time. John, have you any idea how many strings I had to pull to get the traffic diverted and bodies on the ground, to say nothing of getting a firearms unit in place."

"I'm sorry, of course. I'm just . . . Mike, what's going on?"

"Hedgecock popped up when they were still fifty yards shy of the rendezvous. No one can get a clear shot. Jude seems to be . . . Jude seems to be doing something extremely brave. Or extremely stupid."

He was up high with two of the firearms officers, but from his angle he could glimpse only the side of Hedgecock's head and the bright red of Jude's coat. "What the hell's she doing?"

"I think, sir, she's trying to lead him out of cover," one of the officers told him.

"Can you get a clear shot at him?"

"Not yet. Not yet."

Mike could hear the chatter on the radio as each position called in, as each confirmed what he'd already guessed, that no one could get a clear sight on Hedgecock.

Jude, he thought. *I don't know what you've got in mind, but whatever it is, you'd better do it fast.*

* * *

She could feel his rage, a physical thing that crawled up her spine and caught her breath in her throat. She had her back to him now, a terrifying feeling that weakened her knees and set her heart racing. She still had hold of Paul's arm, forcing him to stumble forward. A glance over her shoulder and she saw Hedgecock with his weapon raised like a javelin thrower, his body tense and taut as he prepared to release.

He can't hit both of us, she thought, as though killing just one of them would be a good thing, but she still had to get him to move.

"Run," she yelled at Paul and dragged at his arm as she suited actions to words and lurched forward, trying to get her legs to move, praying that her own momentum would urge Paul on and, more importantly, force Hedgecock into action.

To her profound relief, Paul threw himself aside and took to his heels. She released his arm, skittering away from him before following Paul's example and shifting as fast as her shaking legs would carry her. No point giving the man an easier target than she needed to. She saw Paul dodge under the flyover, hurl himself between the parked cars and she ran on, feeling the threat between her shoulder blades as Brian Hedgecock screamed his rage and his booted feet made up the ground between them.

Jude had nowhere to go. Instinctively, she jinked and swerved, but still he came on. The square was now only yards away, the original rendezvous point almost in touching distance.

Unfortunately, so was she. She felt his weight and height behind her. His hand on her shoulder. If she was too close to him, the sniper could never take the shot. Instinctively, Jude dropped beneath his grip and threw herself to the ground and Hedgecock fell behind her, his weight tumbling onto her legs. Craning around, she saw the blood blossoming from between his eyes.

Jude heard someone scream and it was only when Paul dragged her from beneath Brian Hedgecock's bulk and wrapped his arms tightly around her that she realised the screams were her own.

EPILOGUE

A few hours after Brian Hedgecock's death, when the lunch-time news was filled with the drama of a police shooting and the extensive debriefing had begun, Mike got a phone call from a woman called Deidre Jones. She'd been passed around for a while until someone thought to put her through to Inspector Croft and Mike could sense her — justifiable — impatience.

"Brian Hedgecock," she said. "When you've done with him, I'll be the one burying him."

Her accent was local, possessed of that soft burr Mike had come to like. She sounded like an older woman, he thought, and her tone was self-possessed and no nonsense. She was not someone used to taking no for an answer.

"And why would you be burying him?" he asked. "Is he related to you?"

"Not by blood, perhaps, but I was the one that raised him. Me and his stepfather. In my book, that makes me family."

She had a point, Mike thought. Half an hour later, Mike and a female officer were sitting in Deidre Jones's kitchen and drinking her tea. She had left them for a moment, steering her walking frame through into the back room where Mike lost sight of her. He heard her thumping about as though struggling to turn the walker in a confined space and he wondered if he should offer some help, but moments later she returned, a briefcase swinging against the bars of her walking frame.

She sat down heavily and placed the bag on the table.

"He left it here," she said. "He thought I'd not seen it, but of course I had. The boy could never keep much from me."

Morgan Springfield's missing case and laptop, Mike thought. "You know who this belonged to?"

"I can guess. Like I told Brian, I watch the news. I've still got all my faculties. Oh, he never told me what he'd done and I never asked. That was their business, him and Jimmy's. I know what he was, but I raised the lad and I loved him. The heart loves what it loves."

This last was said defiantly as though she thought Mike might question her right to do that.

He nodded. *The heart loves what it loves.*

"We'll have to search the house," he told her.

She nodded. "As well I've got plenty of milk and tea, then . . . So, when do I get to bury him?"

"Not yet," Mike told her. "I'm sorry, but not yet."

He had spent an hour with her while the search teams were organised, sitting in her warm, bright kitchen and listening as she reminisced about the boy she had known, the man he had become. He let her talk, the time for formalities would come and he would make sure they were gently handled.

* * *

"So what was the thing with the pens?" Terry Gleeson asked him later when the interrogation of Deidre Jones had been carried out in the presence of two officers and a psychologist. It had taken several days.

"Apparently Hedgecock was a fan of true-crime programmes on television," Mike said. "He heard about serial killers staging their scenes and, according to Deidre Jones, was intrigued by the idea. She says she had no idea he'd actually done it, that he never told her about his work, as he called it, but when we talked to her about the way Morgan Springfield and Gary Gibson were positioned and the pens, she just smiled. She said that sounded like something he might have seen on the telly."

Terry shook his head. "People are just bloody weird."

That's true, Mike thought. The search of Deidre's house had helped to fill in a lot of gaps. Without hesitation she had directed them to a deed box that Brian had left with her years before, other documents he had put in his room when he had come back to stay with her.

"Can't none of it do him harm now," she had told Mike. "Can't nothing hurt him now."

* * *

Tom wrote about Brian Hedgecock. About the old lady, Deidre Jones, crying for a man who had been like a son. Of her neighbours, who said how polite and considerate he always was, the friends and family of the dead who hated the fact he had breathed the same air as their loved ones. Of the police officer who might never go back to work and the young man whose life she had undoubtedly saved. The contradictions of it all.

Then he deleted all that and wrote a more straightforward report. One his editor and his readership would like. The bad guy was dead, the world was a little safer. DS Burnett would be honoured for her bravery. All was well.

Was it ever? Tom wondered. Was it ever well?

* * *

Jude was still on extended leave. Mike had picked her up and driven her to the coast. They walked, as Mike had done with John and Maria, three weeks before, allowing the wind to blast the cold salt air into their faces and blow the dark thoughts away. Or that was how Mike always thought of it. He told Jude so.

She nodded. "That's what Seth says."

"You and he . . . is it serious?"

"I don't know yet. I don't know anything much just now."

They walked a little further in silence and Mike asked, "You think you'll come back?"

"I think so. What else would I do? But not just yet. I couldn't do it yet."

It was his turn to nod and then to leave the questioning alone.

"Johanna Pearson gets discharged from hospital today," he said.

"That's good. I heard from Paul. He and Evie are keeping me up to date with everything."

"And . . ." He hesitated, not sure if she'd want to know the rest or if she wanted to forget about work completely for a while.

"And what?"

"Well, we think we know why Hedgecock killed Morgan Springfield."

"Oh?" She turned towards him, genuine curiosity in her eyes and Mike rejoiced. It would take time, but Jude, his Jude, was still in there. She would be all right. "So why?"

"Well, the information was among the papers Hedgecock had left at Deidre Jones's place. It seems before Morgan Springfield's father killed himself, he wrote a complete statement, itemising everything he knew about Charlie Fairford and Gary Gibson and their association with Jimmy Hargreaves. He'd been around both men for long enough that he'd learned a great deal. He knew, or suspected, Hedgecock would come after him, that he'd probably not make it to court. It seems he wanted to leave a record behind."

"Did . . . that man kill him, do you think?"

"Hard to know. Impossible, probably. But Morgan's father left a record for his son, who took it to the prosecution lawyers."

"Why not do that himself?"

"I don't know. Maybe he didn't get the chance. Morgan Springfield received the records the day he found his father. I spoke to one of the prosecution lawyers who told me Russel Springfield had left a note for his son saying he was sorry and that it was up to Morgan to decide what to do once he was gone. Morgan made his choice and it's likely he died for it.

"Russel Springfield mailed the note and the statement to his son the day he killed himself."

"What a bloody mess," Jude said. "And Brian Hedgecock held on to his anger all that time. Why? What was Jimmy Hargreaves to him?"

"Apparently he viewed Hargreaves as his father," Mike said. "And he believed that those men, Gary Gibson, Charlie Fairford and the Springfields, had ruined him."

"But Hargreaves left him to go, well, wherever he went. He'd be an old man by now. Maybe even a dead man."

"And there's evidence he left Brian Hedgecock well provided for. Perhaps the coincidence of meeting Ross Cahn in prison and him mouthing off about Morgan Springfield having let him down rekindled the desire for revenge. Maybe he kept that alive all on his own. I suppose we'll never know."

* * *

Johanna had managed to pack her bag, but the effort had exhausted her. She sat in the hospital chair, high-backed and institutional green, and wondered what to do next. David had said he would be collecting her and she was grateful for that, the idea of going back to the hostel was not one she could have borne and besides, the doctors had said she was still not capable of looking after herself.

Her head ached abominably and it was still hard to keep her thoughts in order.

"Mum." Evie's voice woke her — she must have dozed off again. "You ready? We've got a wheelchair."

David appeared behind her. "There's a room ready for you at the house," he said.

Johanna smiled wearily. "Thank you," she said. "I promise I won't stay for long. Just until I can shift for myself again."

"Johanna," David said. "Just come home. There's a place for you and you'll be welcome."

She stared at him in shock. Home? Could she really go back?

Evie hugged her tightly. "Let me take your bag," she said.

THE END

THE JOFFE BOOKS STORY

We began in 2014 when Jasper agreed to publish his mum's much-rejected romance novel and it became a bestseller.

Since then we've grown into the largest independent publisher in the UK. We're extremely proud to publish some of the very best writers in the world, including Joy Ellis, Faith Martin, Caro Ramsay, Helen Forrester, Simon Brett and Robert Goddard. Everyone at Joffe Books loves reading and we never forget that it all begins with the magic of an author telling a story.

We are proud to publish talented first-time authors, as well as established writers whose books we love introducing to a new generation of readers.

We won Trade Publisher of the Year at the Independent Publishing Awards in 2023. We have been shortlisted for Independent Publisher of the Year at the British Book Awards for the last four years, and were shortlisted for the Diversity and Inclusivity Award at the 2022 Independent Publishing Awards. In 2023 we were shortlisted for Publisher of the Year at the RNA Industry Awards.

We built this company with your help, and we love to hear from you, so please email us about absolutely anything bookish at feedback@joffebooks.com

If you want to receive free books every Friday and hear about all our new releases, join our mailing list: www.joffebooks.com/contact

And when you tell your friends about us, just remember: it's pronounced Joffe as in coffee or toffee!

ALSO BY JANE ADAMS

RINA MARTIN MYSTERY SERIES
Book 1: MURDER ON SEA
Book 2: MURDER ON THE CLIFF
Book 3: MURDER ON THE BOAT
Book 4: MURDER ON THE BEACH
Book 5: MURDER AT THE COUNTRY HOUSE
Book 6: MURDER AT THE PUB
Book 7: MURDER ON THE FARM
Book 8: MURDER AT THE WILLOWS
Book 9: MURDER AT THE WEDDING

MERROW & CLARKE
Book 1: SAFE
Book 2: KIDNAP

DETECTIVE MIKE CROFT SERIES
Book 1: THE GREENWAY
Book 2: THE SECRETS
Book 3: THEIR FINAL MOMENTS
Book 4: THE LIAR
Book 5: THE NAIL

DETECTIVE RAY FLOWERS SERIES
Book 1: THE APOTHECARY'S DAUGHTER
Book 2: THE UNWILLING SON
Book 3: THE DROWNING MEN
Book 4: THE SISTER'S TWIN
Book 5: THE LOST DAUGHTER

DETECTIVE ROZLYN PRIEST SERIES
Book 1: BURY ME DEEP

STANDALONE
THE OTHER WOMAN
THE WOMAN IN THE PAINTING
THEN SHE WAS DEAD